JOE COLTON'S JOURNAL

Of all the atrocities I've seen during my sixty years on this green earth—and believe me, I've seen plenty!—having my nephew, Jackson Colton, stand accused for my attempted murder has to top them all. The case those dim-witted boys in blue have against Jackson is purely circumstantial. Don't they see that they are wasting valuable time with these trumped-up charges when the real culprit is still out there? I'll put a stop to this if it's the last thing I ever do. Luckily, the star witness, Cheyenne James, is secretly sweet on my nephew and believes in his innocence. Those two put their heads—not to mention their lips!—together and figured out a way to beat the system by getting hitched. So Jackson's clairvoyant bride won't have to testify, and the case will surely crumble! Now it's only a matter of time before those two soul mates fess up their true feelings and make a lifelong commitment....

About the Author

KAREN HUGHES

enjoys writing about men and women who want to commit their lives to each other, share dreams and grow old together. She believes romance lives in everyday life and thinks there is a hero inside every man—he just needs the right woman to bring out his best qualities. Wide open spaces call to her, yet she also likes the bustle and convenience of city life. Experience has taught her that true love can be found anywhere. To research this action-packed thriller, the author drove the California coast and fell in love with the mist-swept, rocky shoreline.

Wed to the Witness

Karen Hughes

Silhouette® Books

Published by Silhouette Books

America's Publisher of Contemporary Romance

Special thanks and acknowledgment are given
to Maggie Price for her contribution
to THE COLTONS series.

SILHOUETTE BOOKS
300 East 42nd St.,
New York, N. Y. 10017

ISBN 0-373-38712-1

WED TO THE WITNESS

Visit Silhouette at www.eHarlequin.com

Printed in U.S.A.

THE COLTONS

Meet the Coltons—
a California dynasty with a legacy of privilege and power.

Jackson Colton: *Lawyer on trial.* Falsely charged with Joe Colton's attempted murder, this loner's only defense is to wed the witness. But now that he's legally bound to this dark beauty, he can only hope that the judge grants him a life sentence...to love!

Cheyenne James: *Native American psychic.* This counselor will do anything to stand up for her convictions—even if it means marrying a stranger who appears to have murder on his mind.

Thad Law: *Man with a mission.* Still assigned to the Colton case, this newly married detective smells something fishy. Could they have arrested the wrong man?

Patsy Colton: *The manic matron.* Masquerading as her sister Meredith, she'd thought she was on easy street, but now she's getting cranky as her house of cards begins to tumble....

THE COLTONS

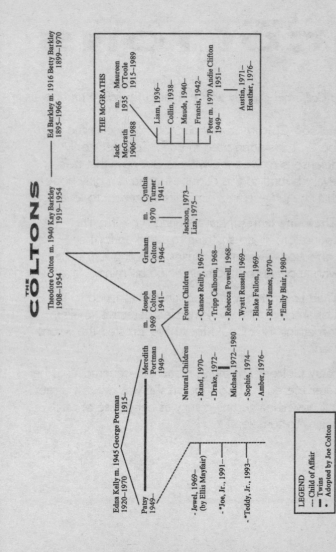

THE McGRATHS

Jack McGrath 1906–1988 m. 1935 Maureen O'Toole 1915–1989

- Liam, 1936–
- Collin, 1938–
- Maude, 1940–
- Francis, 1942–
- Peter m. 1970 Andie Clifton 1949– 1951–
  - Austin, 1971–
  - Heather, 1976–

Ed Barkley m. 1916 Betty Barkley
1895–1966   1899–1970

Theodore Colton m. 1940 Kay Barkley
1908–1954   1919–1954

Graham Colton 1946– m. 1970 Cynthia Turner 1941–
- Jackson, 1973–
- Liza, 1975–

Joseph Colton 1941– m. 1969 Meredith Portman 1949–

Foster Children
- Chance Reilly, 1967–
- Tripp Calhoun, 1968–
- Rebecca Powell, 1968–
- Wyatt Russell, 1969–
- Blake Fallon, 1969–
- River James, 1970–
- *Emily Blair, 1980–

Natural Children
- Rand, 1970–
- Drake, 1972–
- Michael, 1972–1980
- Sophie, 1974–
- Amber, 1976–

Edna Kelly m. 1945 George Portman
1920–1970   1915–

Patsy 1949–

- Jewel, 1969– (by Ellis Mayfair)
- *Joe, Jr., 1991–
- *Teddy, Jr., 1993–

LEGEND
--- Child of Affair
▌ Twins
* Adopted by Joe Colton

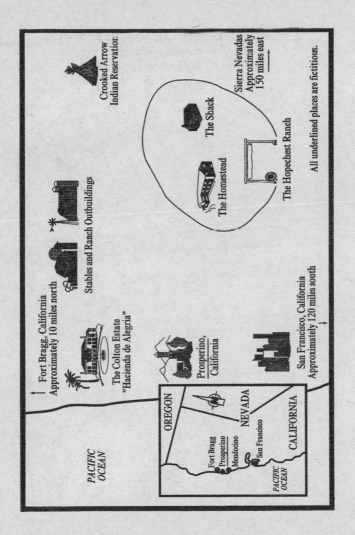

Fort Bragg, California
Approximately 10 miles north

Stables and Ranch Outbuildings

The Colton Estate
"Hacienda de Alegria"

Prosperino,
California

San Francisco, California
Approximately 120 miles south

Crooked Arrow
Indian Reservation

The Shack

The Homestead

The Hopechest Ranch

Sierra Nevadas
Approximately
150 miles east

All underlined places are fictitious.

PACIFIC
OCEAN

OREGON

NEVADA

CALIFORNIA

Fort Bragg
Prosperino
Mendocino
San Francisco

PACIFIC
OCEAN

A special thanks goes to my former colleagues in the Crime Analysis Unit of the Oklahoma City Police Department.

One

Jackson Colton knew all about how cops operated. Although he practiced corporate law, he'd spent two summers during college interning in the Los Angeles County District Attorney's office. He knew that, when fishing for suspects or talking to witnesses who might be less than truthful, the boys in blue preferred to conduct interviews on their own turf. Doing so tended to intimidate people and make them feel like they were a captive audience, whether they legally were or not.

By summoning him to the Prosperino Police Department, Jackson theorized that Detective Thaddeus Law had embarked on a world-class fishing expedition. Which was why he now sat across the scarred table from the sharp-eyed detective in a small interview room that smelled of cigarettes and sweat. The only thing Jackson hadn't yet sorted out was why *he* was the fish Law had chosen to reel in.

Granted, he'd been at his Uncle Joe's sixtieth birthday party nearly a year ago when someone took a shot at the Colton family patriarch. Nevertheless, hundreds of people had gathered in the courtyard of Hacienda de Alegria, where white doves soared, champagne flowed and exotic flowers floated in the bubbling fountain. Jackson knew that just his presence that night shouldn't have put him in a suspicious light. Nor did Law have reason to view him as the guilty party simply because he'd again been at the Colton ranch four months ago when a second shot barely missed his uncle. Yet, for reasons unclear to Jackson, the detective had turned a suspicious eye his way.

"So," Law said, leaning back in his chair. "Not one family member, staff person or guest at your uncle's birthday party can verify your whereabouts at the time the shot was fired."

Jackson regarded the cop. He had a small scar on his left cheek, a bump on his nose from where it had been broken and the bear-size build to knock anything out of his path without breaking stride. A formidable man, Jackson thought. One who obviously believed he had something on him or they wouldn't now be sparring in the stale-smelling room with stark fluorescent lighting and a single pane of one-way glass.

Since Jackson knew *he* hadn't tried to kill Joe Colton, Detective Law was headed for disappointment.

"I didn't know at the time I would need someone to swear to my whereabouts every minute of the evening." Jackson raised a shoulder. "So, I didn't bother interrogating the hundreds of people at my uncle's party. That was your job."

"True. I've talked to a lot of those people lately. No

one remembers seeing you at the exact moment the shot was fired.''

Jackson narrowed his eyes. ''That was almost a year ago. Why are you suddenly asking people my whereabouts?''

''It's my job to get a clear picture of the events that occurred,'' Law said blandly, then glanced at the notepad on the table in front of him. ''You say you'd cut across the courtyard, then took a shortcut through the service hallway to get to the bar. From the angle the slug hit the column behind your uncle, our ballistics expert figures that the shooter was standing a few feet from that hallway. Kind of a coincidence you were right there, too.''

''If you believe in coincidence, you're the first cop I know who does.''

Law's mouth curved. ''I don't. Do you remember seeing anyone on your way to the bar?''

''I saw a lot of people. The courtyard was packed.''

''What about after you reached the hallway?'' Law persisted. ''See anyone coming or going?''

Jackson slid a look at the tape recorder sitting beside Law's notepad. During those summers he'd worked at the D.A.'s office he'd learned never to underestimate cops. Now that he knew where the shooter had stood, he realized Law's seemingly harmless questions were designed to get his taped admission that he was in nearly the same location as the person who made the attempt on his uncle's life.

Which he had been. And, Jackson reminded himself, a certain gorgeous, sexy woman could place him in that exact location until he'd dropped out of sight.

His thoughts went back to the instant he'd spied the woman whose fall of blue-black hair and bronzed complexion attested to her Native American heritage. As if drawn to her by some unseen force, he'd made his way through the milling birthday crowd. When he reached her, he'd discovered she was nearly as tall as he, and wand-slim in the black slide of a dress that hugged her delicate curves. Her nose was slender, her cheeks softly curved, her eyebrows finely arched above eyes the color of rich earth.

When he introduced himself, she'd smiled coolly while the candlelight flickering around them transformed her face into a compelling play of light and shadow. He'd been surprised to discover she was Cheyenne James, sister of River James who'd been Hacienda de Alegria's foreman for years. Throughout the night, he and Cheyenne had talked, drifted apart, yet always seemed to wind up back together. They'd been chatting with River and Jackson's cousin, Sophie, when Cheyenne had turned his way, her mouth curving in a smile he found beguiling. She asked him to get her a drink, then she excused herself to greet a friend. Just then, the band played a flourishing crescendo. Then Jackson's father stepped into the center of the makeshift dance floor and announced it was nearing time to toast the evening's guest of honor. With no waiter hovering to refill their empty glasses, and guests lined up three-deep at the small bars set up around the courtyard, Jackson had decided he would make better time getting drinks from the small wet bar in his uncle's study. With Cheyenne's subtle, haunting scent in his lungs, he wove his way across the courtyard toward the service hallway—the shortest route to the study.

Just before he'd stepped out of sight, he glanced back through the crowd and saw that Cheyenne's gaze had tracked his movements. That she was interested sent a primitive streak of male satisfaction through him. He, too, was interested and he planned to learn a lot more about her than just the fact she was River's younger sister. Maybe, if the chemistry between them was right, he would find out before the night was over exactly what she wore under that curve-baring dress.

Hearing the gunshot's thunderclap moments later changed all that. With a dry mouth and hammering pulse, he'd dashed out of the hallway into the panicked crowd. Keeping one eye out for Cheyenne, he'd shoved toward the dance floor to check on his family. To Jackson's relief, the shot fired at his Uncle Joe had shattered his champagne glass and grazed Joe's cheek, then lodged harmlessly in an ivy-wrapped column behind him. In the resulting confusion, Jackson had tended his shaken family and the panicked guests, then dealt with the swarm of police that had descended on Hacienda de Alegria. He hadn't seen Cheyenne again that night.

Two harried days later, when no leads developed on the investigation, urgent Colton business had required him to return to his office in San Diego. Although he'd felt an innate curiosity about Cheyenne, he'd told himself that getting to know the dark-haired beauty simply hadn't been in the cards. Still, hers wasn't a face a man could easily forget, and he hadn't. Over the eleven months since the party, he'd discovered he had memorized it, feature by lovely feature.

Jackson scowled. As with each time he thought of Cheyenne, he felt the now-familiar restlessness stir inside him, as if everything in his world was a half beat out of sync.

Maybe it was. After all, he hadn't returned to Prosperino three weeks ago only to attend his sister's wedding. He'd taken extra time off from the law office at

Colton Enterprises so he could stay in Prosperino until he made a decision about his life. A decision that wasn't going to get made while he cooled his heels at the cop shop.

Tiring of Detective Law's innuendoes, Jackson locked his gaze with the cop's. "Okay, we've established I was at the ranch both times someone took a shot at my uncle."

"You were more than just at the ranch both times. We also recovered the slug from the second attempt when someone fired a shot into your uncle's bedroom. We know that the shooter was positioned on the south side of the house." Law angled his chin. "I responded to the call, I found you outside the door. Your Porsche—its engine still warm—was parked near the garage. Which just happens to be on the south side of the house. You say you drove in alone from San Diego and parked there right after the incident. That puts you in the shooter's vicinity that night, too."

"Believe me, Detective, I wish I had seen whoever it was who tried to kill my uncle. I didn't, so I can't help you."

A thought occurred to Jackson and he gave the cop a sardonic look. "You jealous, Law? Is that what this is about?"

Law scowled. "I take it you're talking about Heather," he said, referring to the daughter of Peter McGrath, the CFO of Colton Enterprises. And the woman who was now Law's wife.

"That's right. She was staying at Hacienda de Alegria when the second attempt occurred. As I recall, you weren't exactly happy that she and I kept running into each other while I was there. We're friends, Law. That's all."

"Yeah, that's what my wife says." Law leaned in, his eyes stony. "The fact that you're here has nothing to do with her, so leave Heather the hell out of this."

"Fine. Are we finished?"

"Do you own a handgun, Colton?"

Jackson let out a slow breath. "I keep a .32 Walther in my nightstand at home. It's registered in my name. I expect you've done a records check and already know that."

"Do you have any other handguns, registered or otherwise?"

That Law hadn't obtained a search warrant for the Walther told Jackson that the slugs recovered from both crime scenes indicated a different model of gun had been used in the two attempts on his uncle's life. "No, only the Walther."

"I understand several Colton Enterprise subsidiaries have buy-out clauses. Which means if your Uncle Joe died, you'd be closer to inheriting a fortune."

Jackson hesitated. He knew Law's change in rhythm had been intended to throw him off. "My father, Graham Colton, would inherit."

"I said you'd be closer to the money," Law countered, then cocked his head. "Are you familiar with a court case titled Amalgamated Industries vs. Jones?"

The hand Jackson rested against his khaki-clad thigh curled into a fist. Knowing Law had checked so deep into his background that he'd found the obscure, years-old case sent a ripple of unease down his spine. "Since you brought up the case, you know I am."

"Yeah." Law tapped a finger against his pad. "A CEO's son has his drug-dependent father declared incompetent and removed from the company's leadership. Then the son steps in and takes charge. You, Mr. Colton, are listed as the attorney of record on Amalgamated Industries vs. Jones.''

"Make your point, Detective."

"That case proves you know how to use the law to remove a father from a company and put a son in control. It's no secret Joe Colton is both the brains and muscle behind Colton Enterprises, not your father. It's also no secret that Graham Colton likes to drink and party. A lot.''

Jackson learned long ago how to keep his face unreadable, and he did so now. It would only cement the cop's theory if he found out about the blackmail money his father had been paying to his aunt. According to an unrepentant Graham, the money was in exchange for Meredith Colton's promise not to reveal to Joe that Graham had fathered the son Meredith had at first tried to pass off as her husband's.

"To my way of thinking," Law continued, "if your Uncle Joe were to die and your fun-loving Dad inherited, not much would stand in the way of your removing him from control and taking over Colton Enterprises." Law raised his chin. "You drive a Porsche. With your uncle dead, you could drive a fleet of them.''

Jackson felt anger growing inside him, a black heat that bubbled in his blood. "Money and power aren't important enough to me to kill for them.''

"Some people think you can never have too much of both.''

"I'm not one of them. Everything about the Amalgamated case was on the up-and-up. Adam Jones's father was addicted to cocaine, alcohol and gambling. Left in the man's control, Amalgamated Industries would have gone bankrupt in less than a year. Adam did what he had to do.''

"And, by doing so, he wound up a very rich man."

"Are you prepared to charge me with a crime, Detective?"

"Not right this minute."

Jackson rose. "Then I'm ending this chat."

He turned and was halfway to the door when Law said, "If money isn't important to you, why did you take out an insurance policy on your uncle?"

Jackson froze. He blinked, then turned. "I didn't."

"This says differently." Rising, Law drew folded papers out of the inside pocket of his suit coat, then laid them on the table. Locking his gaze with Jackson's, the cop nudged the papers his way. "A policy for one million dollars on Joe Colton's life. Sole beneficiary, Jackson Colton."

A cold fist of dread settled in Jackson's stomach as he walked back to the table. Through sheer will, his hand remained steady when he lifted the policy. "I've never seen this before."

"The insurance agent who sold it disagrees. I put together a photo lineup using head shots from the newspaper's society page. Those pictures are public domain, you know."

"Yes, I know."

"The agent picked your photo. Says he's positive you're the man who purchased the policy."

"He's mistaken."

"Says he'll testify to that in court."

Jackson looked up slowly. "Are we going to court, Detective?"

Law slid a hip onto the edge of the table and crossed his arms over his chest. "Anything's possible."

Jackson's mind worked while he studied the policy. "This is dated three weeks ago. If I'd wanted to collect money on my uncle's death, I would have had to purchase this policy *before* the attempts on his life. The first being eleven months ago at his birthday party.''

''And the second four months ago,'' Law added. ''The timing occurred to me, too. Maybe to deflect suspicion from yourself, the first two attempts on your uncle's life were intended to be just that. Attempts. You wait awhile, take out the policy, then the next time you shoot, you aim to kill.'' Law gave him a slow smile. ''Third time's a charm.''

''You're way off base.''

''Growing up, you spent a lot of time on your aunt and uncle's ranch. You and your cousins used to target shoot on the banks of the Noyo River. Word is, you're proficient with all types of firearms.''

And you're proficient in doing your homework. ''That doesn't prove I tried to kill my uncle.''

''True.''

''How was this policy paid for?''

''Cashier's check. No way to track the money.'' The cop nodded toward the papers still in Jackson's hand. ''The purchaser's signature is on the last page. We could clear up all this tonight if you'd give me a handwriting sample for comparison.''

Jackson braced himself as he flipped through the pages. Even before he saw the signature, the sick feeling in his gut told him it would be close to his. It was. Nearly identical.

He replaced the policy on the table. At this point, he would have advised any person in his same situation to keep his mouth shut and seek counsel.

''This isn't my signature,'' he said.

''Looks like yours.''

''It's not.'' The anger already heating his blood intensified. "Apparently the man who purchased the policy disguised himself to look a great deal like me, too. Someone has gone to a lot of trouble to set me up."

Law cocked his head. "Why would someone do that, Mr. Colton?"

"To divert suspicion away from himself. Someone wants my uncle dead. It will be a lot easier to make that happen if your attention is focused on me."

"An interesting theory."

"It's more than a theory, it's the truth. I know, because I didn't try to murder my uncle." Jackson stared at Law, his jaw rigidly set while his mind worked. "There's no way you stumbled onto that policy," he said after a moment. "And you didn't just happen to find out I'm the attorney of record on the Amalgamated case. Someone tossed all that into your lap. Suppose you tell me who that was? That will go a long way in telling me who's behind this."

Law kept his gaze locked with Jackson's. "I can't give you information acquired during an interview or through investigative procedure. As an attorney, you know that."

"I also know if you were going to charge me with anything, you'd have done so by now."

"That law degree of yours is coming in handy. You're right, I'm not charging you with anything. Not yet." Law plucked the policy off the table, refolded it. "You planning on leaving Prosperino anytime soon?"

Jackson slid his hands into his pockets, then clenched them into fists. At this point, he wasn't charged with anything, nor was he a material witness to a crime. Therefore, Law had no power to keep him in Prosperino. If he walked out the door, climbed into his Porsche and headed back to San Diego tonight, the cop couldn't do anything about it. Legally.

Jackson exhaled a slow breath. All that could change later on. If he did leave town, Law might be able to use his departure as circumstantial evidence that he'd fled the jurisdiction after becoming aware he was a suspect in two attempted murders. Law had the taped proof he'd made his suspect aware of that fact.

"I'm staying in Prosperino," Jackson said evenly. He turned and headed for the door. Pausing, he looked across his shoulder. "I'll be at my aunt and uncle's until I find out who decided I should take the fall for this."

Law nodded while reaching for the tape recorder. "If your travel plans change, give me a call."

The anger he'd strapped in broke free as Jackson walked out of the building and into the adjacent dimly lit parking lot. He took exception at being accused of trying to murder a man he loved and respected. And he had one hell of a problem with being set up!

He unlocked the Porsche, climbed inside; the engine roared to life when he twisted the key. Hands clenched on the steering wheel, he pulled out of the lot, swung in and out of evening traffic, then punched the Porsche into high gear when he reached open road.

Dammit, he didn't need this. He had stayed in Prosperino after his sister Liza's wedding to decide if he wanted to continue working with his father. Now, here he was, contemplating a future that might involve jail.

Jackson shoved a hand through his dark hair as the red Porsche slashed up the highway like a bolt of fiery lightning. To his way of thinking, things were either right or unquestionably wrong; he disliked intensely any murky in-betweens. This evening, Detective Law had

shoved him into dark, murky water. He didn't intend on
getting sucked under.

He was an attorney. He knew how to tear apart a case
to get to the facts. *His* case was no different. All he
needed was to figure out where to start.

As he drove, he began to sift his conversation with
Law around in his head—pulling it apart, dissecting it.
He liked things to fall neatly into place, in their proper
order, according to consequence. Habitually, he worked
puzzles out through long, quiet contemplation. Slow and
meticulous. Over the years, he'd discovered he did his
best thinking in the flickering shadows of a movie theater.

Since his very future now lay on the line, Jackson
figured the faster he settled in front of a movie and decided on a game plan, the better.

Blowing out a breath, he steered the Porsche around
a corner, then headed toward the Cinema Prosperino.

Cheyenne James had better things to do that evening
than take in a movie. Gripping the ticket she'd bought—
and had yet to use—she glanced around the red-carpeted
lobby of the Cinema Prosperino, vaguely aware of the
murmur of conversation and warm, buttery scent of popcorn that filled the air.

She knew that the case files on the three adolescents
she'd counseled in private that morning sat on her small
desk at home, waiting her attention. Her late-afternoon
meeting with her boss, Blake Fallon, had resulted in her
obtaining permission to submit a grant for funding of a
vocational work-training program for several of the teenagers who, like her, lived at Hopechest Ranch.

She had planned on starting a draft of a proposal for
the grant later tonight when she finished updating her

case files. What she hadn't anticipated was turning her back on her work and driving to the remodeled movie theater nestled between an espresso bar and art gallery on Prosperino's main street.

After the vision came, nothing could have kept her away.

Her visions were her legacy, a gift from her mother of the blood through the blood. A gift she had embraced years ago and learned never to discount. The pictures she saw in her mind's eye were not always pleasant, but had always proved accurate. When they came, she accepted them, and responded. Just as she had nearly an hour ago when the vision of the man's eyes slid, cool and clean, into her head.

Closing her eyes, Cheyenne pulled back the memory. Her breath shallowed as she pictured again gray eyes with the same hardness as rocks hacked out of a cliff. Her vision had revealed only the man's eyes, not his face. She didn't know his name. She had sensed only that he was in trouble and needed her help. And that she would encounter him at the movie theater.

Flipping her heavy braid behind one shoulder, she watched as the doors to the still-darkened theater swung open. Several couples emerged, tossing empty popcorn sacks and soda cups into the container outside the door. A pair of teenage girls strolled out, whispering to each other as if trying to keep a secret from the two tall, gangly boys who trailed just behind them.

Seconds later, a lone man emerged from the theater's dim depths, his hands thrust deep in the pockets of his khaki slacks. Cheyenne's heart took a hard leap into her throat and snapped it shut.

Jackson Colton looked tall, rangy and intimidatingly fit, like a long-distance runner at his peak. His sharp-featured face, full of planes and angles, looked as darkly handsome now as it had at his uncle's birthday party. Yet, she noted the changes in him. Eleven months ago he'd stood relaxed, gazing down at her with smoky silver eyes while he oozed charm and sex appeal with an easy smile. Now his shoulders looked wire-tense beneath his deep-blue linen shirt, his mouth was set in a grim line and his eyes were no longer the color of cool smoke, but the gray, rock-hard agates from her vision.

The instant his gaze met hers, recognition flashed across his face. His chin rose. Turning with catlike fluidity, he veered from the exit and strode toward her.

Cheyenne's pulse raced with the knowledge that fate had brought her to the man who had filled her thoughts so often since that long-ago night.

"Cheyenne." He said her name soft and low, as if he couldn't quite believe she was there.

"Hello, Jackson. How are you?" Just his nearness had her pulse thudding at the base of her throat.

"Surprised to see you. Especially now."

"Now?"

He raked his fingers through his jet-black hair. "After so long," he amended. "It's been nearly a year since my uncle's party."

"Yes." Once or twice, she had even caught herself wondering if he would come back to Prosperino again this year to help celebrate his uncle's birthday. And if she would see him if he did.

His gaze dropped to her hand. "I see you have a ticket for the next show."

"That's right."

His gaze swept the lobby. "Are you here with someone?"

"No."

"Meeting someone, then?"

"I didn't make plans with anyone."

"You haven't used your ticket yet. We could get you a refund."

She tilted her head. "Was the movie that bad?"

"No." His smile came and went. "To tell you the truth, I was working something out in my mind. I didn't pay attention to what was on the screen."

"That alone doesn't say a lot for the movie."

"I guess not."

Her vision had brought with it the sense that he was in trouble, yet his eyes had cleared and told her nothing. He knew how to keep his thoughts to himself, she realized.

As did she. Her gift might have brought them together again, but she was under no obligation to tell him that. There was a richness to her power, as well as bitterness. Her heart had learned well just how devastating relationships could be when people were unable to accept others for what they were.

"At my uncle's party," Jackson continued, "I promised you I'd be back so we could have a drink together. That didn't happen."

She arched a brow. "What happened was someone fired a shot at your uncle. I didn't hold your not keeping your promise against you."

"How about if I keep it now? I hear the espresso bar next door brews a mean latte."

The same warm, musky scent that had infused a pang of desire into her blood so long ago slid into her lungs. Jackson Colton was attractive, magnetically sexual and she had lost count of how many times she had thought about him since they'd met. Now, as she always did, she reminded herself she was giving far too much importance to a man in whose presence she'd spent so little time.

Yet, tonight fate had brought her to him. She didn't know why. The answer would come. It always did. Until then, she would not—could not—turn away from him.

"I'd love some coffee."

"Great." When he reached and slid the ticket from her grasp, his fingers grazed hers. "I'll see about getting you a refund."

"Fine," she said, struggling to ignore the quick jumpiness in her stomach. "I'll wait here."

When he walked away, she closed her eyes and waited for her system to level.

Two

What were the chances, Jackson wondered, that just hours after his being questioned by the police, the one woman would walk back into his life whose testimony could put him behind bars? He had left her and dropped out of sight moments before someone took a shot at his uncle. Cheyenne James had seen him in almost the exact spot where the shooter stood. If she told Law that, the cop would have one more piece of circumstantial evidence against him.

An important piece.

Jackson gazed across the small table they'd settled at in the cozy espresso café that was cluttered with people and thick with noise. He had forgotten nothing about her, he confirmed as he watched Cheyenne sip a latte from an oversize cup. Not the high curve of her cheeks, her softly defined mouth, the dark eyebrows above those arresting brown eyes, or the jet-black hair that tonight was pulled back into a loose braid.

As he sipped his cappuccino, it occurred to him how striking the resemblance was between her and her brother, River.

"Marriage to River has made Sophie happier than I've ever seen her. That and motherhood."

At the reference to her niece, Cheyenne's smile tipped into a grin that sent heat into Jackson's stomach and made him wonder if her mouth tasted as passionate as it looked. He didn't make a habit out of wanting the hell out of a woman the minute he laid eyes on her. Yet, that was the very thing that had happened at his uncle's party. He felt the same way tonight. He didn't know exactly why. He had no idea what made Cheyenne James different from any other woman he'd met. He just knew she was.

"Sophie has promised to let me baby-sit soon for Meggie," Cheyenne said. "I can't wait."

"That's understandable. That kid's a real charmer. All it took was one of her dimpled smiles, and Meggie had me hooked."

Laughing, Cheyenne tossed her braid across her shoulder. "You sound like River. He goes around, grinning like an idiot day and night. He'll have Meggie spoiled rotten before she can even crawl."

"I don't blame him."

Jackson caught the whiff of Cheyenne's warm scent and thought of the tea roses that bloomed in his aunt's garden. His gaze dropped to the hand Cheyenne rested on the table beside her cup. Her fingers were long and as wand-thin as the rest of her. Her nails were oval and perfect, with the gleam of clear polish. She had hands made for rings, he thought, but wore none.

"It's a shame you and I didn't meet until my Uncle's party. And that I was out of the country on business when River and Sophie got married. I would have liked to have seen you again."

Cheyenne arched a brow. "Actually, you and I met years ago, Jackson."

"We did?"

"Yes. River and I grew up apart. He was nearly sixteen when he came to live on your family's ranch. That was the same year he and I reunited. Your uncle used to pick me up from the reservation on the weekends and bring me to Hacienda de Alegria so I could spend time with River. You and your sister stayed at the ranch on some of those same weekends."

Jackson narrowed his eyes. "I have the image of a skinny girl with long legs and a dark ponytail trailing around the stables on River's heels. That was you?"

"Yes." Cheyenne tilted her head. "I was about eleven years old when you and I first met. You were in high school. Some of your friends used to come to the ranch to ride horses when you were there. Your taste seemed to run to voluptuous blond cheerleaders."

Chuckling, Jackson leaned his forearms on the table. After the hours he'd spent in Detective Law's presence, it was hard to believe someone could make him laugh. "Miss James, are you implying I have a reputation to live down?"

"It depends on if what I heard about you when I got to high school is to be believed."

"What did you hear?"

"Among other things, that you always dated a handful of girls at the same time. You had a Monday night girl, a Tuesday night girl and so on. One time you got your days confused and showed up at your Tuesday girl's house on the Wednesday girl's night.''

"Although I'll point out all that is hearsay, I'd better plead the fifth," Jackson countered, resting one of his hands near hers. "With the stipulation that things get blown out of proportion over time."

But not too much out of proportion, he thought wryly. He'd learned early not to take relationships seriously. After experiencing firsthand his parents' farce of a marriage, then watching his aunt and uncle's relationship slowly disintegrate, he'd resolved to never bring that kind of misery down on his own head. Even in high school he'd made a point to get involved only with females who knew how to laugh and to love without undercurrents. Whatever emotions came into play in those associations only skimmed the surface. That was the way he'd always wanted things. Nothing had happened over the years to change his thinking.

Until now. Now, he found himself incomprehensibly drawn to a woman who seemed to hold some underlying mystique for him.

Although that knowledge sent a stab of unease through him, Jackson pushed it back. Those moments he'd spent with Cheyenne at his uncle's party had played in his mind too often for him to shrug off her having walked back into his life.

"I'm remembering something else about that skinny little girl who followed her brother around like a shadow."

"That she was desperately shy?"

"That, and she read palms." He creased his brow in thought, trying to bring back the long-ago memory. "Or maybe it was minds?"

The words were barely out of his mouth when her

eyes went cool and remote. Her chin angled like a sword. "I don't do either."

"My mistake." He'd hit a nerve. *Which* nerve, Jackson had no idea. All he knew was that it was a sensitive one. Judging from the absolute stillness about her, he knew it would be wise to change the subject.

"You said my Uncle Joe used to pick you up at the reservation. Do you still live there?"

"No." She looked away, her gaze settling on a glass display case that bulged with cakes and cookies. Beside the case, a waiter worked a hissing espresso machine while steam rose from the metal pitcher he held.

Jackson laid his hand on hers. "Cheyenne," he said quietly, and waited until her gaze re-met his. "I apologize if I offended you."

"You didn't. You reminded me of something important. To answer your question about where I live, I'm a counselor at Hopechest Ranch. I live in one of the small staff houses there."

"Hopechest." His thumb moved lightly up and down the length of her finger. "My aunt and uncle used to be involved with the kids there. They've probably lost count of how many kids from Hopechest Ranch they've been foster parents for over the years."

"One of those kids being my boss, Blake Fallon. He thinks a lot of your Uncle Joe. The exact term he uses is 'walks on water.'"

"I agree with Blake." Jackson paused. At one time, most people had also held his Aunt Meredith in equal esteem. That was years ago before she'd undergone a personality change that had the whole family wondering what had happened to transform the once sweet, sensitive wife and mother into a woman whose severe mood swings could on occasion rock the entire household.

For Jackson, living half the state away in San Diego had insulated him from the majority of the family tremors caused by his aunt. That is, until his recent discovery that Meredith had blackmailed his father into paying her two million dollars to keep secret the fact he'd fathered her son, Teddy. The revelation had been even more bitter for Jackson because he remembered the caring, generous Meredith who had lavished love and attention on himself and his sister when their own parents left their upbringing in the hands of nannies and housekeepers.

That he remembered—and mourned—the woman he'd once adored was the thing that had prompted him to confront his aunt weeks ago about the blackmail. Maybe he'd hoped to see some regret in the dark eyes that had once sparked with love. Perhaps a softening in the brittle shell she'd built around herself. All sentimental feelings he'd harbored for his aunt had died when she'd displayed even less remorse than his father had over their affair. Faced with her cold aloofness, Jackson had warned her he would report her extortion to the police if she didn't end it.

And now, he thought, he had his own problems with the police. Serious problems.

"Is something wrong?" Cheyenne's quiet question told him his face mirrored his grim thoughts.

"Just some things I need to work out." He massaged his fingers across her knuckles. "Tell me about Cheyenne James. Why did she wind up counseling kids from troubled homes?"

"My reasons have a lot to do with River. Our mother was full blood Mokee-kittuun, our father white. When she died giving birth to me, my father let my aunts raise me on the rez as long as they sent me to Anglo schools. He took River to live with him on his ranch. I lost contact with my brother after that," she said with an edge of regret. "Before either River or I were born, our mother had another son, Rafe. My father adopted him, but because Rafe is full-blood Indian, my father shunned him when our mother died. From the stories Rafe tells me, our father was an alcoholic. A mean drunk. For years Rafe took the brunt of his anger to save River. That changed after I was born and our father left Rafe and me on the rez and took River away."

Jackson shook his head. "Rough life for a kid."

"Yes. One day, River showed up at school covered with bruises. A social worker took him to live at Hopechest. Your aunt and uncle later became his foster parents and River moved to their ranch."

"So, was it a happy coincidence that you and River found each other again?"

Cheyenne matched his gaze. "Some people have called it that."

Jackson cocked his head. Those rich, dark eyes held secrets, he realized. Perhaps that was why she was beginning to fascinate him. "What do you call your finding your brother again?"

"Destiny," she said almost reverently. "Living with the Coltons was the first time River had ever known a real family life. Your uncle encouraged him to work with his horses and that built River's self-esteem."

"Uncle Joe's good with people."

"Yes." Cheyenne played her index finger along the handle of her cup. "When I realized the foster care the Coltons gave my brother saved his life, I knew I wanted to help kids who had no control over the circumstances they were born into. I went to college, got a Masters in Social Work. I've been at Hopechest about a year. I counsel the kids, help them get the work skills they need to support themselves. I also teach a sport.''

"What sport?"

"Archery."

"Archery?"

She rolled her eyes. "Go ahead and make your comment. I'm used to hearing them."

"What comment?"

Her mouth curved. "About how I must have reverted back to ancient days when my people rode swift ponies and hunted with bows and arrows."

"Now that you mention it," Jackson said with consideration while his hand stroked hers, "You riding bareback, armed with a bow and arrow while all that dark hair flies behind you conjures up an interesting image."

"Sorry to disappoint you, but an image is all it is. I didn't learn archery on the rez. I learned it at the college."

"Really?"

"Really."

"Actually, I didn't think about Indians or bows and arrows when you mentioned archery." As he spoke, he cupped his hand around her bare, tanned forearm.

She was tense, muscles tight. What would it be like, he wondered, to loosen her, to get to the soft woman beneath the tenseness?

"Jackson?"

He skimmed his thumb up until he felt the pulse inside her elbow skitter. "Yes?"

"I…" She took a deep breath. "What did you think about when I told you I teach archery?"

Hearing her voice hitch gave him a small thrill of power—and pleasure. He smiled. "I thought that you must be stronger than you look." He squeezed her arm. "You are. You fascinate me, Cheyenne. I'm not quite sure why."

He saw a brief, uneasy flicker in her dark eyes before she shifted away, forcing his hand from her arm.

"I've told you about myself. Why don't you tell me something about Jackson Colton?"

"You're changing the subject."

"Why are you a lawyer?"

Resigned with her distance for the time being, he leaned back in his chair. "Because my father groomed me to be one," he replied, then hesitated. He had never thought of things that way, but it was the truth. His mother had barely acknowledged his existence, which had made him as pliable as clay in his father's hands. Jackson supposed he would have agreed to a career of digging ditches if that would have gained him the love of the one parent who'd paid him any attention.

That he'd never felt truly satisfied working at his father's side had been something Jackson had chosen to overlook. Until last month when he'd discovered Graham's affair with Meredith. Learning his father had paid for his aunt's silence not out of remorse for his actions, but from fear that Joe Colton would write him out of his will if he found out the truth had put a sick feeling in Jackson's gut.

"Is that what you wanted, too?" Cheyenne asked. "To be a lawyer?"

"I thought I did until recently." He moved his shoulders carelessly. "I don't know. Could be I'm just in the wrong area of the law. One reason I'm hanging around Prosperino for a while is to figure that out."

She sipped her latte. "What's another reason?"

For the space of a heartbeat, he considered telling her

that the police suspected him in the two attempts on his uncle's life. That he could be arrested. Go to jail. And that she might be in a position to help the cops put him there.

Just as quickly, Jackson pushed away the urge. He was innocent and he planned to clear his name—maybe as early as the following day if the trip he planned to make to L.A. paid off. If it did, there wouldn't be any reason for Cheyenne to know he'd even been questioned by Detective Law. No reason for this woman, who had slid into his thoughts so easily and often over the past months, to have cause to avoid him.

He took in her fine-boned features, dark eyes, the seductive arch of her throat. She looked…elegant, he decided. A kind of inner elegance that wasn't the least diminished by the simple blouse and slacks she wore. Granted, he'd always preferred more flamboyant women, but this was the first time in his life he'd felt so intensely drawn to *one* woman. Right now, he didn't know why. He was only sure that he wanted her in his world where he could see and touch her. And find out just what those secrets were he saw in her eyes.

"I've thought about you a lot since my uncle's party," he said quietly. "I'm not going to let you get away this time. I have to go into L.A. tomorrow. Will you have breakfast with me the day after?"

She regarded him steadily. He had the uncomfortable feeling she knew more was going on than what he'd said.

"I have an early archery lesson," she said after a moment. "And a counseling session later that morning."

"I'll come to Hopechest Ranch. We can squeeze in breakfast between the two." He linked his fingers with hers and thought of how good her hand felt against his. "Say yes, Cheyenne. I need to see you again. Say yes."

"Yes, Jackson, I'll have breakfast with you."

Never before had she fascinated a man.

The thought tightened Cheyenne's belly as she walked at Jackson's side along the neat sidewalk illuminated by streetlights that took on the hazy glow of tiny moons.

When they'd sat across from each other at the café's small table, it had not been a simple matter to ignore the heat that raced up her arm when he touched her. His hand wasn't soft, but hard and callused. That had been the first wayward thought that stumbled into her brain. Now, with that same hand pressed against the small of her back, she felt the pressure of each of his fingers, the strength. Power.

Jackson Colton might make his living as a smooth, sophisticated attorney but he knew how to work with his hands. And the feel of those hands made her knees go weak.

She rubbed an unsteady palm across her throat. She knew she was breathing too fast. Feeling more than the brief contact of a man's palm against her back warranted.

"Which car is yours?" he asked when they turned a corner and stepped into the parking lot on one side of the Cinema Prosperino.

She tried not to think about the fact that his arm was brushing hers.

"The white Mustang."

As they neared the car, she dug in her purse for her keys. Very deliberately, she turned enough away from Jackson that he was forced to drop his hand.

Cool, common sense was the order of the day, she

reminded herself. He was in trouble—*that* was the reason her vision had brought her to him. She didn't yet know why, but she doubted fate had reunited her with Jackson Colton just so she could get a reminder of how a man's touch could stir her. She'd found that out years ago. That knowledge had left her with a bruised heart. She wasn't likely to ever forget that experience.

She shoved the key into the door's lock, then swung it open. Before she could slide behind the wheel, Jackson's hand settled on her shoulder.

"Cheyenne?"

She closed her eyes for an instant, then turned to find him standing only inches away. His face was bathed in a mix of moonlight and shadows; the woodsy scent of his cologne drifted to her on the cool, night air.

"Yes?"

"I'm glad we had the good luck to run into each other." As he spoke, he ran a fingertip down her jawline.

The lightning response of her body to his touch sent a wariness through her that had her wanting to back away. Even if she chose to retreat, it wasn't an option, she realized. She was trapped with him in the small V formed by the side of the car and the open door.

Her breath shuddered. Her gift of sight, not luck, had brought them together tonight. Destiny would guide them from here. "I enjoyed talking with you, Jackson."

"Talking was good." His fingers closed over one of her hands. "At my uncle's party, I wondered if your skin felt as soft as it looks. Tonight I found out it does. Now I'm wondering if your skin tastes as rich as it feels." Moonlight glittered in his gray eyes when he pressed his lips deep in the center of her palm. "It does," he murmured.

Her heart shot straight up and lodged in her throat. "I

don't think..." Her voice trailed off when his lips brushed across hers, soft as a whisper.

"You don't think what?" he asked, touching his mouth to hers again with a lightness that had the blood pounding in her head.

She had ignored her physical needs for so long, she had forgotten what it was to want a man. One man. "I...don't know...what to think."

"Me, either." One of his hands slid beneath her heavy braid to cup the base of her neck. His fingers felt cool and strong against her heated flesh. He lowered his lips to within a whisper of hers. "Why don't we forget about thinking and just let ourselves feel?"

Softly, slowly, his mouth roamed over hers, sending thick, liquefying pleasure seeping into her. Her eyes fluttered shut. Her hands went limp; in the recesses of her mind she heard the jingle of metal when her keys hit the pavement.

"You stir something in me, Cheyenne," he murmured as his mouth took hers, warm and coaxing. His fingers stroked the back of her neck. She didn't need a vision to see the teasing image of what his hands could do to her body.

Her arms moved upward; her fingers locked tight on his shoulders. Beneath her hands she felt the bunch of muscles that veered toward a hard, dangerous strength. Passion came to life inside her like a fire that had been smoldering beneath cold ash. Her lips parted beneath his, opening, accepting, urging.

His arm slid around her waist, drawing her closer until she fit tightly against his hard, lean body. His mouth became more greedy, taking her deeper, demanding equal response. Her legs trembled, and blood swam so fast in her veins that she could hear the roar of it in her head. A low moan sounded in her throat while reason slipped against the pull of need.

Desire gripped her as if it had claws. His mouth continued its assault on hers, seducing her senses, peeling away the layers of caution that guarded her secrets.

An alarm sounded somewhere in the recesses of her dazed mind.

The will to survive smothered the yearning for pleasure. She hadn't come here tonight to be kissed. She was here because the man whose mouth was currently ravishing hers was in trouble and fate had brought her to him.

"Stop." She dug her fingers into his shoulders. "Jackson, we need to stop."

"Why?" His voice was a raw whisper as his mouth trailed down her jaw, nuzzled her throat.

"I... Because." She flattened her palm against his chest, forced him back. Breathing jerky, she stared at him while every pulse point in her body hammered. "Just...because," she managed in a hoarse whisper.

"Well." He expelled a ragged breath. "I guess that's as good a reason as any."

"I..." She waved a hand vaguely. "We don't even know each other."

His smile was slow and potent. "Seems to me we're working on changing that."

When he reached to touch her cheek, she jerked her head back. "I have to go. Now. Right now."

"I didn't mean to come on so strong."

He bent down, scooped up her keys, then stood with them in his hand while his concerned eyes skimmed over her face, lingering on each feature. "It's just that you've been in my thoughts for so long. I still can't quite believe you're here tonight.'' He handed her the keys, his fingers sliding against hers. ''With me.''

She stared into his face, the shadowy lights of the far-off street lamps emphasized his ruthless good looks. She scraped her teeth over her bottom lip, bringing his taste back to flood her mouth…and a swell of fresh desire into her system that made her legs go weak all over again.

''Good night.'' It didn't matter that her voice was unsteady. What mattered was that she get into her car before her wobbly legs gave out.

''Good night.'' The eyes that had looked so rock-hard in her vision were now the color of smoke. ''I'll see you the day after tomorrow.''

''Yes.'' She was reasonably sure her system would have settled by then.

It wasn't until she pulled the Mustang out of the lot that she released the breath she'd been holding. Whatever trouble Jackson Colton was in, it had brought her to him. Until she knew why, she needed to keep a clear head. Then, when the knowledge came, she would be capable of putting two rational thoughts together. Unlike she had been while wrapped in Jackson's arms.

When she turned onto the winding coast road she flexed her fingers against the steering wheel, pleased that her hands no longer trembled. Her breathing had evened. Finally.

Before this night, only one man had ever rocked her senses and taken her so swiftly toward the edge of control. After she'd given herself to him and told him about her gift, he'd looked at her as if she were crazy. Even now, the memory of the names Paul called her had her blinking back tears.

Holding a part of yourself back wasn't deception, she

reminded herself. It was self-preservation—as she'd learned through hard experience.

With Jackson, she would let fate take her hands and lead her.

And she would hold her secrets close.

Three

———

Jackson knew the drive along the dark coastal highway should have calmed him, helped his thoughts steady. Instead, his mind was as restless as the sea that churned against the ragged cliffs edging the shoreline.

How many women had he kissed? Slept with? He neither knew nor cared. He'd indulged in nights of mutual pleasure, then walked away unscathed. Tonight he and Cheyenne had shared a few kisses, nothing more. They'd been exceptional kisses, but kisses all the same.

Why, then, while he held her in his arms, had he been hit with aching desire when he had expected to feel the usual careless, carefree passion? The memory of her hot, unrestrained mouth pressed against his crept into his mind like a seductive phantom. He wanted her taste again. Wanted to hold her. Wanted her. Just her.

"Dammit."

Something was happening inside him. Because he

wasn't precisely certain what that something was, he felt a tug of worry. He'd always been sure of his ground when it came to the opposite sex, yet he could have sworn he'd felt the earth move beneath his feet when Cheyenne's mouth opened beneath his, inviting him in.

He just needed to get his balance back, he told himself as he steered the Porsche off Highway 1 onto Colton land. After all, his usual afternoon and evening didn't include having the cops accuse him of two attempted murders, then running into—and ravishing—the woman whose testimony could place him in almost the exact spot a wannabe killer had stood during one of those attempts.

No matter how perverse, right now dealing with the dilemma of how to keep his butt out of jail was preferable to trying to figure out what was going on inside him where Cheyenne James was concerned.

In Jackson's mind, the first order of business was to tell his uncle that the cops suspected *he* was the person who'd tried to put a slug into him. Twice.

"Can't wait," he muttered.

Blowing out a breath, he swung the Porsche around a corner. In the distance, the barn, stable and bunkhouses huddled in shadowy outlines against the starry night sky. The neat white-railed fence that lined the two-lane road stood ghostlike beneath the moon's silver glow. Beyond the fence, shadowy trees dotted the hillside pastures. Jackson knew the security cameras his uncle had installed after the second attempt on his life were recording the Porsche's progress along the private road. Monitors had been installed in his uncle's study that displayed the views picked up by the cameras placed in strategic spots across Colton property.

Moments later, Jackson eased to a stop in the drive-

way that curved in front of the sprawling two-story
house painted in soft white with jutting balconies, a
terra-cotta roof and high-columned porch. Colorful lakes
of flowers and shrubs pooled nearby. Swinging open the
car door, he breathed in the salty tang of the ocean that
lay just past the steep face of rough rock bordering the
house's manicured back lawn. The beat of his footsteps
against the driveway mixed with the pounding of the
surf.

Out of the corner of his eye he caught movement at
the right of the porch. An armed security guard nodded
to him, then melted back into the shadows.

Twin carriage lamps on either side of the towering
front door cast overlapping puddles of light onto the
porch. Twisting his key in the lock, Jackson pushed open
the door, closed it behind him, then veered across the
tiled foyer. He paused beneath the arched doorway that
marked the entrance to his uncle's beamed study.

As always, Jackson was struck by the coziness of the
room with its leather sofas and chairs, polished brasses
and thick rugs that spread vibrant color across the wood
floor. The walls were paneled in oak mellowed by time,
housing row after row of shelves lined with leather-
bound books. Across from the stone fireplace in which
flames ate greedily at logs to ward off the cool night air
was a mahogany desk almost as imposing as the man
who sat behind it.

Joe Colton was over six feet of solid muscle with a
linebacker's shoulders and a square-jawed face softened
by kind blue eyes. The gray that had begun peppering
his dark brown hair only a few months before his sixtieth
birthday lent the Colton patriarch a distinguished air.

As a rule, his uncle worked alone in his study after
dinner. Tonight was clearly an exception, Jackson noted.

On the far side of the room, his Aunt Meredith curled like a cat on the leather sofa, her beautiful face framed by the wavy, golden-blond hair that cascaded to her shoulders. As she thumbed idly through a magazine, the diamond broach on the lapel of her sleek black jumpsuit caught the flash of the flames in the fireplace.

Jackson remained in the doorway, his brow furrowed. He remembered other long-ago nights when his aunt and uncle sat in silence together in this room. Then, an unspoken contentment had existed between them. The sense of companionship they had once shared had vanished years ago. Even now, Jackson had a hard time accepting that the woman who'd lavished so much love on him and his sister was the same person he'd confronted weeks ago and warned he would go to the police if she didn't stop blackmailing his father.

As if sensing his presence, Meredith raised her bored gaze from her magazine and glanced toward the doorway. Annoyance flashed in her eyes like lightning, then was instantly replaced by concern.

"Jackson," she said, laying her magazine aside. "Thank goodness."

Joe Colton snapped his gaze from the panel of security monitors installed in the wall near his desk. "Glad you made it back, son," he said, his voice booming across the study.

"Finally," Meredith added as she uncurled off the couch. "We've been worried sick about you."

"Why?"

"*Why?*" Meredith repeated, arching a perfect blond brow. "It's not every day a Colton gets called to police headquarters for questioning."

Jackson winced. "River wasn't supposed to tell you about that phone call."

"River didn't." When Joe leaned back in his leather chair, Jackson noted the shrewd assessment in his uncle's eyes. "Sophie overheard you tell River that the police called and asked you to come to the station. She blurted it out at dinner."

"Good going, cousin," Jackson muttered. When he stepped into the room the scent of leather and wood smoke settled around him.

Meredith flicked a wrist. "Never mind about Sophie, Jackson. We've been worried to death about you."

"Sorry. If I'd known, I would have called."

"You've been gone for hours," she persisted, glancing at her husband. "Joe wouldn't let me phone the station to check on you. He kept saying you're a lawyer and if you needed us, you'd call."

"That's right, I would have."

She took another step toward him. "Have the police been questioning you all this time?"

"No. After I left the station, I went to a movie. Then I..."

With thoughts of Cheyenne crowding in on him, Jackson hesitated. It was impossible to pin down what he thought about her, what he already felt about her. Instinct told him she was capable of igniting a spark in him that he wasn't sure he wanted stirred to life.

"Then you what?" Meredith prodded.

"Stopped and had coffee."

"You saw a movie," Joe said, tilting his head. Jackson knew his uncle was aware of his penchant for losing himself in heavy thought while a movie played on the big screen. "Is everything okay?"

"I handled things." Shrugging, Jackson walked to the desk, slid one hip onto the front edge. "Uncle Joe, there's no easy way to tell you this, so I'm just going to say it. Thad Law thinks it's possible I'm the person who tried to kill you. Both times."

In the silent seconds that followed, Jackson watched the initial shock in his uncle's eyes veer to anger.

"Has the man lost his mind?"

"I didn't get that impress—"

"I don't care if he is married to my foster brother's daughter, he's crazy," Joe protested. "There's no way Law has reason to even look at you. I've got a good mind to call Peter McGrath and tell him his Heather has married a blockhead. Then I'll call Mayor Longstreet and let him know exactly what I think about his police force."

"His police force is doing its job," Jackson countered. "And Law isn't a blockhead. He has what he believes are solid reasons to suspect me."

"What reasons?" Meredith scooted behind the desk to stand beside her husband. "You mean *evidence?* Thad Law claims he has some sort of evidence that proves you're the one who shot at Joe?"

"He doesn't just claim to have evidence," Jackson stated, then told them about the insurance policy on his uncle's life and the years-old court case the detective alluded to.

As Jackson spoke, a log in the fireplace broke apart and fell with a shower of sparks. "At the birthday party," he added, "I was a couple of feet from where the suspect stood only seconds before he or she fired the shot."

"Can someone say they saw you there?" Joe asked. "In that spot?"

"Yes." Jackson thought about the undercurrents that had pulled at him while his mouth ravaged Cheyenne's. Undercurrents, he reminded himself, had a habit of dragging in the unwary. He had spent his life avoiding just that.

"Who?" Meredith asked. "Who told the police they saw you in the same spot as the person who shot at Joe?"

"Actually, I told Law I was near that spot."

His aunt's eyes widened. "*You* told him? Why?"

"Because that's where I happened to be," Jackson said, giving her a mild look. "I'd cut through the service hallway to get a drink refill. I was there when I heard the shot."

Joe shook his head. "Did it occur to Law that hundreds of other people were milling around the house and courtyard that night?"

"I pointed that out. It didn't seem to make a difference."

"The man ought to stop harassing innocent people and find some real evidence." As he spoke, Joe stabbed holes in the air with an index finger. "Like the gun the bastard used to take those shots at me. Find that, and you've got some real proof."

"I agree." Jackson raised a shoulder. "Meanwhile, someone appears to want me as the scapegoat for the shootings. He or she has done one hell of a job of setting me up. I have a real problem with that."

"You're not alone," Joe huffed. "And we're not going to stand for it."

"Of course we're not," Meredith said with a flip of her slender, flame-tipped fingers. "Jackson, pour us all a brandy. Joe, we need to get Jackson the best criminal lawyer money can buy."

Joe's gaze shot up to meet hers, his brow creased in annoyance. "If you're referring to our eldest son, I doubt Rand will send us a bill for services."

"It was just an expression, darling."

Jackson noted the way his aunt's shoulders had gone rigid beneath her black jumpsuit. It was as if he could almost see the wall of tension shoot up between husband and wife.

"I don't need a lawyer." Rising off the front of the desk, Jackson walked to the wet bar built into a small alcove between bookcases. He poured two snifters of brandy, reached for a third glass, then changed his mind. The last time he'd tasted alcohol was two weeks ago at Liza's wedding reception. The one drink he'd had hit him like a ton of cement. He didn't want to chance that happening again, especially now when he needed to keep a clear head.

"At this point, I'm not charged with anything." He crossed the room with the two snifters of brandy. "Yet," he added as he offered a glass to his aunt.

"It might be a good idea for me to call your cousin and put him on notice," Joe said, accepting the snifter Jackson handed him. "Just in case."

"That's not necessary," Jackson said. "Rand has his hands full in D.C. trying criminal cases. Besides, there's nothing for him to do, except tell Law his evidence isn't solid enough to make an arrest. I already delivered the message."

Joe inclined his head Jackson's way. "If you don't feel like brandy, I can have Inez bring in coffee," he said, referring to the longtime housekeeper.

"No thanks."

"Bam! Bam!" The shouted words echoed off the high ceiling just outside the study. "You're gut-shot, slime-ball!"

Meredith rolled her eyes, then looked at Joe. "Those boys were supposed to be in bed an hour ago."

Joe's mouth curved. "Sounds like another war interrupted their sleep. Joe! Teddy!" he said in a booming voice. "Get in here now!"

Seconds later, two barefoot boys clad in camouflage pajamas and toting toy rifles skidded through the door side-by-side.

"Yes, sir?" they asked in unison.

Joe sent a stern look across the desk. "Your mother informs me you were supposed to be in bed an hour ago."

"Aw, Dad, we just needed to see who wins the war," Joe, Jr. said, his sandy brown hair looking as if it had been combed by a hurricane.

Jackson held back a smile. Nearly ten years ago, Joe, Jr. had been abandoned on the Coltons' front porch. His uncle and aunt had taken in the infant and raised him as their own. As far as everyone was concerned, the kid was one hundred percent Colton.

"Yeah, and I'm about to win," Teddy boasted.

Joe, Jr.'s gaze swung sideways, his green eyes flashing. "It's not over till it's over, as Mama always says," he commented, then gave his mother a knowing grin.

"I'm glad someone around here listens to me," Meredith murmured, then checked her slim gold-and-diamond watch. "All right, you two, pay attention. The war must be won in five minutes or this general is calling a draw."

"Yes, ma'am," Teddy replied, giving her a military-precise salute. Shifting his gaze, the boy flashed Jackson a grin. "Hi ya, cousin."

"General Colton," Jackson replied mildly. "It appears the war is going well for you."

"Yeah, I'm winning."

"Are not!"

Jackson had known for three weeks that Teddy was the product of a one-night stand between his father and his aunt. Still, Jackson couldn't quite get used to the idea that the mischievous eight-year-old standing before him with tousled blond hair and sparkling blue eyes was his half brother.

The thought had Jackson glancing at his uncle in time to see Joe beam at both boys as they raced out of the study, their bare feet slapping against the wood floor.

Years ago a bout of mumps had rendered his uncle sterile. What had it done to him, Jackson wondered, when he found out Meredith had been unfaithful? That she'd conceived another man's child? What inner strength did Joe Colton possess that had compelled him to continue his marriage with Meredith and raise Teddy as his own son?

And what, Jackson wondered as a fist knotted in his gut, would the family patriarch do if he ever found out his brother, Graham, was the boy's father?

"I'd better make sure our troops brush their teeth," Meredith said. Setting her snifter on the desk, she met Jackson's gaze. "I'm sorry to hear about your problems with the police, Jackson. No one should have to endure something like that."

He slid a hand into the pocket of his khakis. It didn't take a genius to figure out she was referring to his promise to turn her in to the cops if she didn't stop blackmailing his father.

"Not when they haven't done anything wrong," he commented. "I'll get it resolved, Aunt Meredith. One way or the other."

"I'm sure you will." She dropped a kiss on top of her husband's head, then walked toward the door, her grace perfect in her black spiked heels.

Remaining silent, Jackson watched his uncle's expression while his gaze tracked his wife out the door. He felt a twist of sorrow at the dull resignation that clouded the man's eyes.

"Well," Joe said after a moment as he leaned back in his chair and swirled the brandy in his glass. "I figure while you sat through that movie you came up with a plan on how to deal with this mess?"

"The start of one." Jackson dropped into one of the leather visitor chairs in front of the desk and stretched out his long legs. "First thing in the morning I'll call Adam Jones at Amalgamated. I want to know if someone's been asking questions lately about the lawsuit I filed for him against his father. If so, I want to know who that person is."

"Good. After that?"

"I need to go to L.A. I plan to pay a visit to the insurance agent who's ready to swear I was the one who took out the policy on your life. It wasn't me, and I'm hoping his seeing me in person will convince him he's wrong."

"Take the corporate jet."

"I planned on hopping a commuter."

"Nonsense." Joe sent a wry smile over the rim of his snifter. "I'm not only your uncle, son, I'm your boss."

"Who's talking to an employee taking a leave of absence to decide if he wants to continue in his job."

"You're a fine lawyer, Jackson, and I'm proud you're a part of Colton Enterprises. But if it's not a job you can put your heart into, you'll never be happy." Joe shrugged. "Until or unless something changes, you work for me and I'm ordering you to take the corporate jet tomorrow. Is your mother in L.A. these days?"

Jackson frowned. "Last I heard." His parents had always maintained an arrangement that suited them. Graham lived near Jackson in San Diego; Cynthia Colton, a high-powered entertainment attorney, kept an office and condo in L.A. Throughout their marriage they had led their lives, together and separately. Mostly separately.

"If Cynthia's there, take some extra time if you want and drop by to see her."

Jackson thought about the impersonal air kiss and polite "how are you?" he'd received when his mother arrived at Hacienda de Alegria for his sister's wedding. That had been the first time he'd seen her in nearly a year. He didn't see a point in stopping by her office for another token kiss and disinterested greeting.

"I'll take the jet, Uncle Joe. Thanks."

"No need to thank me, son. We're family. Family sticks together."

"Yeah." Jackson rubbed at the muscles knotted in the back of his neck while his gaze drifted to one of the bookshelves where picture frames and books vied for space. A woman with a wavy mane of chestnut hair and dimples smiled out from a pewter frame. Emily Blair Colton, the youngest of Joe and Meredith's daughters, adopted as a toddler, had disappeared months ago in what had initially been thought of as a kidnapping. After receiving a ransom note, Joe had paid a heart-stopping amount of money for Emily's return. Days later, Joe had informed the family that he'd heard from a trusted source that his adopted daughter had fled Prosperino after an intruder tried to kill her. All Joe would tell anyone was that Emily was safe. If he knew her whereabouts, he wasn't saying. The FBI was still trying to get a lead on the person who had sent the fake ransom note and collected the money.

"Uncle Joe, I'm sorry to bring my problems to your doorstep," Jackson said quietly. "You've got enough to worry about with someone taking potshots at you and all that's happened to Emily."

"I'd have been hurt and insulted if you hadn't brought your problems to me." Joe ran a hand through his thick hair. "I want Emily home. More important, I want her safe."

"We all want that."

"Everyone, except the person who tried to kill her."

"True."

Joe plucked a brass paperweight shaped like an oil rig off his desk blotter. "Emmett Fallon gave this to me when the first wildcat well we dug in Wyoming came in," he said, hefting the paperweight in his palm. "Back then, I was young, headstrong and arrogant enough to think nothing bad could happen to myself and the people I cared about." Sighing, Joe resettled the paperweight on the blotter. "These past ten years, life has proved me wrong."

The look of genuine sorrow in his uncle's face prompted Jackson to veer the subject in a different direction. "Speaking of Emmett, I ran into a woman tonight who works for his son, Blake, at Hopechest Ranch."

"Who?"

"Cheyenne James."

"River's little sister," Joe said, his face instantly brightening. "I used to pick her up from the reservation and bring her to stay here on the weekends. She was so shy, she barely spoke to me. Would hardly even look at me. Years went by and I didn't see her. When she walked up to me at my birthday party and introduced herself, you could have knocked me over with a fingertip. She's a beautiful woman. Took my breath away just looking at her.''

"Yes," Jackson agreed quietly.

Joe stared down into his drink, his brow furrowing. "Later at the party, I saw the two of you talking. I remember thinking I wasn't surprised, seeing as how you'd never been one to bypass a gorgeous woman. That wasn't too long before all hell broke loose." Joe's gaze rose slowly to meet Jackson's. "Is Cheyenne the one who saw you a couple of feet from where the person who shot at me stood?"

"Yes. Although I doubt she's aware of the suspect's location."

"Did you tell her the police questioned you?"

"No." Jackson raised a shoulder. "Maybe I will."

Joe's mouth curved. "So, you plan to see her again?"

"We're having breakfast the day after tomorrow."

"Can't say that surprises me. Like I said, I've never known you to let a beautiful woman get away."

He'd let Cheyenne get away once, Jackson acknowledged silently. Then spent months with thoughts of her chasing through his brain. No other woman had ever had that effect on him, ever captured his thoughts for so long. Maybe that was why—until his sister's wedding—he'd made only one short visit to Prosperino. Maybe somewhere in his subconscious he'd known if he had stayed in Prosperino for any length of time, he would seek out Cheyenne. And maybe, just maybe, he harbored a small lick of fear that she was the one woman he couldn't walk away from unscathed.

So, he'd avoided her. Successfully. Until tonight when he walked out of a dark movie theater and found her in the lobby. It was as if she'd been waiting for him. Just him.

Dammit, he could still taste her. And he wanted to taste her again. Soon.

Jackson let out a long breath. What in the hell was he going to do about Cheyenne James?

Patsy had watched the climactic end of Joe, Jr. and Teddy's war game, then kept a sharp eye on both boys while they brushed their teeth. After that, she'd herded them into their separate bedrooms in the north wing and kissed them good-night, leaving them both with a prediction of dire consequences if they didn't stay in bed this time.

Now, an hour later, dressed in a robe of shimmering white silk, she stood in her dark bedroom before the expansive wall of windows that faced the sea. The moon was full and high, cutting a swath of light across the black water.

"What do you mean you're going underground?" Patsy hissed into the cell phone she'd crammed between her shoulder and cheek. She wasn't concerned over the prospect of Joe walking in during her phone call. He hadn't stepped foot into her bedroom in years. "I'm paying you to kill Emily Colton, not lay low while she disappears again," she added.

"Look, the sheriff in this fleabag town—Atkins is his name—has his men working overtime trying to find the bitch's attacker," Silas Pike answered. "I show my face in Keyhole, Wyoming, I'm dead meat."

"What you are is incompetent. I hired you to *kill* Emily in her bed, in this house. You screwed that up and let her get away. Then, you chased her across the country for heaven knows how many months. By some miracle of God you stumble on her whereabouts, attack her, yet still can't manage to kill her. Now, you expect me to continue to *pay* you while you hole up somewhere for who knows how long?''

"Ain't gonna be *that* long," Pike countered. "Just long enough for that sheriff to figure some dude just passing through town is who jumped her. Once that happens, I'll go back for her."

"And fumble things again."

"And kill the bitch. You don't want to pay me to lay low for a while then finish her off, just say the word and I'll go home. Makes no never mind to me."

Patsy closed her eyes, blocking out the moonlight that shimmered on the dark water.

Dammit, was she the only person who could do anything right?

Silas Pike couldn't kill Emily, the private investigator she'd hired to track down her twin sister Meredith had run into a dead end, and the other investigator hadn't been able to locate her sweet baby, Jewel. No, Patsy corrected herself. Not a baby. Jewel was a grown woman now. It had been so long, she thought. So many years since she'd held her darling daughter.

"You still there?"

Pike's voice set Patsy's teeth on edge. Joe Colton had her on such a tight budget she couldn't afford to hire anyone else to find Emily. She didn't have *time* to hire anyone else. It was as if a force had been set in motion that she couldn't control. She could feel all of her carefully laid plans coming apart, slowly, thread by thread, yet she couldn't seem to pull them all back into place.

"I'm still here." She kept her voice calm and even. "I'll wire you more money in the morning. I warn you, Pike, I'm tired of paying for nothing. I want results, positive results. *Soon,*" she added, then clicked off the phone and dropped it on the French directoire reading table that sat to one side of the windows.

All of her senses screamed it was a matter of time before the police closed in on her. Meredith was her sister, her *twin.* If she'd died years ago a homeless vagrant like the P.I. had tried to convince her, Patsy would *feel* it. Bitter regret flooded over her. If only she had gone through with her initial plan and killed Meredith on that long-ago day when she'd run her sister's car off the road and assumed her identity. If only seeing the mirror image of herself after so long hadn't stirred some emotion deep inside her.

Instead, when Meredith came to and Patsy realized a blow to her head during the accident had left her with amnesia, she'd dumped her twin on the grounds of the clinic where Patsy had finished the twenty-five year sentence she'd served for murder. Where the hell had Meredith gone after she'd left the clinic? Patsy wondered for the thousandth time. And how long would it be before Emily, who had been in the car with Meredith on that fateful day remembered what she'd witnessed?

Emily had been a child then. Now, she was a woman whose nightmares about seeing her "two mommies" right after the accident had intensified over the years. Months ago, Patsy had heard Emily sobbing for her real mother during a nightmare. Patsy had jolted into action, knowing it was inevitable Emily would soon realize the truth of what she'd seen.

And eventually share that truth with the police. As far as Patsy was concerned, that nightmare had sealed Emily's fate.

Patsy dragged in a shaky breath. All Thad Law had to do to discover her deception was run her fingerprints. He would then know she wasn't Meredith, but the twin sister who'd served time for murdering the man who'd fathered—and sold—their daughter, Jewel. And that, for the past ten years, Patsy Portman had deceived the entire Colton clan.

Patsy suspected the clout carried by the Colton name was why Law had yet to request her fingerprints. He had to know she wouldn't have consented willingly to being fingerprinted. And it was doubtful any judge in the state would force her to do so. Still, Law wasn't the type of cop who gave up.

With unsteady hands, she snatched the gold pill case off the table beside her, popped open the lid and scooped up two Valium. She lifted a crystal tumbler full of vodka, and washed down the Valium with one deep swallow. She'd been a fool for not killing both Meredith and Emily that day, Patsy chided herself viciously, slamming the pill case back on the table. If she had, maybe she wouldn't now feel the sickening sensation that they were both getting closer. So close she could almost feel them breathing down her neck.

More money, she thought, fighting back a wave of panic. She needed more money in case she had to leave Prosperino in a hurry. She couldn't support Joe, Jr. and Teddy by herself.

Her eyes narrowed as her thoughts focused on Jackson Colton. He'd been so damn cool and forthright when he'd confronted her about blackmailing his father. Even as Jackson assured her he would go to the police if her extortion didn't end, she had seen a flash of regret in his eyes. It was as if he couldn't believe his Aunt Meredith had stooped so low.

Meredith, who had refused to cover for her own sister when Patsy had killed Jewel's father in a fit of rage. Meredith, who'd been too good to lie to the cops. Instead, she'd let her twin rot in prison for twenty-five years.

Patsy wrapped her arms around her waist, hugging the silk robe closer to her flesh. She would show Jackson Colton just how low she could stoop when she went after what was owed her. His father, Graham, had sniffed around her for years trying to bed her before she'd given him what he wanted. Now she intended to see that he continued to pay her the money he'd agreed to.

She had no doubt that, with his son cooling his heels in prison, Graham would continue making the payments she'd demanded. He would most likely do anything to keep her from telling Joe that his brother had sired Teddy. After all, the two million Graham had agreed to pay for her silence was peanuts compared to what he would lose if Joe wrote him out of his will.

"Evidence," she said, her voice a whisper on the still, night air. The evidence she'd already collected and sent anonymously to Thad Law had clearly caused Jackson some bad moments this afternoon.

She intended to cause him a lot more.

Gone momentarily was the feeling of impending doom that had dogged her for months. Having a good, solid plan—along with the Valium and alcohol that had just begun creeping into her system—calmed her nerves.

She smiled as she pictured the scene earlier in the study when Joe stabbed the air with his finger while he pronounced, *"Like the gun the bastard used to take those shots at me. Find that, and you've got some real proof."*

"No problem," Patsy murmured.

She had the proof. It was a matter of time before she could deliver it to the police.

Then she would have Jackson out of her way and his father's money would start flowing back in.

Four

The May morning was bright and clear, with the hills sporting color so bold and vivid that Cheyenne had shoved on her sunglasses the instant she walked out of her house. Now she stood in the center of the small archery range near a rushing stream that cut a jagged path across Hopechest Ranch.

"Stance is everything," she reminded the tall skinny-as-a-rail teenager standing a yard away. At her side was a high table fashioned out of native stone on which she'd laid the bows and the quiver filled with arrows that she'd picked up from the counseling center on her way to the range.

"Yeah, stance." Johnny Collins gave her an intense look across his shoulder. Repositioning his right foot a half inch, he raised a bow formed out of a curve of polished hickory. Dressed in faded jeans, a white T-shirt and ball cap swiveled backward to keep his dark shaggy hair out of his eyes, Johnny was beginning his second month of lessons.

The kid showed promise.

Cheyenne knew Johnny's growing skill as an archer coincided with an increase in the self-confidence that had eroded after his mother abandoned the family. His father started drinking and got fired from his job. Earlier that year, the fourteen-year-old boy had lied about his age to get hired at a fast-food restaurant. Days later, he had been caught stealing money out of the register. When a social worker discovered he'd taken the money to buy food for him and his father, she arranged for Johnny's stay at Hopechest Ranch.

Since then, several counselors and volunteers had worked with Johnny to increase his reading and math skills. Thanks to Drake Colton, he'd learned to ride and take responsibility for a horse's care. Cheyenne knew that with a lot of hard work and equal luck, Johnny Collins's life might turn around.

As hers had when she'd come to Hopechest.

Even though she worked there as a counselor, the ranch provided as much a sanctuary for her as for the young children and teens who wound up there through the efforts of various social workers, cops and the courts. Established by the Hopechest Foundation on vast acres of prime real estate a few miles outside of Prosperino, the ranch sometimes represented the only stable environment some of its occupants had ever known. To others, who associated home and family with physical or emotional abuse or both, Hopechest stood as a safe haven where no one had cause to cower, scared and alone.

Growing up, Cheyenne had sometimes done just that.

Although her mother's people had raised her with love and a deep understanding of the legacy she'd inherited from the woman she had no memory of, Cheyenne had sensed early that her father had sent her away because she was different. How different became apparent at the first Anglo school she'd attended when she tugged on her teacher's sleeve one sunny morning and predicted an accident would happen on the playground. When the teacher dismissed the warning and the event Cheyenne had seen so vividly in her mind's eye occurred moments later, her classmates had begun taunting her, calling her Princess Voodoo and She-Who-Knows-It-All.

Her most intense memories of that school year were of the hours she'd spent cowering at a desk in the back of the classroom, wishing desperately she were like everyone else.

Over time, she had grown accustomed to being different. She learned the value of using discretion with outsiders, understood that the only people she could trust were those of her mother's blood who accepted and revered her gift of sight. Only once since that day on the playground had she misjudged. During her final year of college she had fallen in love with Paul Porter, a man she had trusted with her heart and her secrets. Like her father, Paul could not deal with the fact she was different, and wanted no part of her after she'd told him about her heritage. So, he'd walked away, leaving her to deal with a raging, tearing hurt. In the year she'd been at Hopechest, her battered heart had healed and she'd settled into a content, safe existence.

Until the night before last when she'd stepped into Jackson Colton's arms. Even now, while she watched her student fit an arrow's nock into the bowstring then slowly draw it back until his right hand came even with the side of his mouth, Cheyenne felt a frisson of need stir deep inside her. A need she knew well she could not risk feeling.

So, she wouldn't risk. After all, she and Jackson had shared only a couple of kisses in a dimly lit parking lot. Nothing more. Just because she'd allowed her control to slip for a few mind-numbing minutes didn't mean she would ever again try to crawl up the man's chest.

The thought of the blatant way she'd opened her mouth in invitation, of how her body had melted against his put a heated flush into her cheeks that had nothing to do with the warmth of the morning sun that slanted across her face.

She knew next to nothing about the man.

Granted, she knew a lot about his family—her brother had married Sophie Colton—but Cheyenne had no clue what kind of man Jackson was. And there she'd stood, making out with him in a parking lot for God and everyone to see!

Behind the dark lenses of her glasses, Cheyenne narrowed her eyes. Sophie had once mentioned that Jackson had broken an ample number of hearts after he'd graduated from law school and moved to San Diego to work in the law offices of Colton Enterprises. Cheyenne didn't doubt it. With his arresting good looks and charmer's grin—and the talent to kiss a woman until her bones melted—Jackson was a man countless women would be drawn to.

Just because she was drawn to him didn't mean she had to act on that attraction. She had no intention of winding up on the list of another man's spoils.

If it had been anything other than fate that had brought them together, she would have phoned Jackson and canceled this morning's breakfast plans. Only her deep understanding of the responsibilities that went hand in hand with her gift had prevented her from making the call. The vision that had slid inside her head and sent her to the Cinema Prosperino had told her the man she would meet there was in trouble. That he needed her help. She could not turn her back on Jackson any more than she could reject her gift.

So, she would deal with her responsibilities. This morning she and Jackson would share a civilized meal. Eventually she would know why the vision had sent her to him. She could then act accordingly, do what was in her power to help him.

After that, she would settle back into her calm world with her secrets safe and her heart intact.

"How's that?" Johnny asked.

Feeling a tug of guilt, Cheyenne forced her thoughts back to her pupil. Taking a step forward, she focused her gaze on one of the straw-filled targets positioned on an easel in the distance.

"I'd say three arrows a quarter inch from a target's bull's-eye is a great way to end today's session," she said, her mouth curving. "I'd like you to compete on my team at the Memorial Day competitions," she said, referring to the county-wide event Hopechest Ranch sponsored each year. "If that's what you'd like to do."

Wariness slid into Johnny's eyes as he laid the bow on the stone table beside her. Even now he didn't quite believe in his ability.

"Maybe I could do that. No big deal." Lowering his gaze, he began unhooking the elastic straps of the leather guard that covered the inside of his right arm.

"It is a big deal, Johnny." While she spoke, Cheyenne pointed a finger toward the target. "See those three arrows a hair away from the bull's-eye?"

After a moment, the teenager's gaze followed hers. "What about 'em?"

"*You* put them there. And if you think I ask all my students to be on my team, think again. You've got a real talent for this sport. You can be as good an archer as you make up your mind to be."

"The audience thinks that, too."

At the sound of Jackson's voice so close behind her, Cheyenne nearly gasped. The rush of the nearby stream had prevented her from hearing his approach. Taking a deep breath that did nothing to settle her pulse, she turned to face him.

One glimpse of the grin on his tanned, rugged face—and those incredible gray eyes—made her knees weak.

"I...didn't know you were here." He wore crisply starched jeans and a blue polo shirt opened at the neck to expose dark curling hair. The thought of swirling a fingertip through that hair had her shoving her sunglasses higher up the bridge of her nose. "You didn't need to come all the way out here to find me. I'd have met you at the dining hall."

"I ran into Blake Fallon out repairing fence. He told me I could find you here."

"The boss is working on the fence line?" she asked.

"Not just the fence. One of the regular ranch hands is down with a stomach virus, another has a broken arm. With Memorial Day less than a week away, repairs can't wait." Jackson angled his chin while his gaze did a slow slide down her body. "I let Blake coerce me into helping him and his dad repair hail damage to the horse barn's roof after you and I finish breakfast. You look great," he added quietly.

She felt her flesh heat beneath her khaki shorts and

red T-shirt monogrammed with the Hopechest Ranch brand.

Clearing her throat, she nodded toward her student. "Jackson Colton, this is Johnny Collins."

"Great shooting," Jackson said, extending his hand.

"Thanks," the teenager muttered, returning the handshake.

Cheyenne looked back at Jackson. "While your cousin, Drake, was home on leave, he taught Johnny to ride."

"Is that so?" Jackson asked. "Can the tough Navy SEAL ride a horse these days without getting tossed off onto his butt?"

"Yeah. He gave me some good tips."

Nodding, Jackson narrowed his eyes. "Are you the Johnny who Teddy and Joe, Jr. keep harping about? The one they say can rope almost anything?"

Johnny raised a shoulder. "Drake gave the three of us some lessons. I can sometimes get a rope around stuff."

"Like you can sometimes put an arrow into the center of a target," Cheyenne commented, then glanced at her watch. She knew Johnny had a reading lesson in less than an hour. "Go ahead and head for breakfast. I'll take care of stowing the equipment."

"Okay." Sticking his thumbs in the front pockets of his jeans, the teenager turned and headed up the dirt trail that led to the dorms and dining hall.

"Seems like a nice kid," Jackson commented.

"He is." Cheyenne watched until Johnny's gangly, stoop-shouldered form disappeared from sight. "No one ever believed in him, so it's no surprise he has a hard time believing in himself. He still has trouble accepting the fact he can accomplish something worthwhile."

Jackson cocked his head. "Was what I just witnessed an archery lesson or a counseling session?"

"A little of both. With kids, you can only sit so long in an office and talk. You have to *do* something. Show them there's a way to deal with their problems, even sometimes solve them."

"So, you use archery to build Johnny's self-esteem."

"Archery, riding and roping lessons and other skills along those lines. Like all the kids at Hopechest, he has daily chores to do, too. Everything is geared to teach them a sense of responsibility, accomplishment and self-worth."

"From what I saw this morning, things appear to be working for Johnny."

"I hope so. I hate to think about what might have happened to him if a social worker hadn't referred him to Hopechest."

Jackson's gray eyes measured her for a silent moment. "Your job makes a difference. That must be a nice feeling."

"It is." She thought of how his father had groomed him to be an attorney, that one of the reasons he was staying in Prosperino was to decide if he wanted to continue his work as a lawyer. Her brow furrowed. Did the aura of trouble she had sensed so strongly in her vision stem from his uncertainty over his career? Or was it something unconnected?

The thought had her angling her head. "How was your trip yesterday to L.A.?"

"A waste of time." His eyes narrowed as he shifted his gaze to the table. "So, these are the tools of an archer's trade."

His change of subject had her hesitating. Clearly, he didn't want to discuss his trip. "Some of them," she said after a moment. "I use other types of bows, depending on a student's progress and strength."

When he slicked a fingertip along the curve of the bow Johnny had used, Cheyenne felt her stomach turn over. Two nights ago, Jackson had brushed that exact fingertip down the length of her cheek just moments before he'd kissed her.

"What type is this?"

She blinked against the memory. "What?"

"The bow. What type is it?" The slow smile he gave her just about stopped her breath. "Since there's an expert handy, I might as well learn something about archery."

"Sure." Struggling to pick up the thread of the conversation, she lifted the bow off the table. "This is called a recurve."

Jackson regarded the bow's curved ends. "Looks like Cupid's weapon of choice."

"Exactly. Have you ever used a bow and arrow?"

"Sure, when I was a kid, playing cowboys and Indians with my cousins, Rand and Drake. Even your boss sometimes joined us. Our arrows had rubber suction cups on the ends, which was a good thing since Drake's aim was deadly."

Cheyenne smiled at the image. "Real archery is a little different."

"It appears so." Pursing his lips, Jackson slid one of the arrows from the quiver then tested its sharp metal point with a fingertip. His gaze slowly raised to meet hers. "You any good, teach?"

She lifted her brow. "Extremely."

Taking a step toward her, he offered the arrow. "How about giving me my first archery lesson?"

"My pleasure." As she accepted the arrow, the warm

breeze stirred, bringing his remembered subtle scent into her lungs. She took a deep breath to calm her jittery nerves, stepped away then turned toward the row of distant targets.

"Archery begins with the feet," she commented evenly. If she approached this as teacher to pupil, she might manage to keep her mind focused.

"The feet?"

"A stable stance is the foundation for a good shot," she explained. "If you get into the same position each time you shoot, you'll be more consistent."

"Makes sense." His voice was smooth as silk on the warm morning air.

"It's a matter of concentration," she said for her own benefit as much as his. "You have to concentrate on what you're doing."

With the ease of long practice, she shifted into position, the wind picking up strands from her loose braid as she moved. The rush of the stream faded from her consciousness while the target she'd chosen filled her vision. Slowly, she slotted the arrow's nock into the bowstring, drew back the string, sighted, then released the arrow with a smooth roll off her fingertips. The arrow zinged through the air, impaling neatly into the target's bull's-eye.

Jackson let out a low whistle. "I'm impressed, Miss James. Mind if I try?"

She slid him a look. "What about breakfast? And roof repair?"

"On the agenda, too."

"Fine." She handed him the bow and arrow then shifted behind him. In a gesture that came automatically with teaching, she reached around him, guiding his arms into position.

"The bow should be held about forty-five degrees above the horizon," she said across his shoulder as she used her fingertips to nudge up his right elbow.

"Hmm."

"Place the arrow's nock, or notch, on the bowstring then draw the string back slowly." She stepped in closer so they could move as one while he pulled the string taut. It wasn't until her breasts were pressed against his back and her hips against his that she realized what she'd done.

Her eyes went wide; the lesson suddenly lost its importance as her blood heated in instant response. Her pulse picked up speed. The gilded sunlight was suddenly too hot, her throat abruptly too dry.

"What's next?" he asked softly.

"Release it. Just release it." Her spine as taut as the bow's string, she skittered back two steps as if she'd been scalded.

At the same instant, Jackson took the shot. Cheyenne watched the arrow slice the air then disappear into the stand of redwoods that edged the range.

"Missed." He turned, took a step toward her. She saw desire in his eyes—a reckless desire that had her heart thudding painfully. "Guess that's what you meant about concentration. I think both pupil and teacher had their minds on something else."

"I...guess so." She retreated two more steps, halting when the stone table jabbed into the small of her back.

Keeping his gaze locked with hers, he moved to where she stood. Reaching around her, he laid the bow on the table. "What are we going to do about this, Cheyenne?"

She closed her eyes. She'd never known her name could sound like that—soft and smooth and vaguely exotic.

"You should try another shot," she said almost desperately. Only moments before she had resolved that nothing physical would again happen between them. So, how had she come to be backed against the table, his body brushing hers, his mouth so close, so temptingly close, that she could all but taste it?

"You need to concentrate this time," she managed to add in a hoarse whisper.

"I did." Reaching out, he slid off her sunglasses, laid them beside the bow. He trailed his fingers down her cheek to her chin, along her jaw, then down to where the pulse in her throat beat hard and erratic. "I concentrated on the woman who had her body pressed against mine."

"I'm sorry. I...shouldn't have done that. I didn't think—"

"I've thought." He drew her into his arms, touching his lips to hers. "For two nights and a day I've thought about the way you look. The way you smell, taste. The way you feel, pressed against me," he murmured, then quick as lightning, he deepened the kiss.

The jolt, the heat, the yearning all melded together to swim in her head, through her whole body. As she whirled quickly into passion, she forgot to think about her resolve to protect her secrets, to keep him at arm's length. How much easier it was to move into him, to press close and let all of her caution slide away.

Her heart pounded a primitive beat through her blood. Her palms slid up his arms; she felt the power in the smooth, muscled contours of his shoulders before she linked her fingers behind his neck.

His hands dove into her hair, loosening her braid as he arched her head farther back. His mouth moved from hers to ravage her throat. Against her belly she felt his hard arousal.

Somewhere deep inside her, enough sanity remained that she knew she should pull back, step away before she was lost.

The wild ruthless kisses that raced across her flesh only made her crave more.

One of his hands cupped her breast, kneading, tormenting. "I want you." His mouth moved against her throat, coaxing, enticing, relentless. "Now. Let me have you now."

She had heard those same words in another lifetime, had succumbed to the hot, aching desire. She had learned the hard way that the depth and suddenness of passion held its own special danger. That she was opening herself to emotions she'd learned to lock out had reason breaking through the smothering desire with sharp clarity.

"No." Even to her own ears, her voice sounded thin and far-off. "Jackson, no."

"All right." His voice was steel, with rough edges as his arms slid around her waist. He rested his forehead against hers. "You're not ready."

"We should..." How could a man's lips grind her mind to mush so quickly? "We should..."

"Acknowledge the chemistry between us, then decide how far we want this to go?" he suggested, gazing down at her with eyes that had gone the color of smoke.

"No farther."

"Cheyenne—"

"I don't know you," she blurted even as the fire he'd kindled inside her blazed red hot. "I don't even know you. You don't know me."

"I know how I feel."

"It's all physical—"

"Damn right it is."

"Emotions." She pressed her palms against his chest. "They cloud your judgment, make you do things you wouldn't normally do. I don't trust emotions, Jackson."

His eyes focused on her face, narrowed. "And you don't trust me."

"I don't *know* you." She took an unsteady step back, forcing him to drop his arms. "In college, I got involved with a man I thought I knew. Turns out, he wasn't anything like I'd imagined."

A crease formed between Jackson's dark brows. "I take it you were in love with him."

"Completely. Totally." She pressed a shaking hand to her throat. "When we met I didn't *think,* didn't take time to get to know him. I went with my emotions and jumped into the relationship. He…didn't share my feelings. When he walked away I felt as if I'd taken a flying leap off a cliff and landed on jagged rocks. I don't ever want to feel that way again."

"I don't plan to hurt you, Cheyenne."

"Neither did he. It happened anyway."

Blowing out a breath, Jackson nodded. "So, we cool things off and take some time to get to know each other. Is that what you want?"

"Our getting to know each other might not change anything." She looked away, staring down the length of the empty range while she willed herself to ignore the sharp twinge of regret that settled in her chest. "I like my life. I'm content. I don't know if I *want* anything to change."

Reaching out, he took her chin in his hand, forced her gaze back to his. "Wanting something and getting it are two different things."

"Sometimes."

"Most of the time." He tightened his grip when she tried to pull away. "Let me tell you what I want, Cheyenne. I want to get you out of my head. I've tried like hell to do that for two nights and a day," he continued, his intense gaze locked with hers. "Nothing I've done has worked. That's never happened before with any other woman and I can't say I like the feeling. But the fact is, it's there. My entire life I've made a point to avoid any kind of serious relationship. I don't like what they do to people." As he spoke, his fingers gentled on her chin. "Despite that, I find myself wanting something with you. I'm not sure what that something is."

"I…" She had to press her lips together to stop their trembling.

"You want me to keep my hands off you?" he continued. "Fine, I'll deal with that," he said before releasing her chin. "All I'm asking is to spend time with you. Just some time so we can get to know each other. Figure out where we go from here. If anywhere."

She swallowed around the lump in her throat. With her senses still clouded by desire, she told herself there was no way she could be sure what she thought, what she wanted. *Him,* her traitorous heart whispered before she could steel her resolve.

In the space of the next dozen heartbeats, a brilliant burst of color flashed before her eyes, bringing with it an image of her and Jackson lying naked together, sweat slicking their flesh as candlelight flickered softly. Lovers. Her nerves vibrated even as the vision vanished like a ghost.

She understood now that what they had begun would not be broken. They were destined to be lovers. And she had no clue if that was what she wanted.

It was to be, she reminded herself. Her heritage had taught her she couldn't change destiny any more than she could hold back her visions.

Accepting fate, she lifted her gaze to meet his waiting one. "All right, Jackson. I'll give us some time to get to know each other."

Hours later, Jackson still wasn't sure how he was going to manage to keep his hands off Cheyenne.

He would figure out a way, he assured himself, using his forearm to swipe sweat out of his eyes while he knelt on the roof of Hopechest Ranch's towering horse barn. Overhead, the late afternoon sun beat down with blazing intensity. Waves of heat rose off the cut sheets of metal he'd used to patch hail damage to the structure's roof. Earlier he'd sweated through his shirt and stripped it off. Now he could feel the beginnings of a sunburn across the back of his neck and shoulders, but he didn't give the discomfort much thought.

He was thinking about Cheyenne. About what had happened between them that morning on the archery range.

Dammit, he'd been close to getting on his knees and pleading his case. Would have done just that, if that had been what it took to get her to agree to continue seeing him. He shook his head. Never before had he begged a woman for anything, and he wasn't comfortable with the knowledge he'd been close to that point.

Ready to beg, just so a woman he barely knew would spend time with him!

He thought without smugness of the females who regularly tossed offers at him to join them in bed. He sure as hell didn't have to beg any of them to spend time with him.

He narrowed his eyes behind the sunglasses that fought a losing battle against the sun's glare. The problem was, he didn't want to spend time with just *any* woman. He wanted Cheyenne James.

The instant edge of desire that had hit him this morning when she pressed her body against his had been so sharp, so blinding that it had made him wonder if there was some outside force that had jumbled his system so thoroughly.

No, he told himself as he hammered a nail through metal into the roof's wood frame. He couldn't blame his reaction on some outside force. Whatever change had occurred had taken place inside of him, he needed to accept that. Just as he'd finally accepted the fact he wasn't going to get the woman out of his head.

So, he had talked her into taking time to get to know him. And he would keep his hands off her. Somehow.

He dug nails out of the tool belt strapped to his waist, clamped them between his teeth. Laying another piece of metal over a sizable hail dent, he positioned a nail, swung his hammer.

That Cheyenne might not give him the chance to touch her again was a thought that hummed in his mind like an unrelenting gnat. He wasn't a man who in good conscience could let her walk deeper into any kind of a relationship with him without knowing how things stood. During the hours he'd toiled beneath the sun's searing rays he had made the decision to knock on her front door and lay everything on the table the minute he climbed down off the barn's roof. What happened after that was up to her.

Once she knew the cops had questioned him about the two attempts on his uncle's life—and considered him a suspect—she might tell him to get lost.

A fist tightened in his chest. Not until his trip yesterday to L.A. had he realized to what lengths someone had gone to frame him. He had no idea what other bombs sat quietly ticking in the murky shadows, but he suspected there were more. And that they were timed to go off at planned intervals.

As a lawyer, he knew how bad things already looked. Knew his situation would get even worse if the police questioned Cheyenne. Jackson was certain Thad Law would get around to doing that since the cop had given him the impression he was re-interviewing all those who'd attended Joe Colton's birthday party. It wasn't hard to envision the gleam that would settle in Law's eyes when Cheyenne told him she'd seen his prime suspect drop out of sight in almost the same location where, moments later, the person who'd taken a shot at the Colton patriarch had stood.

The anger Jackson had held in since the previous day strained at his control. Dammit, he was innocent—it shouldn't matter what Cheyenne told the cops. Just because he was at a certain place at a certain time didn't mean he was guilty. Still, add that to the insurance policy he'd supposedly purchased on his uncle's life and his knowledge of how to unseat an inept CEO in order for a son to take over a company and its assets, and the pile of circumstantial evidence against him took on an impressive appearance.

Things were going to get a hell of a lot worse—he *felt* the premonition like footsteps of the devil crawling up his spine.

"Damn miserable job."

Jackson raised his head from his work, his gaze going to the man kneeling on the roof a few feet away. Sweat saturated Emmett Fallon's white hair and mustache; his plaid shirt and tan work pants were soaked and clinging to his skin. Emmett had worked as Joe Colton's right-hand man from the day Colton Enterprises had been founded until earlier that year when he'd retired. Jackson had heard rumors that Emmett's drinking was the reason his uncle had nudged his longtime friend into early retirement. Emmett's red-splotched face and bloodshot eyes sent the message that he was still involved with the bottle.

"The heat's miserable," Jackson agreed. He glanced around, decided they had a quarter of the roof left to patch. "Guess we'll have to let Blake talk us into finishing this tomorrow."

"Guess so."

Emmett laid down the hammer he'd wielded for the better part of the afternoon and leaned slowly back, as if trying to unstiffen his spine. "Teach me to offer to help out my boy at his place of business." Emmett pulled off his leather work gloves, then dug a wrinkled pack of cigarettes and lighter from his shirt pocket. "You see Blake up here helping us like he said he'd be?"

Jackson grinned. "I noticed he ran out on us over an hour ago. Didn't he mention something about being right back when he left to take that phone call?"

"That's what he said. He probably paid his secretary extra to invent that conference call she said he had." Emmett lit his cigarette, jabbed the pack and lighter back into his pocket, then expelled a stream of smoke. "I'm not used to manual labor. My back's aching like a bad tooth."

"I know the feeling." Jackson tugged off his leather gloves, stuffed the fingers into the back pockets of his jeans. While he rolled his shoulders to unkink his tired muscles, he gazed out at the view. In the years since he'd moved to San Diego he'd become accustomed to the sight of high-rises and choked highways. Now, he studied the rolling hills covered with emerald green grass where cattle were fattening in pasture, the fields of waving wheat and the occasional pond that gleamed a dazzling blue beneath the sun. In the distance, he could see the edge of the reservation where Cheyenne grew up. Farther off, towering redwoods speared, straight and strong, into the sky.

Jackson wondered if his recent discontent with his job was the reason that the space, the solitude, the land now called to him when it never had before.

He glanced at Emmett who sat quietly puffing on his cigarette. "The other night I was in my uncle's study. He still has the brass paperweight shaped like an oil rig you gave him when the first wildcat well you dug in Wyoming came in." Jackson cocked his head. "I bet you and Uncle Joe have some stories to tell."

"Yeah. Problem is, not all of the facts in our stories jibe." Emotion flickered in Emmett's eyes, then disappeared. "Guess that's to be expected after the passage of forty years. I say we call it a day."

Just then, Blake Fallon's head appeared over the eave of the barn's roof, followed by the rest of him as he deftly scaled the metal ladder that leaned against one side of the barn.

"I was about to suggest that very thing," Blake said, glancing at his watch. He had worked hours on the roof before he had left to take his call and the jeans and dark shirt that covered his tall, lean frame were close to the same state as the two other men's. "Sorry I didn't make it back. The Hopechest Foundation's attorney decided to go over the annual budget line-item by line-item."

"Damn lawyers," Emmett muttered. "Can't get nothing done because of them."

Blake winced. "Your timing's off, Dad. You might want to rethink that statement."

Emmett glanced at Jackson, his eyes widening as if he'd suddenly remembered Jackson's profession. Clearing his throat, Emmett crushed out his cigarette on a piece of metal, then rose. "Didn't mean nothing personal, son."

"No harm done." Sliding his hammer through the loop in his tool belt, Jackson grabbed his wrinkled shirt, then stood. He met Blake's gaze while he swept his hand toward the section of roof behind them. "In case you're too shy to ask me to come back, I'll be here tomorrow to help finish the job."

Blake grinned. "Since I now know I don't have to resort to blackmail to get that to happen, I'll have Holly dig your Porsche's distributor cap out of my desk drawer."

Jackson chuckled. "You always did know how to work things so they'd go your way."

"I'm proud to say I learned that from your Uncle Joe," Blake commented.

"Guess I'll be back, too, if you want me," Emmett said, taking cautious steps toward the roof's edge.

"Of course I do." Blake turned, a frown furrowing his forehead as he watched his father step onto the ladder. "I appreciate the hard work, Dad. Holly has some fresh lemonade waiting in the office."

"My tastes run more to cold beer," the older man said before disappearing out of sight.

Expelling a breath, Blake shoved a hand through his dark hair, then turned to Jackson. "I'm sorry about the remark about lawyers. Dad's never been one to think before he speaks. I expect you already know that."

"Not a problem." Jackson squeezed his friend's shoulder. "My hide's been toughened by hundreds of lawyer jokes."

"A few of which I made up," Blake added, then grinned. "Thanks for the help today, Jackson. I appreciate it."

Jackson glanced at the roof where metal lay nailed on top of metal. Despite his aching muscles—and what now promised to be a blazing sunburn—he appreciated the fact he could actually see the results of a hard day's work. That happened only seldom when he sat behind a desk. Suddenly, he craved more of the space, the openness he'd felt that day.

He looked back at Blake. "I'll make you a deal."

"What?"

"You keep your hands off my Porsche and I'll show up here every day this week to help you with work."

Blake's eyes widened. "Do, and I'll kiss you."

"Do, and you're a dead man."

"You serious, pal?"

"Totally. The Memorial Day competition is something I used to look forward to every summer. I haven't been to one in years, so I'm due to sweat a little to help you get ready for this one."

Blake nodded, his expression sliding to somber. "Has something happened that has to do with your job?"

"I took a leave of absence." Jackson lifted a shoulder. "I'm trying to decide if I want to stay at Colton Enterprises." He gazed out at the rolling, peaceful landscape. "Hell, I don't even know if I still want to practice law."

"I don't want to get on Joe Colton's bad side and make him think I'm trying to steal you from behind his back. But if you decide you want to leave Colton Enterprises and still practice law, Hopechest Foundation just lost its attorney who acted as legal advocate for the kids it handles. They want to fill the vacancy within the month.''

"I'll keep that in mind."

"That's all I can ask. How about we get off this roof and have some lemonade?"

"I'm all for getting down from here," Jackson said, edging his way toward the ladder. "What I'd like in addition to that glass of lemonade is to borrow your shower and a clean shirt. I need to drop by Cheyenne's house before I head home."

Blake raised his chin. "I didn't know that was the way the wind blew around here these days."

Jackson gripped the top of the ladder, swung a leg around. Pausing, he met his friend's gaze. "I don't know if the wind's blowing that way or not, Blake. Cheyenne and I are trying to figure that out."

"Well, Cheyenne might have her hands full when you get there."

"Why's that?"

"I saw your cousin Sophie pull up to Cheyenne's house about fifteen minutes ago. I helped her unload a playpen, a diaper bag and a portable swing while Sophie carried Meggie. Seems Aunt Cheyenne is baby-sitting this evening while Sophie attends a meeting and River takes care of one of his mares that went into labor."

Jackson nodded. He figured he might have to wait until Meggie settled down for one of her frequent naps before he and Cheyenne got to talk.

He would wait however long it took.

Five

Thirty minutes after Sophie Colton James drove her sleek Jaguar away from Cheyenne's small frame house, three-month-old Meggie James began screeching like a storm-warning siren.

Cheyenne checked her niece's diaper. Dry, and clean as a whistle. She tried to give Meggie the warmed bottle of breast milk Sophie had packed in the quilted diaper bag. Then the rattle shaped like a fluffy white sheep. All the while, Cheyenne sang a soothing lullaby in her native Mokee-kittuun. Nothing did the trick.

"It's okay." Feeling more and more frazzled by the minute, Cheyenne brushed her fingers over soft black curls and continued patting Meggie's back while she wailed. "It's okay, angel."

Wishing fervently for a rocking chair and earplugs, Cheyenne paced her living room, her red-faced, howling niece hugged to her chest.

"She trying to break the sound barrier?"

Cheyenne whirled at the sound of Jackson's voice coming through the screen door. "I think she's already done that and is on her way to setting a new record."

"The obvious question is, did you check her diaper?" Without waiting for an invitation, he pulled open the screen door and stepped inside.

"Yes," Cheyenne said, then winced when Meggie's fingers snared in the hair that rained down to her waist. Big mistake, she realized, to not have re-braided her hair after she showered. "Meggie's diaper is as pristine now as when Sophie put it on her right before she left."

"Is she hungry?"

"I don't think so. She didn't want the bottle I offered. Or the rattle. I sang her a lullaby, but I doubt she heard any of it."

Gently, Jackson freed Meggie's tiny fingers from Cheyenne's hair and nudged the thick fall behind her shoulders. "She for sure has healthy lungs," he observed. "Want to let me have a shot at her?"

Feeling a scrape at her pride, Cheyenne raised her chin. "Do you know anything about babies?"

He lifted a brow. "I've got a ton of younger cousins and foster cousins. At one time or another they all howled like crazed wolverines in my presence. I managed to get them quiet."

"That makes you the expert here." Cheyenne transferred the screaming infant into Jackson's arms. "I wish I knew what was wrong so I could help her."

"No fever," he said, touching his fingertips to Meggie's cheek.

"No, her skin feels cool."

"Did you check her gums for swelling?"

Cheyenne blinked. "She's barely three months old. Isn't she too young to be teething?"

"Who knows? For the sake of our eardrums and to prevent the noise from stampeding every cow within hearing distance, I say we don't discount anything."

"Good point."

"I saw my Aunt Meredith use this trick a couple of times," he said as he nudged a knuckle against Meggie's lips. "Come on, sweetheart, try wrapping your gums around this," he murmured. "That's my girl," he added when Meggie drew in a choked breath and began to gnaw.

He nodded toward the diaper bag in the portable crib beside the sofa. "Did Sophie bring something for her to chew on?"

"If she didn't, I'll make something," Cheyenne said. She rummaged through the bag, found a plastic case. Inside was a freezer pack and a couple of teething rings. "Here," she said a second later, offering one of the taffy-pink rings.

Jackson slipped the cold ring into Meggie's mouth to replace his finger. Whimpering, she gummed the ring while staring up at him with wide eyes, her tiny face red and tear-streaked.

"This is the first time I've kept a baby on my own." Shoving her hair behind her shoulders, Cheyenne moved to Jackson's side and peered down at her niece. "Sophie will never let me keep Meggie for a weekend if this is what happens when I have her for less than an hour."

"Sure she will." Jackson flashed a grin that Cheyenne felt all the way to her toes. "To cinch the deal, the three of us will swear a secret pact." He looked down at Meggie and got a drooling smile in return. "Nobody mentions 'crying jag.' Got that, doll face?"

Cheyenne was suddenly aware of the tall, lanky man smelling vaguely of soap, his black hair damp and slicked back from his tanned face, his faded work shirt with the sleeves rolled up past the elbows of well-toned arms. And in those arms was a now cooing Meggie, cradled so naturally Cheyenne couldn't help wonder if he held a baby every day.

Touched at his gentleness, Cheyenne swallowed around the lump in her throat and glanced toward the window where early evening sunlight suffused through gossamer curtains. "I didn't realize what time it was," she said, looking back at Jackson. "Did you hear Meggie screaming all the way up on the barn's roof and decide to come to her rescue before you left for the day?"

"No." He blew out a breath as the humor abruptly left his eyes. "I planned to drop by and see you. There's something I want to talk to you about. The sooner, the better."

The grimness in his eyes made her mouth go dry. Her thoughts scrolled back to the vision that had first sent her to him two nights ago. The gray eyes now staring down into hers looked as hard as those she'd pictured in her mind's eye.

Her vision had revealed he was in trouble. Instinct told her that trouble was the reason Jackson had come to her.

"We can talk as soon as I get this angel to sleep," Cheyenne said.

"Fine." Jackson planted a light kiss on top of Meggie's head before he passed her to Cheyenne.

While Cheyenne cooed her niece toward sleep, Jackson took the opportunity to check out his surroundings. The living room was small, done in cool clay and cozy warm wood. Pillows in shimmering earth tones lined a tan sofa that looked as if it would welcome afternoon naps. Beneath the window that nudged out onto the house's front porch sat a table that held a pewter pitcher from which flowers burst with wild and careless color. A rustic hooked rug covered the gleaming, wide-planked oak floor.

Through a door past the couch was a small, neat kitchen where an assortment of baskets and dried herbs hung on wood pegs over the sink. What he supposed was a bedroom lay at the end of the dim hallway to his right.

The house was as tidy as its owner, he decided, shifting his gaze to Cheyenne while she settled Meggie into the portable crib. And as seductive, he thought, taking in the white T-shirt that fell over the swell of her breasts, her legs long and brown and soft coming out of black shorts that skimmed down her slender hips.

He watched in silence as she draped a daffodil-yellow blanket over her niece's tiny body. When Cheyenne turned from the crib, she absently brushed the heavy fall of black hair from her cheek. His reaction to her transformed to sheer lust, so basic and raw that he took one deliberate step in retreat.

"Is something wrong?" she whispered, her whiskey-dark eyes serious and watchful. Secret eyes, he reminded himself. Would he ever find out what those secrets were?

"No." Tucking his thumbs in the front pockets of his jeans, he waited for the need clawing in his stomach to ease. He had given his word he would keep his hands off her until she wanted them on her again. *If* she wanted them on her again. He intended to keep his promise...even if it killed him.

"I noticed a couple of chairs on the front porch when I came in," he said. "Want to talk out there?"

"Fine. We'll be able to hear Meggie if she wakes up."

"We'll hear her, even if we go to Oklahoma to talk," he commented, then moved to the door and pushed open the screen.

Cheyenne smiled, but her eyes stayed sober as she crossed the room. When she stepped past him onto the porch, Jackson caught the drift of her soft scent and thought again of the tea roses planted in his Aunt Meredith's garden.

The sun hung low, casting long, graceful shadows across the wooden porch lined with a simple, sturdy rail. Beyond the porch were bushes of yellow roses and a postage-stamp-size lawn edged by a picket fence painted the same soft yellow as the house.

Because he wanted to watch her face, her eyes, Jackson leaned against the rail while she lowered onto one of the wicker chairs padded with floral cushions. The waning summer sunlight turned her skin the color of gold.

"I haven't offered you anything to drink," she said. "I have wine, beer."

"No, thanks. The last drink I had was at my sister's wedding. It knocked me out cold. I haven't touched alcohol since."

"I can make some iced tea."

"I'd rather talk."

"Okay."

He flexed his fingers against his thighs and listened to the soft lowing of cattle that carried on the warm air.

"I've spent all day thinking about what happened between us on the archery range," he began. "I meant it when I told you I've never wanted a serious relationship. Never had use for one. Now I'm pretty sure that's what I want with you.''

He watched nerves slide into her eyes, and silently cursed the man in her past who had hurt her so deeply.

''Jackson, I told you I don't know if that's what I want. I just don't know. And I won't be pushed where I don't choose to go.''

''I'm not pushing. I understand you've been hurt. You want to take things slow. I'm content with that, for now.''

''For now?''

He raised a dark brow at the challenge in her voice. ''For as long as you need,'' he amended. It wasn't often a beautiful woman insisted he keep his distance. Doing so was taking some getting used to.

She pulled her bottom lip between her teeth and regarded him across the span of the porch. ''Is that what you wanted to talk to me about?''

''I'm getting there.'' He shifted his gaze past the picket fence to the gravel road that dipped and curved around soft rises of green. In the distance he could see the house that doubled as Blake Fallon's office. Beyond that were the barns, stable, paddocks and weathered post-and-rail fence that marked the property line.

Not for the first time that day, he wondered if a big-city lawyer could find contentment in a ranch's open spaces.

''Jackson, where have you gone?''

Cheyenne's soft question brought his gaze back to hers. ''Sorry.''

''Why don't you just tell me what you came here to say?''

"All right. We want to get to know each other. That won't happen unless we're up-front about things."

"Up front." Beneath her T-shirt, he saw her shoulders stiffen. "About what?"

"Everything." Taking a deep breath, he crossed his arms over his chest, then dove in. "Are you aware that the same person who tried to kill my Uncle Joe at his birthday party made a second attempt about four months ago?"

"Yes, Sophie told me. She said her dad was in his bedroom, getting dressed for dinner. Just as he bent to tie his shoe, a bullet crashed through one of the windows."

"Right. It was my bad luck that I chose that day to drive up from San Diego. I pulled into the driveway a few minutes after the shooting occurred."

Cheyenne tilted her head. "Why was that bad luck for you?"

"Because the Prosperino cops—Detective Thad Law in particular—think I'm the person who made both attempts on my Uncle Joe's life."

Jackson had the satisfaction of seeing sheer astonishment settle in her face. "They... He *what*?"

"As far as I know, I'm Law's prime suspect."

"Why? Why would he even think that?"

"Last time we spoke, he had three reasons. First, if my uncle dies, my father inherits Colton Enterprises. That includes all of its assets if he exercises his option to purchase Uncle Joe's stock." Jackson paused, his thoughts veering to his father's lack of remorse over sleeping with his aunt and fathering Teddy—the son Graham could never acknowledge as his own. Then there was the two million dollars in blackmail Graham had readily agreed to pay Meredith to ensure she kept the name of Teddy's father secret.

"My father and I have never been what you would call close," Jackson continued. "Our relationship has gotten even shakier lately. Let's just say Graham Colton has the brains to run the company, but not the heart. With him at the helm, it wouldn't be long before he'd have Colton Enterprises in financial trouble. Big trouble."

"How would your father's inheriting the company be reason for you to try to kill your uncle? You don't directly profit if Joe Colton dies."

"At first, I didn't get Detective Law's implication either. Then he brought up a lawsuit I filed years ago, right after I passed the bar. The suit was on behalf of a friend whose father had gotten hooked on drugs and alcohol and was in the process of bankrupting the family's business. The court ruled in my friend's favor, which resulted in his father's removal as CEO. The son took over control of the company. Law pointed out that my being attorney of record on the case proves I know how to legally put the reins of Colton Enterprises into my own hands if Uncle Joe were to die."

"Knowing that doesn't prove you tried to kill him," Cheyenne said quietly.

"You're right, it doesn't. Law and I both know he's basically blowing smoke on that point." Jackson raised a shoulder. "The second reason he gave for considering me his prime suspect is more problematic. About three weeks ago, a man who apparently could be my twin walked into the office of a Los Angeles insurance company. Using my name, he purchased a one-million-dollar insurance policy on Uncle Joe's life."

"It wasn't you?"

"It wasn't me."

A crease formed between Cheyenne's dark brows. "The second attempt on your uncle's life happened months ago. The one at his birthday party was almost a year ago. If you planned to gain by his death, you'd have had to take out the policy *before* the attempts."

"I pointed that out to Thad Law. He seems to think the two attempts were intended to be just that—attempts. My alleged motive for buying the policy at this late date is that all along I've planned to take a third shot at Uncle Joe. And I'll make sure that one hits the target."

Cheyenne blinked. "Could you do that? Are you that good of a shot?"

Jackson gave her a grim smile. "Growing up, I spent all my summers on my aunt and uncle's ranch. I practiced target shooting, hunted, put down injured cattle and horses. I'm as accurate with a gun as you are with a bow and arrow. That's another bit of information about me Law picked up. If anything, the cop is thorough."

"Is this insurance policy the reason you went to L.A. yesterday?"

"Yes. I planned to walk into the insurance company, introduce myself to the agent who sold the policy, then get him to admit it wasn't me whom he'd done business with a couple of weeks ago."

Jackson shoved a hand through his hair. Twenty-four hours later, his stomach felt just as sick as it had when he'd ended his meeting with the agent.

"The man insisted I'm the person who took out the policy on my uncle's life. The signature on that policy looks enough like mine that I'd be a fool to give the cops a voluntary handwriting sample for comparison."

"If it wasn't you who bought the policy, who did?"

"Los Angeles is full of starving actors and celebrity

look-alikes. I imagine it would be easy to find an actor so desperate for money that he'd impersonate someone for a couple of hours and not ask questions about why he was hired to do the gig. The risk of doing so would be minimal.''

"Because he was disguised to look like you no one could identify him.''

"Only the person who hired him, who isn't likely to talk since doing so would implicate him or her in the scam,'' Jackson concurred. "Chances are, the guy who pretended to be me couldn't have fooled someone who knew me, but that's not what he needed to do. The insurance agent had never laid eyes on me—the real me—until yesterday. The man who walked into his office and handed him a cashier's check told him he was Jackson Colton. The agent didn't have reason to think otherwise.''

"So, where were you when the policy was purchased? Can you prove you were somewhere else? With someone?''

"It was a couple of days before my sister's wedding. I was here, in Prosperino. I had a lot of thinking to do that day, so I got up early, left without telling anyone where I was going and just drove. I paid cash for my gas and meals. If I had known I would need an alibi, I'd have made sure I had one.''

Cheyenne nodded, her gaze locked with his. "You said Detective Law has three reasons to suspect you. What's the third?''

"It's the most damaging,'' Jackson said while dread tightened his chest. "And it involves you.''

"*Me?* How could it involve me?''

"At the birthday party I told you I was going to refill our glasses so we could toast Uncle Joe. When I left you, I headed across the courtyard to take a shortcut to the bar through the service hallway. Right before I stepped into the hallway, I glanced across my shoulder. You were watching me. I liked knowing that.''

"Yes, I watched you." Her cheeks blushing, she dropped her gaze to the fingers she'd entwined in her lap. "I remember hoping you wouldn't be gone too long."

"I had every intention of getting back to you in a hurry." He hesitated. "Cheyenne, has Detective Law questioned you about what happened that night?"

"No, not Law. None of the guests could leave until they'd given a statement to the police. I gave mine to a uniformed officer. He asked if I had noticed anyone acting suspicious, if I'd seen anyone with a gun. Things like that."

"From what I gather, now that Law suspects me, he's re-interviewing everyone who was there that night. He'll probably get to you soon."

"Which will be a waste of his time. I didn't see who fired the shot at your uncle."

"No, but you did see me near the service hallway. You did watch me disappear inside."

"Yes. So?"

"So, did you keep watching the hallway after that?"

"No." She frowned, as if pulling back memories of that night. "I started talking to Rebecca Powell. Then Rafe came up," she said after a moment. "Not long after that, we heard the gunshot and Rafe dragged us to the floor." She raised a hand, palm up. "How am I involved in this, Jackson? Is it because I can give you an alibi for where you were right before the shooting?"

"That's one way to look at it," he said, his mouth curving into a sardonic arch. "And I wish that were the reason I'm here talking to you, but it's not. The police have determined the trajectory of the bullet fired at Uncle Joe. They know that whoever shot at him stood a few feet from the entrance to the service hallway. You can place me near there right before the shooting."

"I can also say that I saw you go into the hallway."

"Then you shifted your attention to Rebecca. You wouldn't know if I'd stepped back out seconds later, pulled a gun and shot at Uncle Joe."

He saw the flash in her eyes as awareness settled in. "I guess it would be safe to say that your situation is likely to get worse if I tell Detective Law where I saw you and when."

"That about sums things up."

"I see."

She rose, walked to the far end of the porch and stood, arms crossed over her chest, to stare out at the small lawn. Her hair rained down her back, as black as a moonless night.

"So, here you are," she said after a moment. "Jackson Colton, who professes to have never wanted a serious relationship with a woman, claims to suddenly want one with me."

"I do—"

"Is it just a happy coincidence that I'm the one woman who can maybe prevent you from going to jail if I keep my mouth shut about where I saw you that night?"

He closed his eyes. As an attorney, he had anticipated her reaction. As a man whose feelings for her seemed to deepen by the minute, he'd dreaded it. He shifted against the rail, then settled back again to study her profile.

"I didn't come here to try to sweet-talk you into keeping me out of jail."

"Really?" She turned and gave him a steady stare. Her burnished skin carried a flush of anger; her mouth had thinned. Jackson saw the full power of her heritage in her face. "A woman involved in a serious relationship might think twice before implicating her lover in an attempted murder."

"Am I going to be your lover, Cheyenne?"

Her chin rose. "That's exactly what you tried to become this morning. But you discovered I'm not a woman who's easily seduced. Your Plan A didn't work. You've had all day to come up with a new course of action. Is this Plan B, Jackson? Have you come here this evening, expecting to cajole me into not telling the police where I saw you?"

Understanding her reaction didn't stop anger from churning inside him. Jaw set, he pushed off the rail and walked across the porch to face her.

"Listen to me," he said, forcing a steadiness into his voice he was far from feeling. "I didn't want what happened between us this morning to stop with a kiss. I'm sure that was obvious. I want you, Cheyenne. Every time I see you, get close to you, smell you, that need deepens. Like now."

"I…" When she took a step back, he took one forward. "I don't want—"

"I do," he continued quietly. "I want to take you someplace quiet where the only light comes from flickering candles." Slowly, his eyes skimmed over her face, lingering on each feature. "I want to drink sweet wine with you and listen to you sigh while I peel every piece of clothing off your body. Then I want to make love with you until I'm the only man who ever has, or will, exist for you. That's what I want, Cheyenne."

Her lips parted, trembled. "Don't. I can't think straight when you say things like that."

"Good, because I'm having a hard time thinking straight when I get around you, too." He blew out a breath. "My kissing you this morning had nothing to do with the problems I've got with the police. And I'm not here now to try to 'cajole' you into keeping quiet when Thad Law contacts you. I expect you to tell the man the truth about that night, just like I did."

She slicked her tongue over her lips. "You *want* me to tell him I can place you in almost the exact spot as the person who fired a shot at your uncle?"

"Hell, no, I don't *want* that." Jackson jabbed a hand through his hair. "But it's the truth, so there's nothing I can do to change it. I didn't try to kill my uncle that night. I was halfway to the bar when I heard the shot. I ran back into the courtyard where all hell had broken loose. It's my bad luck no one saw me in that hallway. Just like it was my bad luck months later to be alone when the bastard took a second shot at Uncle Joe. Those are facts *I* have to deal with. Just like I've dealt for almost a year with thoughts playing in my head of the time you and I spent together at the birthday party."

"Maybe I..." Her voice was ragged, unsteady.

"Maybe you what?"

Dragging in a breath, she wrapped her arms around her waist. "There's no maybes about it. Since that night, I've dealt with those same kind of thoughts about you."

Jackson acknowledged the streak of primitive male satisfaction that came with her words. "So, maybe you understand why I'm asking for a chance at a relationship with you?" he asked evenly. "There's a reason we've stuck in each other's heads, Cheyenne. Maybe you'd like to know that reason as much as I would?''

"Maybe. Maybe just the thought of knowing scares me.''

"Doesn't do much for my nerves, either. Hell.'' He ran his hands over his face, then gave her a considering look. "I have to say, though, that taking time to get to know each other does have its intriguing moments.''

Her eyes came to his, dark and curious. "Meaning?''

"Meaning, you're tougher than you look. There's a streak of steel inside you.''

"I take after my mother in many ways. Her people were warriors.''

A fact, he thought, that only heightened her underlying mystique that had fascinated him since the moment he'd laid eyes on her.

He studied her profile, both angular and soft. "Despite all that's going on, I consider myself lucky.''

"Lucky?'' She slanted him a look. "The police suspect you of trying to murder your uncle. Twice. What could you possibly find lucky about that?''

"When I have a lot of thinking to do, I take in a movie. Losing myself in front of the big screen usually helps me work things out.'' Without thinking, he raised a hand, intending to slide his palm down the tempting length of all that silky black hair. Remembering his promise to her, he let his hand drop to his side.

"I went to the movie the other night after I left the police station,'' he added softly. "When I walked out of the theater, there you were. Lucky for me.''

"Lucky,'' Cheyenne repeated softly, then drew in a quiet breath. She'd had no idea a man could entice so deeply, so completely with mere words. Not until Jackson's voice had skimmed along her flesh, leaving a heated trail of magic with promises of candlelight, wine and seduction. She hadn't known how intimately he could touch her, without ever laying a hand on her.

Oh, how she wanted to pull those words to her heart, hold them close. Yet, she couldn't. Couldn't let down the barrier that protected all she was. Couldn't let her deepening feelings for him take root in her scarred heart.

"I appreciate you telling me about the police," she said quietly. "About their suspicions."

"I don't want secrets between us."

His words tightened her throat. He had come to her and bared the truth. Yet she would not afford him the same openness about her gift.

The sun setting at his back cast shadows over his face, darkened his eyes to the color of pewter. "I didn't try to kill my uncle. I hope someday you'll know me well enough to believe that."

Cheyenne struggled to get a grip on her tumbling emotions. The hurt that had ignited her anger and wounded her pride just moments ago had clouded her thinking. After the police had questioned Jackson, after he *knew* the harm she might bring to him, he had not sought her out, intent on seducing her into silence. Instead, he had gone to the movie theater.

Where fate had sent her in search of him.

She closed her eyes. With the first breath she'd drawn she had understood that she possessed the power to help people, that her gift of sight was linked solely to goodness. She had been sent to Jackson because he was in trouble. Because somehow, someway, it was in her power to help him.

Because he's innocent.

Looking up, she met his eyes calmly, so that he would

understand she spoke the truth. "I believe you, Jackson. I know you didn't try to kill your uncle."

His eyes narrowed. "How do you *know* that?"

"I just do."

He shook his head. "Not good enough, Cheyenne. This morning you were ready to walk away because you hardly know me. Now you're taking my word I didn't try to kill Uncle Joe. What's changed?"

"Nothing." She tilted her head. "I see the truth in your eyes."

"My eyes?"

"Yes."

He stared down at her, his brow creasing. "I suspect this is one of those situations where it's best to quit while I'm ahead."

"I'd say so." She gazed out at the small lawn where a slate-blue twilight had settled. "Do you have any idea who's made the two attempts on your uncle's life?"

"No. Find him or her, and you'll find the person who's gone to a hell of a lot of trouble to set me up to take the fall for two attempted murders." As he spoke, his hands clenched into fists, unclenched. "Whoever that is, isn't finished with me. I can *feel* there's more to come. Dammit, it's like walking through a field infested with snakes. You know they're there, but there's no way to predict where they'll strike next."

And she couldn't see them, Cheyenne thought. She could not will the visions that came to her any more than she could change what she saw.

The wind picked up, whispering the secrets of the coming night. Absently, she rubbed her hands along her arms to ward off the chill. Although she was still uncertain how fate intended her to help the man standing beside her, she knew, with time, the answers would come. They always came.

"You're cold," he said quietly.

She looked up, unaware he'd been studying her. "A little." She glanced across her shoulder toward the front door they'd left ajar. "I should check to make sure Meggie hasn't wiggled out from under her blanket."

"Probably should," he agreed, keeping his eyes on hers. "Now that you know there might be a jail cell in my future, do you still want time to get to know me?"

The vision that had come to her that morning replayed in her mind like a seductive phantom. She and Jackson, lying together on cool sheets while candlelight flickered softly against their heated flesh. He wanted to give her candlelight and warm, sweet wine.

Cheyenne felt her chest tighten. Even as her mind cautioned her to go slow, desire poured through her.

"If I told you I changed my mind about getting to know you, would that keep you away?"

"No," he answered instantly. "I'd have to try to over-rule whatever objections you had to my presence. And I'll be present a lot, because I volunteered to help Blake get this ranch ready for the Memorial Day competition. Starting tomorrow, I'm staying in one of the spare rooms in his house. Since I can't seem to keep away from you, why don't you plan on seeing me tomorrow night?" He flashed her a grin. "In case you can't tell, I'm trying to cajole you into letting me take you to dinner."

Cheyenne fought a smile. He had walked into her life two days ago, and already so much had changed. Just, she supposed, as it was meant to.

She walked across the porch, pulled open the screen

door, then met his gaze across her shoulder. "I'll cook. Dinner will be ready at seven. Don't be late."

"I'll be here."

Six

For the next five days, most of the work done on Hopechest Ranch was geared toward getting ready for the Memorial Day all-around rodeo competitions. During that time Jackson worked beside Emmett Fallon to finish repairs on the roof of the horse barn, then they plied similar labor to the stables. After that, Jackson supervised a paint crew consisting of Johnny Collins and several other Hopechest Ranch teens while they swiped brushes and rollers dipped in glistening white paint over the dorm-style lodge known as the "Homestead," the counseling center and expansive dining hall. Working beside a grizzled ranch hand, Jackson restrung more barbed wire than he knew had existed. He'd even labored over a tractor that threw a rod.

During the years he'd spent in law school, then sitting behind a desk in a climate-controlled office, he'd forgotten the grueling, exhausting work that went hand-in-hand with the operation of a ranch.

And the satisfaction derived from doing that work.

Even falling into bed each night with new blisters, scrapes and muscles that ached from the inside out didn't dampen that feeling of satisfaction.

Now, as Memorial Day dawned in hazy swirls of pinks and gold, he stood on the porch of Blake Fallon's combination home and office, wishing he felt the same contentment with his life as he did with the work he'd done over the past days.

Sipping coffee from the thick mug he'd carried from the kitchen, he acknowledged that his peaceful surroundings were in direct contrast to the churning going on inside him. The time was fast approaching when he would have to make decisions. Some with life-changing impact.

Just the thought of returning to his job in San Diego made his brow furrow. Working with his father no longer held appeal. In truth, the only thing that had kept Jackson at the law offices of Colton Enterprises over the past months was the loyalty he felt to his uncle.

Joe Colton had phoned several times to assure his nephew he was under no obligation to stay in a job for which he no longer had any heart. Jackson knew those calls had been made to ease the guilt he felt that came with the thought of walking away from the business his uncle had built with his own grit and sweat.

If he decided to move on, Jackson knew he also had to figure out if he wanted to continue practicing law. Or try something new. If that were the case, he had no idea what the hell that something would be. Or where it might take him.

He shifted his gaze down the gravel road while a distant rooster crowed a greeting to the dawn. Through the early morning haze, he could see the outline of the simple frame house that sat amid the other small houses in which the ranch's counseling staff resided.

For the past five evenings, he had knocked on the door of Cheyenne's pale yellow house. Twice, she'd opted to cook, so they'd eaten dinner in. They'd driven into Prosperino and dined at dim, elegant restaurants. Last night he'd charmed the ranch's cook into packing a basket of sandwiches, potato salad and apricot cobbler. He and Cheyenne had driven to the coast, spread a blanket on an empty stretch of beach and shared the meal while the moon slid into the sky to cast pale light on the sea.

To Jackson, it hadn't much mattered if they'd stayed in or gone out. As long as they were together. He just wanted—*needed*—to be with her.

And he wasn't quite sure why.

"Hell," he muttered.

The sense that everything inside him was undergoing change made him feel off-balance. Unsteady. Not only was his career up in the air, for the first time in his life he had found that just any woman wouldn't do. That desire for one woman could completely obliterate desire for anyone else.

He wanted Cheyenne James. Wanted her with a growing fervor that was like a sickness. Yet, he hadn't done anything about that want. He'd kept his word. Over the past five days, he hadn't touched her.

Dammit, if he didn't get his hands on her soon, didn't again taste that cool, gold flesh, he was going to put his fist through a wall.

Setting his jaw, he tamped down on his churning emotions. Still, it wasn't easy to ignore the tight wire of control that stretched inside him to near breaking point.

He had wanted women before, lots of women. But never with a force that bordered on violence. That was another thing about him that had changed, he acknowledged. And he wasn't quite sure what to do about it—or about the woman at the center of those unsettled feelings.

Jackson's hand clenched on the mug's handle. Always in the past he would ease away from a relationship before emotions became tangled and messy. No damage done, no hard feelings. With Cheyenne, he found that the only way he wanted to ease was into a future with her.

Problem was, he couldn't. Not while two attempted murder charges hung over his head. He had heard nothing further from Thad Law. Still, Jackson sensed that nothing good would come from the detective's silence.

During the evenings he and Cheyenne had spent together, she hadn't broached the subject of the police investigation. Hadn't mentioned the possibility of his being charged with the attempts on his uncle's life. She just seemed to have accepted a simple, unquestioning belief in his innocence.

He was sure as hell innocent, he thought, dumping the remains of his coffee off the side of the porch. Trouble was, he couldn't *prove* it.

Until he could, he wasn't free to make promises to Cheyenne. Couldn't ask her to make promises to him. Not as long as he could hear the sickening clank of a prison cell door slam behind him.

Rand Colton strode into his D.C. law office early Memorial Day morning, after having thoroughly kissed his wife and promised to be home by noon. That's when he and Lucy planned on taking his five-year-old stepson,

Max, to the zoo. Although Rand looked forward to the outing, Max was so revved with anticipation that Rand knew home was not the place to spend a couple of hours catching up on work.

Dressed in khakis and a sport shirt, he sipped coffee at his desk while reading the deposition of a nighttime jogger who claimed he'd spotted a client of Rand's sneaking a can of gasoline into the rear of the client's failing hardware store. Half an hour later, the store had been engulfed in flames.

Fire investigators determined the blaze had been purposely set, using gasoline as an accelerant.

A background check on the jogger revealed the man was divorced twice and had four convictions for domestic assault. A plan was brewing in Rand's mind on how to get that information in front of a jury—hopefully made up mostly of women—when the cell phone clipped to his belt rang.

"Colton," he said.

"Rand?"

"Emily?" The sound of his adopted sister's voice shoved all thoughts of the case from Rand's mind. It had been three days since he'd heard from her. "How are you?"

"I'm fine. Okay."

Although her words sent a wave of relief through him, the thready fatigue in her voice didn't sound convincing. Not when she'd recently survived a second attempt on her life.

"Where are you?" As he spoke, Rand opened a drawer on his desk, pulled out a road atlas and flipped it open.

Eight months ago, a man had broken into Emily's bedroom at Hacienda de Alegria and tried to kill her.

Terrorized, she'd fled into the night. The Colton family had spent torturous days believing she'd been kidnapped. When a ransom note arrived, Joe Colton paid the money demanded. Eventually Emily phoned Rand to tell him she hadn't been kidnapped. Instead, she'd run away and was hiding out in the small town of Keyhole, Wyoming. After swearing him to secrecy, she related an almost unbelievable story about their mother, Meredith. Although skeptical, Rand had promised Emily to check out her theory, just to ease her mind.

The information he'd found to date had been heart-stopping. As was the call he'd received from Emily three days ago after her attacker caught up with her in Keyhole and made a second attempt on her life.

"I'm in Red River, Montana," Emily said. "It's small—right across the Wyoming border."

"I'm looking at a map," Rand said. His finger paused on a small dot on a thin strand of a road while his other hand balled helplessly on the desk. She was so far away. So vulnerable.

"Got it. Does Wyatt know where you are?" he asked, referring to Wyatt Russell, a close friend and attorney who as a child had lived on Hopechest Ranch. Wyatt had given up the high-paced life of D.C. to live in Keyhole after reuniting with his high-school sweetheart.

"Yes, Wyatt knows. Now you. You're the only two." Emily paused. "Wyatt told me the deputy in Keyhole—Toby Atkins—has his men working day and night to hunt down the man who attacked me. Her voice broke. "Rand, everyone in that town has been so good to me. My staying there puts them in danger. That man… If someone tries to help me, he'll kill them, too."

"He's not going to kill you," Rand shot back. Scrubbing a hand over his face, he dragged in a calming breath. "Emily, we've talked about this," he said quietly. "You know you can come here. I'll take care of you."

"If I come there, he'll find out. He'll follow me. I won't put you and Lucy and Max in danger."

He pictured his sister with her wavy mane of chestnut hair and dimples...and that stubborn line her jaw took when she intended to do things her way. Now, he heard that same unbending determination in her voice. Nothing, he knew, could change her mind. "Do you need money?"

"No, I'm fine. I'm working here at a diner," she said, then gave him the phone number.

Rand jotted the number on a slip of paper. "Look, tomorrow I'm flying to Sacramento on business. I can shift my schedule, come up there and check on you. I would feel a hell of a lot better if I could just see you."

"Rand, you can't come. We've agreed that whoever hired the guy to kill me might be watching you and other members of the family. We can't risk meeting."

Rand nodded. "You're right. I know you're right. It's just that a big brother is supposed to take care of his little sis."

"You are taking care of me, and I love you, too."

"I just wish I could do more."

"You are. You've got Austin McGrath working on this. Has he found out anything yet about Mother?"

"Not yet. Emily, Austin might not find anything. At this point, everything is supposition on our part. We might be wrong."

"We're not. And Austin has to find something, Rand. If he doesn't, this nightmare we're all caught in won't ever end."

* * *

Cheyenne had hired on as a counselor at Hopechest only two days before last year's Memorial Day competition, so she'd missed out on the planning. This year she'd jumped at the chance to organize and schedule all of the events.

She had her hands full and was enjoying every minute of it.

"So far, the barrel-racing and bronc-busting competitions started on time," she informed Jackson when he caught up with her just before noon.

"With you in charge, I had no doubt."

"Bull riding starts after the lunch break." She flipped through the pages on the clipboard angled into the crook of one arm. "So do the roping and target shooting competitions. The archery and pie-eating contests are also this afternoon."

"Thanks to you, everything's running smoothly," Jackson commented as they squeezed into a spot near the corral where the bronc busting was in full swing. "And it looks like everyone is having a good time."

In her haste to leave her house that morning she'd forgotten her sunglasses, so Cheyenne used a hand to shade her eyes while she surveyed the people crowded on and around the newly painted fence. A roar sounded as onlookers cheered for the cowboy who had a one-handed death grip on a rope bridle while a furious bronc bucked him around the corral.

"Some are having a better time than others," Jackson amended when the cowboy flew from the saddle and landed on his butt in a puff of dust.

Out of the corner of her eye, Cheyenne saw Jackson tip his head toward Johnny Collins who was across the corral, straddling the fence with a couple of other Hopechest teens. Johnny nodded, then shifted his attention to a chaps-clad cowboy who had scrambled onto a nearby chute to bark instructions to the next rider.

Cheyenne glanced at Jackson. "You've made an effort this week to choose Johnny to help on the work crews you've supervised. That's good. He needs to know he's not the failure his father always made him out to be."

Jackson shrugged. "Johnny's a good kid who deserves a break. Besides, he works like a demon when he's pointed in the right direction."

Deciding she could take a few minutes from her duties to watch the action, Cheyenne slid her pen in the back pocket of her snug jeans, tucked the clipboard beneath one arm and propped a booted foot on the rail beside Jackson's. Seconds later, the chute sprang open and another horse leaped out, bucking like a hellhound. Its rider had one hand locked to the saddle, another reaching for the sky...then he sailed into the air.

Cheyenne tilted her head. "I understand that flying through space is a part of the enjoyment of bronc busting."

"I prefer having a plane under me when I fly," Jackson said and gave her a grin that had her smiling back at him. He was wearing a white shirt with its sleeves rolled up on his forearms and faded jeans that molded his long legs. The week he'd spent in the sun had given his skin a healthy, golden tan that added to his rugged handsomeness. "I'll get my enjoyment later judging the target shooting match," he added.

She furrowed her brow. "I wish you could have signed up to compete. I would have liked to have seen you in action."

"Taking Thad Law's suspicions of me into consideration, I didn't think it would've been smart to show off my shooting skills just now.''

"You're right." Without thinking, she placed her hand on his and squeezed. "I'll help you judge the match.''

"Then I'll enjoy myself even more." Smoothly, he turned his hand over to grip hers. "In case you haven't noticed, I like having you around.''

She felt the same about him, Cheyenne thought. Over the past week they'd eaten meals on her small porch, dined at elegant restaurants, even shared a moonlit picnic on a beach. They'd talked for hours, about anything and everything.

The whole time, Jackson hadn't touched her. Hadn't even tried.

And each night after he'd left her, she had lain awake, staring at her bedroom ceiling, driving herself crazy wondering what it would be like if he had been there with her. The knowledge that she'd asked him to keep his distance, insisted he give her time to get to know him had done little to ease the desire that thickened round her like a spiderweb whenever he got near. Like now.

For the first time in her life, she fully understood the power—and allure—of greed. She wanted Jackson Colton, more than she had known she could ever want a man. Any man.

Even as desire tightened its grip on her senses, she felt the familiar niggling fear begin to surface. She could imagine herself trusting Jackson with her body, perhaps even her heart.

But not with her secrets.

An involuntary shudder coursed through her. What if she told him about her gift of sight, and he looked at her as if she were crazy, as Paul had? She had no idea how deep her feelings for Jackson went, yet she knew his rejection would be devastating.

"Cheyenne, what's wrong?"

"Nothing."

"I felt you tremble."

"I'm fine."

Keeping her hand firmly in his, Jackson leaned in, his eyes grave. "Have you changed your mind about me?"

She blinked. "Changed my mind?"

"Maybe you've decided Law's suspicions about me might be true. Maybe now you're afraid for me to even touch you." Enough bite sounded in his words for her to recognize hurt.

She stared down at their joined hands, wishing she weren't so moved by the tone of his voice, by the touch of his flesh against hers. But she was. He stood beside her, handsome as sin, the bright sunlight gleaming on his dark hair while the woodsy scent of his cologne filled her lungs.

And she wanted.

She raised her eyes to meet his somber gaze. She didn't need a vision to tell her that he cared for her. "I know you're innocent, Jackson. And I'm not afraid for you to touch me."

"You're afraid of something," he countered quietly. "I see it in your eyes."

"I…" She shook her head and found she could no longer resist the whisperings of her heart. No longer wanted to resist. "I want us to be together."

His eyes narrowed. "Are you saying what I think you're saying?"

"Yes."

His gaze remained steady on hers as he tugged her

out of the crowd and away from the corral. "Let me get this straight," he said when they were far enough away so they couldn't be overheard. "Are you saying you want us to be lovers?"

"Yes."

"What brought this on? Why now?"

"I don't know." She let out a long breath. "It just hit me. You took my hand in yours, and I knew."

With his free hand he toyed with a wisp of hair that had come loose from her braid. "So, you think you know me now? You think we know each other well enough?"

"I think." A thought hit her, along with a wave of embarrassed heat. Up until a few moments ago he hadn't touched her in nearly a week. Maybe he had decided he no longer wanted to. Maybe he just hadn't mentioned that *he'd* changed his mind. She pulled the clipboard from under her arm and hugged it to her chest like a shield. "That is, if you still want—" She gnawed her bottom lip. "Maybe you've decided you don't—"

"Not a chance." His fingers laced with hers while his gaze flicked to the corral, then came back to her. "I don't suppose there's any way you could get away right now?"

While the shaky heat of anticipation settled in her belly, she checked her watch. It was almost noon—she needed to go by the dining hall to make sure they'd begun serving the mountains of potato salad, fried chicken, biscuits and desserts that the cooking staff had slaved over. After that, it was her responsibility to see that all the events scheduled for the afternoon started on time. And she hadn't yet had a chance to check the temporary bandstand that had been erected for that evening's dance.

She nearly groaned out loud. "I can't get away for hours," she said, her mouth curving with regret. "I guess my timing's not the best."

"It sucks." He rested his forehead against hers. With that one gesture, he closed off everything in her world but him. Only he existed.

"Tonight," he murmured. "We'll be together tonight."

His closeness had her pulse thudding. "Yes—"

"Thought we'd never find you!" a voice boomed from behind them.

They turned in unison to find Joe and Meredith Colton standing only inches away.

"Mr. and Mrs. Colton," Cheyenne said while heat rushed into her cheeks at the possibility they'd overheard her and Jackson's plans. "Welcome to Hopechest Ranch. I'm glad you could make it."

"Joe and Meredith." From beneath the brim of his Stetson, the older man beamed at Cheyenne and gave her arm a squeeze. "The only time I ever missed a Hope-chest competition was during the years I served in the Senate and lived in D.C." Turning to Jackson, he gripped his nephew's hand in a hearty handshake. "You doing okay, son?"

"Things are looking up," Jackson said, then gave Cheyenne a wink that sent her heart whacking around in her chest.

Pulling in a breath, she forced her thoughts away from lust and to the couple who'd joined them. The Colton family patriarch had dressed for the day in an unassuming plaid shirt, worn jeans and scuffed boots. His wife had opted for skintight designer jeans that highlighted her lean, leggy figure. Tooled black boots covered her feet; her yellow silk blouse sported silver trim that matched the band on her white-as-snow hat. A small leather purse hung from a silver chain looped across one shoulder. Diamond studs the size of gumdrops glittered coldly at her earlobes.

Her blond hair slid behind one angular shoulder as Meredith shifted her attention toward the corral. "We'd barely been here fifteen minutes when Teddy and Joe, Jr. dashed off. That was ages ago. Have either of you seen them?"

"Sorry," Jackson answered.

Cheyenne ran her tongue around her teeth. "Actually, I ran into them earlier behind the pole barn."

Using a red-tipped nail, Meredith slid her designer sunglasses down her nose and gave Cheyenne a look over the tops. "I'm almost afraid to ask what my boys were doing *behind* the pole barn."

"Nothing dastardly," Cheyenne answered. "Just teaching Priscilla Cooper how to make noises with her armpit."

"Hell's teeth." Meredith rolled her eyes, then shoved her glasses back up the bridge of her nose. "I can't let them out of my sight for a minute."

Joe shook his head. "Sweet thundering Jesus, Meredith, they're just being boys!"

"That's right, Aunt Meredith," Jackson commented. "You remember what you did when you caught Rand and me doing the same thing."

Cheyenne saw a look cross the woman's face, a quick shadow, that cleared instantly. "Of course I remember. Cheyenne, do you have any idea where Joe, Jr. and Teddy are now?"

"I sent them over to the kids' area near the dining hall." While she spoke, Cheyenne was pointedly aware that Jackson's gaze had narrowed on his aunt's face.

"Sophie, River and some of the Hopechest counselors are in charge of the three-legged races. There's also milking, roping and greased pig contests for the kids. I'm sure Joe, Jr. and Teddy have found plenty there to keep them busy."

"No doubt. I'm going to check just to make sure." Meredith looked at her husband. "Coming, darling?"

"I'll catch up with you later." Joe glanced at Jackson. "Right before we left the house I got a call from your dad. He and your mother are coming in this evening to spend a couple of days with us. Graham has some business to discuss. I know you're officially on a leave of absence, but I need to go over a few details with you before I talk to him."

Jackson nodded. "Sure."

"See you later, then." Meredith turned and sauntered off down the gravel path that led to the dining hall.

"She doesn't remember," Jackson said almost to himself.

"Doesn't remember what?" Cheyenne asked while his gaze tracked his aunt.

"That day Aunt Meredith found Rand and me in the backyard, making noises with our armpits. She thought what we were doing was so hilarious that she had us teach her our technique."

Only after Meredith moved out of sight did Jackson meet Cheyenne's gaze. "She and Rand and I have joked with each other about that day off and on over the years. There's no way she could have forgotten about it. But she has. You could see it in her face."

"The accident," Joe said. "She's never been the same since she and Emily were in that car wreck."

"No." Jackson angled his head. "I guess not."

Joe raised a shoulder. "That's not something I want

to think about today." He looked back at Cheyenne and smiled. "Mind if I steal my nephew for a while?"

"Go ahead." She looked up at Jackson. "I need to go by the dining hall." She flipped a page on her clipboard. "I've got a ton of other things to check after that."

"You're one busy lady," Joe commented. His gaze shifted in the direction of the corral. "There's Emmett and Blake Fallon. I haven't seen Emmett in a while. Guess I ought to visit with him, see how he's enjoying retired life."

"Go ahead, Uncle Joe," Jackson said. "I'll catch up with you in a few minutes."

"Take your time, son," Joe said, then gave Cheyenne a wink before striding off.

"Alone at last." As he spoke, Jackson nodded in the direction of a nearby towering oak. "Want to meet there about half an hour before the target shooting competition? We can walk over to the range together."

"That sounds good."

He curled a finger under Cheyenne's chin, nudged it up. "There's one other thing I want you to plan on."

"What's that?"

"Save me every dance tonight," he said quietly, then dipped his head. His lips brushed hers, as light as a wish. "After that, I'm going to take you home and make love with you. All night."

Patsy clenched her trembling hands into fists as she made her way along the gravel path that led to the ranch's dining hall. Inside her, desperation rose like floodwater. She hadn't known what the hell Jackson was referring to. Didn't have a clue how Meredith had reacted when she'd found him and Rand years ago making noises with their armpits. Armpits!

Behind the oversize lenses of her sunglasses she kept her eyes straight ahead, nodded only slightly to people coming the opposite way along the path. She didn't want to talk to anyone, *couldn't* talk right now. Not while she felt so vulnerable. So alone.

She needed to think.

She dragged in air, but couldn't seem to get enough in her lungs. Years ago, when she had assumed her twin sister's identity, she had handled anything and everything that had come along. References to the past hadn't knocked her off-balance. Only lately had she begun experiencing the ice-pick jabs of panic in her chest that she felt now.

Pulling her purse off her shoulder, she dug inside, fished out the small gold case and opened its lid; her hands shook so badly she almost fumbled the pills it held onto the path. She'd recently discovered one Valium was no longer enough to calm her nerves, so she popped two into her mouth and swallowed them dry.

On impulse, she veered off the path, forcing her trembling legs to carry her into the small clearing she spotted behind towering redwoods. There, she dropped onto one of several large rocks that had been pushed together to form a rustic bench. She gave scant notice to the swatch of colorful wildflowers that spread across the floor of the clearing.

She could still feel Jackson's eyes on her, looking down in a way that sent the message she wasn't being looked at, but into. His gray gaze had been like a cold wave against her flesh. What did he know? Something about Emily?

Patsy closed her eyes against a rising sense of panic

that made breathing almost impossible. She had covered her tracks, she told herself. No one—including Jackson—knew that she'd hired the man who had broken into Emily's bedroom that night. If only Silas Pike hadn't bungled the hit. If only Emily hadn't gotten away and now was who-knew-where, living on the lam.

The unfairness of it all rose inside her, swamping Patsy's mind. What if the nightmares Emily had suffered since the accident finally revealed the answers that had been locked for the past ten years inside the little bitch's head? What if Emily realized her image of seeing "two mommies" was no image? What if she remembered she'd actually witnessed Patsy and Meredith together? What if Emily suddenly recalled seeing Patsy dump an injured, unconscious Meredith on the grounds of the clinic?

What if? What if?

For a moment, the shapes and colors in the small clearing seemed to shift out of sync. Patsy felt droplets of sweat break out on her skin. For the millionth time she cursed herself for not having finished things after she'd run Meredith's car off the road. If she had killed Meredith and Emily, she'd be free and clear. Instead, here she was, desperate to hold on to the cushy lifestyle she'd created for herself and her two sons. A lifestyle all of her senses screamed she was in danger of losing. She *had* to find Meredith. And Emily. She could feel them out there, hostile eminences. They deserved to die. *Had* to die.

Patsy dragged off her hat, dropped it onto the bench. Despite the additional money she had wired Silas Pike, he had yet to track down Emily. Yesterday, Patsy had spoken to the private investigator she had hired to find

Meredith. The idiot still insisted her sister had died years ago, homeless on the street.

Patsy had told him in no uncertain terms she would believe that only after she saw her twin's cold, dead body on a slab in the morgue.

The P.I. then responded that he was out of leads and closing the case unless she paid an additional retainer.

Dammit, she needed more money!

Patsy's right hand went up, her fingers skimming the diamond stud in her ear. She couldn't sell her jewelry— wouldn't sell it. Not when she might need to spirit away Joe, Jr. and Teddy at a moment's notice. To support them, she needed all the jewelry and money she could get her hands on. To make matters worse, damn Joe Colton had her on a strangling budget and the bastard hadn't bought her any new baubles in years!

Money. She had to get more money. Suddenly, she felt almost quiet inside and she realized the Valium had kicked in. She was still in control, she assured herself. No reason to panic.

Maybe it was fate that Graham was coming to Prosperino for a couple of days. Even though he was bringing ice-bitch Cynthia with him, Patsy knew she wouldn't have a problem getting Graham alone—he and his wife spent even less time together than she and Joe. Yes, Patsy thought, she would have ample opportunity to talk to Graham. When she did, she would force him to agree to resume paying her to keep quiet about the fact he'd fathered Teddy.

Before she could do that though, she had to get rid of the one obstacle that stood in the way to her getting Graham to agree to whatever she wanted.

Jackson.

Timing was everything, Patsy thought as she plucked

up her hat and stood. Just as it had been the evening four months ago when she'd stormed into the backyard just before dinner. Who would have thought that her needing to calm down over Heather McGrath's failure to dress appropriately for dinner would have turned into a gold mine?

Patsy smiled to herself. If she hadn't been outside the instant the gunshot sounded, she wouldn't have seen the figure clad in black and gripping a gun race down the staircase built against the face of the rocky cliff. She'd remained out of sight, while the dark figure disappeared into the shallow alcove that stared out at the sea. Seconds later, the shooter stepped back into sight, hands empty, then disappeared into the shadows.

It had been dusk—too dark to get a good look at the man who'd fire the shot. Even if she had, she wouldn't have told the police what she'd seen. Lord knew she wanted the person to keep trying until Joe was dead. Then, she would inherit a trust fund worth more money than Fort Knox ever thought about having. Even while she was being questioned by Thad Law, she had formulated possibilities on how to use this latest development to her advantage. Later that night, after the cops had gone, she had retrieved a small flashlight, gone down to the beach and slipped into the alcove. She'd searched until she found the well-concealed gun, then slid it into her coat pocket and crept back to the house through the oozing shadows.

She had hidden the gun, thinking she might use it to her advantage down the road.

That advantage had arisen when Jackson threatened to go to the police if she didn't stop blackmailing his father. During his sister's wedding reception, it had been a simple matter to slip Jackson a drink loaded with Valium. Then, when he'd shown the effects, she'd played the dutiful hostess and concerned aunt and taken him to his bedroom.

Having already wiped the gun clean of prints, she donned gloves and crept to his bedside. While he lay in a drug-induced sleep, she'd pressed his hand around the weapon's grip, then slid the gun back in the knapsack where it now lay hidden. Jackson had no clue.

Now she needed to get him out of her way. With him cooling his heels in a cell, he would spend his time trying to figure out how the hell his fingerprints got on the gun used in the attempts on Joe's life. The last thing Jackson would give a damn about was Graham's resuming his payments to buy her silence.

Patsy glanced at her watch while a plan clicked in her brain. She knew Joe intended for them to stay at Hopechest Ranch through all the boring afternoon competitions. Knew, too, he would keep a fatherly eye on Joe, Jr. and Teddy, but he wouldn't lift a finger to even look for her until he was ready to leave. His indifference toward her was convenient, considering what she had to do.

She settled her hat back on her head, her glossed lips curved in a smile. It would take only a couple of minutes to go by the dining hall and check on her sons. After that, she would get the car, swing by Hacienda de Alegria and unearth the knapsack that held the gun. Then she would make the short drive into Prosperino. With the town's entire population doing their holiday celebrating at Hopechest, little chance existed that anyone would see her.

Rechecking her watch, she stepped out of the clearing and resumed her trek along the gravel path. The final phase of her plan to set up Jackson for the two attempts on Joe's life shouldn't take long to put into motion.

It didn't.

A little over an hour later, a smug Patsy steered along the winding curves of the coast highway like a five-time winner at Le Mans. Everything had gone without a hitch. The instant she got back to Hopechest Ranch she would make an anonymous call to the cops.

Then she would sit back and watch everyone play into her hands.

Seven

The sun was stretching the afternoon shadows when Cheyenne crossed the grass-covered rise toward the temporary bandstand that several off-duty Prosperino firemen had built. As she moved, the wind picked up, bringing with it the mingling scents of fresh hay, animal flesh and earth. From the corral below she heard the crowd cheering their picks in the bull riding competition.

While she checked the flame-red bunting stapled to the edges of the raised dance floor, she again assured herself she had been right to tell Jackson she was ready to become his lover. Right to follow her emotions. Right, too, not to tell him about her gift of sight. Her holding back wasn't deception, it was self-preservation—she'd learned that through hard experience. While her own heart had lain ripped open and bleeding she had come to the understanding that, no matter the love she felt for a man, she was under no obligation to tell him about her heritage. So, she would not tell Jackson. She simply wouldn't. Couldn't.

The slide of guilt tugging at her conscience had her worrying her bottom lip with her teeth. Forcing her thoughts to her duties, she retrieved her clipboard off the edge of the bandstand and jotted a note. The sound system was in place. The strands of twinkle lights that would illuminate the dance floor when night fell stretched above her like spiky vines of ivy. The table was already in place to display the trophies Blake Fallon would present to the winners of the competitions. Cheyenne had spoken to the bandleader that morning and he had assured her his group would be there in plenty of time to set up for the dance.

Save me every dance tonight. After that, I'm going to take you home and make love with you. All night.

The memory of Jackson's soft words had her fingers trembling against the clipboard as weakening, seductive anticipation settled shaky heat in her belly. It had been so long since she'd stepped into a man's arms and let herself feel. Just feel. She couldn't wait—

"Miss James?"

Cheyenne jolted at the deep male voice coming from just behind her. She turned to find a powerfully built man with black hair and piercing midnight-blue eyes standing inches from her. He had a small scar on his left cheek and his nose didn't quite line up with the center of his mouth.

She thought she had seen him before, but she couldn't place him. "Yes, I'm Cheyenne James."

"Detective Thad Law." As he spoke, he tugged a gold shield from the snug front pocket of his faded Levi's and clipped it onto his belt beside a cell phone.

Cheyenne realized she'd seen him at the Colton estate after the first attempt on Joe Colton's life.

"I need to ask you a couple of questions," Law added.

"Welcome to Hopechest Ranch, Detective Law." She forced a smile while dread shredded her insides. All week she'd desperately hoped this moment would never come. "I trust you're enjoying today's activities."

"I am, though I'm mixing business with pleasure. You attended Joe Colton's birthday party nearly a year ago."

"That doesn't sound like a question, Detective."

"It wasn't." He smiled and surprised Cheyenne with a flare of charm. "I have a copy of the guest list. Several people I've spoken to recently confirm seeing you there that night."

"It was crowded. I imagine a lot of people can confirm I was there."

"Did you go to the party with a date?"

"No, with my half brother, Rafe James."

"Did you hear the shot fired at Joe Colton?"

"Yes."

"Where were you when you heard the shot?"

"In the center of the courtyard."

"Alone?"

"No, I was talking to Rebecca Powell and Rafe."

"How long had you been with them?"

"A few minutes."

"Whom did you talk to before Rebecca and your brother?"

Cheyenne hugged the clipboard to her chest. She sensed the cop knew the answer to every question before he asked it. "My other brother, River and his wife, Sophie Colton. Her cousin, Jackson Colton, too."

GET 2

HOW TO GET YOUR
2 FREE BOOKS AND FREE GIFT!

1. Peel off the MIRA sticker on the front cover. Place it in the space provided at right. This automatically entitles you to receive two free books and an exciting mystery gift.

2. Send back this card and you'll get 2 "The Best of the Best™" novels. These books have a combined cover price of $11.00 or more in the U.S. and $13.00 or more in Canada, but they are yours to keep absolutely FREE!

3. There's no catch. You're under no obligation to buy anything. We charge nothing – ZERO – for your first shipment. And you don't have to make any minimum number of purchases – not even one!

4. We call this line "The Best of the Best" because each month you'll receive the best books by some of today's hottest authors. These authors show up time and time again on all the major bestseller lists and their books sell out as soon as they hit the stores. You'll like the convenience of getting them delivered to your home at our special discount prices . . . and you'll love your *Heart to Heart* subscriber newsletter featuring author news, horoscopes, recipes, book reviews and much more!

SPECIAL FREE GIFT!

We'll send you a fabulous surprise gift, absolutely FREE, simply for accepting our no-risk offer!

5. We hope that after receiving your free books you'll want to remain a subscriber. But the choice is yours – to continue or cancel, anytime at all! So why not take us up on our invitation, with no risk of any kind. You'll be glad you did!

6. And remember...we'll send you a mystery gift ABSOLUTELY FREE just for giving "The Best of the Best" a try.

Visit us online at
www.mirabooks.com

® and TM are trademarks of Harlequin Enterprises Limited.

BOOKS FREE!

Hurry!

Return this card promptly to GET 2 FREE BOOKS & A FREE GIFT!

The Best of the Best ™

▼ DETACH AND MAIL CARD TODAY! ▼

Affix peel-off MIRA sticker here

YES! Please send me the 2 FREE "The Best of the Best" novels and FREE gift for which I qualify. I understand that I am under no obligation to purchase anything further, as explained on the opposite page.

385 MDL C6PQ

(P-BB3-01)
185 MDL C6PP

NAME (PLEASE PRINT CLEARLY)

ADDRESS

APT.#   CITY

STATE/PROV.   ZIP/POSTAL CODE

Offer limited to one per household and not valid to current subscribers of "The Best of the Best." All orders subject to approval. Books received may vary.

©1995 MIRA BOOKS

The Best of the Best™ — Here's How it Works:

Accepting your 2 free books and gift places you under no obligation to buy anything. You may keep the books and gift and return the shipping statement marked "cancel." If you do not cancel, about a month later we will send you 4 additional novels and bill you just $4.24 each in the U.S., or $4.74 each in Canada, plus 25¢ shipping & handling per book and applicable taxes if any.* That's the complete price and — compared to cover prices of $5.50 or more each in the U.S. and $6.50 or more each in Canada — it's quite a bargain! You may cancel at any time, but if you choose to continue, every month we'll send you 4 more books, which you may either purchase at the discount price or return to us and cancel your subscription.

*Terms and prices subject to change without notice. Sales tax applicable in N.Y. Canadian residents will be charged applicable provincial taxes and GST.

If offer card is missing write to: The Best of the Best, 3010 Walden Ave., P.O. Box 1867, Buffalo, NY 14240-1867

THE BEST OF THE BEST
3010 WALDEN AVE
PO BOX 1867
BUFFALO NY 14240-9952

BUSINESS REPLY MAIL
FIRST-CLASS MAIL   PERMIT NO. 717   BUFFALO, NY

POSTAGE WILL BE PAID BY ADDRESSEE

NO POSTAGE
NECESSARY
IF MAILED
IN THE
UNITED STATES

"How long did you spend with Mr. Colton?"

"Ten minutes. Maybe."

"This was before you started talking to Rebecca and Rafe?"

"Yes."

"Do you know where Colton went after he left you?"

The air in her lungs seemed to thicken. "To get us drinks from the bar in his uncle's study. It was nearing time to toast Mr. Colton's birthday."

"Were you in the center of the courtyard when Colton walked off?"

"Yes, near the fountain."

"Which way did Colton go?"

"Toward the house."

"There were several small bars set up on the grounds. Why didn't he go to one of those to get a refill?"

"As I said, it was nearing time to drink a toast to Mr. Colton. People had lined up in front of all the bars. Jackson said it would be faster if he went into the study and fixed our drinks there."

"I need a reference point, Miss James. Do you know where the service hallway is that connects the house to the courtyard?"

"Yes." Cheyenne smoothed her hand over a section of red bunting the wind had flipped back.

"Is that the direction Colton went?"

"Yes."

"Did you see him step into the hallway?"

"Yes."

"And then?"

"I started talking to Rebecca. Then Rafe came up."

"Did you keep your eyes on the hallway after that?"

"No."

"So, Colton could have come right back out."

"There wouldn't have been a reason for him to do that. He went inside the house to fix our drinks."

"How long after you saw Colton duck into the hallway did you hear the gunshot?"

"Maybe two minutes." She shrugged. "I'm not sure."

"So, you can say positively that Colton was near the service hallway a couple of minutes before someone tried to kill his uncle."

Cheyenne kept her eyes locked with Law's. "I can say that Jackson was with me until a minute or two before I heard the gunshot."

"That's a good try at alibiing him, Miss James. But there's a space of time you can't account for his whereabouts. People can do a lot of things in a minute or two."

"Detective Law, it's obvious you suspect Jackson is the person who tried to kill Joe Colton. You're wrong."

"I expected you to say that."

"We've never met. What makes you think you would have any idea what I might say?"

He angled his head. "Earlier, I watched you with Colton by the corral. Considering the way you look at each other, touch each other, I figure you've got a relationship going. People close to each other usually try to protect the other person."

Knowing that Law had watched her and Jackson sent a chill up Cheyenne's spine. After she and Jackson parted, Law must have followed her to the dining hall, she reasoned, where there had been a horde of people and nowhere for a private talk. So, he'd waited until he could get her alone, on the small rise where the deserted bandstand stood. She looked beyond Law, her gaze sweeping the paddocks, the corrals, the buildings, the houses and farther to the ranch's property line where giant redwoods stabbed into the sky. She felt small and alone and suddenly vulnerable—which she guessed was intentional on the cop's part.

"Yes, Jackson and I are close. But I'm not trying to protect him. I don't need to. He's not the person who fired the shot."

"Can you prove that?"

"No." A distant cheer rose from the crowd watching the bull riding.

"I can't either," Law stated. "Jackson Colton was present at his uncle's birthday. He was at the Colton ranch seven months later when someone took a second shot at his uncle. In a case like this, proximity and accessibility to the intended victim mean a lot."

She felt as if a stone had lodged in her chest. "Just because Jackson was in the general vicinity both times someone tried to kill his uncle doesn't mean he's guilty."

"True." The wind whipped Law's dark hair into his eyes, but he didn't seem to notice. "In my mind it's a stretch to think it's just a coincidence that no one can vouch for his whereabouts during either attempt."

"That's exactly what it is. A coincidence."

"I've been a cop a long time, Miss James. I've learned the more I can't prove someone innocent, the greater chance they are guilty."

"Try harder. Jackson is innocent."

"Everyone's entitled to his own opinion." Law raised a shoulder. "You're an intelligent woman, Miss James. You do good work here with kids who need help. Backing off from Colton might be smart for you, at least until this investigation's completed."

"I have no reason to back off."

"That's your choice."

Law's cell phone rang. He pulled it off his belt, flipped it open and answered. He listened for a moment, his brow creasing. Then his gaze lifted to meet Cheyenne's. "I'll be in touch, Miss James."

Turning, he strode away, the phone clamped to his ear.

Jackson caught a glimpse of Cheyenne in profile as she waited beneath the oak where they had agreed to meet before the target shooting match. She had one shoulder propped against the trunk of the towering tree, her gaze focused on the bull riding competition in full swing a few yards away.

He glanced toward the corral, saw that Johnny Collins and a couple of other Hopechest teens were again straddling the same section of gleaming white fence they'd claimed that morning during the bronc busting. At that instant, the chute sprung open and Johnny whooped a cheer for the cowboy holding on for dear life while a snorting black Angus bull kicked and bucked beneath him.

Shifting his gaze back toward the oak, Jackson took time to study the woman who, somehow, someway had become a permanent part of his thoughts. He took in her endlessly long legs clad in snug denim, the sleeveless red blouse that fell over the curve of her breasts then cinched at her narrow waist. As he watched her, he realized he had never before seen Cheyenne James so unaware. The faintest line of concentration showed at the corner of her eye and mouth. Her lips were slightly parted. The wisps of hair that had fallen out of her braid fluttered against one high, sculpted cheekbone.

She took his breath away. Just like that. And before the night was over, she would be his.

A pang of desire, then something deeper and stronger than he'd expected stirred inside him as he walked to her. What that something was, how deep it went, he didn't know.

"Cheyenne."

She started at the sound of his voice, then turned. Concern overrode everything else when he saw the bleakness in her dark eyes.

"What's wrong?"

"Detective Law's here. He questioned me. Jackson, he already knew we spent time together at your uncle's birthday party."

Jackson fisted a hand against his thigh, unfisted it. Anger would get him nowhere. "We were standing in the courtyard, surrounded by hundreds of people. It's not a surprise a few of them mentioned to Law that they saw us together."

"I doubt any of them know exactly when it was you left me to go get us our drinks. No one else but me remembers that. And I had to tell Law. I had to tell him I saw you near the service hallway only minutes before someone near there shot at your uncle."

"Yeah." Jackson pulled in a slow breath. "Cheyenne, we knew this was going to happen. It was a matter of time before Law got around to talking to you."

When she raised her chin, sunlight filtering through the oak's leaves patterned her burnished skin. "I wanted to refuse to talk to him. I wanted to just tell him to get lost."

"No." Gripping her arms, Jackson leaned in. "You'll only make problems for yourself if you give Law a bad time. You have to talk to him. You have no reason not to.''

"He thinks you tried to kill your uncle. He wants to use me to try to prove it.''

"Let him.''

"I don't want to let him—''

"Dammit, I didn't do it!'' The frustration growing inside Jackson flexed in his words. "Law can try all he wants, but he can't *prove* anything.''

Her hands came up, her palms pressing against his chest. "I know you didn't do it, Jackson. I know.''

The certainty in her voice twisted something in his gut. He pulled her against him, buried his face in her hair and swore.

"I'm sorry I put you in the middle of this. If I could change things, if I could go back to that night, I wouldn't have come anywhere near you.''

Tipping her head back, she met his gaze. "We were meant to talk to each other.''

"Maybe.'' He furrowed his brow at the stillness that had settled in her voice. "If there's such a thing as fate, it wasn't doing you any favors at that party by hooking you up with me.''

"I'm not sure of that.''

A roar rose from the crowd watching the bull riding. Cheyenne's gaze slid toward the corral. In a crystallized moment Jackson saw the color drain from her face. She stiffened against his touch.

"Cheyenne—''

"No!''

"What—''

Her hands gripped the front of his shirt as her gaze swung back to his. Her face was ghost-pale, her eyes wide and filled with fear. "Johnny!''

Jackson jerked his head toward the corral. The smiling teenager still straddled the fence, cheering the cowboy riding the back of a ferocious Brahma bull. "What about him?"

"The bull! He'll go out of control, get too close to the fence, to Johnny." She was talking so fast that her words tripped over each other. "We've got to get him off the fence."

"Cheyenne—"

"Now!" She clamped her hand on Jackson's wrist, yanked him forward.

"All right." He sprinted with her across a gravel path, then a section of grass, driven by pure instinct that told him to ask questions later.

On the far side of the corral, Johnny and his pals continued cheering and clapping for the cowboy atop the livid bull.

Out of the corner of his eye, Jackson caught movement. He whipped his head around just as the cowboy went airborne. The man smashed onto the ground. Instantly, he rolled several times as the fire-eyed, snorting Brahma went after him, its back hooves shooting up clumps of dirt like bullets.

A murmur went up from the crowd when the angry animal dipped its head and aimed both horns at his former rider. To Jackson, the black, red-eyed bull looked akin to the devil.

"Move! Move!" Cheyenne shoved her way through the mass of watchers. The urgency in her voice invaded Jackson's system as they plowed toward the corral.

He saw the cowboy regain his feet. With fifteen hundred pounds of incensed bull charging after him, the man bolted toward the closest section of fence where the teenagers sat. The rider scrambled up the side of the corral and over, barely evading the Brahma's horns.

The animal spun, kicking and bucking. Its back hooves smashed into a support post. Once. Twice.

Jackson heard a crack of wood splinter the air. Cheyenne screamed Johnny's name. A look of horror crossed the teen's face as his body teetered. A half second later, he pitched forward into the corral. The bull bucked, a roar of motion and sound as both hind legs kicked into the air.

Jackson saw the hooves crash into Johnny's side, heard the boy's startled bark of pain.

Short, rusty breaths scraped at Jackson's throat. Adrenaline surged through his body like fire. He levered over the corral's top rail, snagged the back of Johnny's belt. Using both hands, Jackson jerked the boy's limp body up at the same instant the snorting bull's deadly hooves trampled the earth where he'd landed.

"Give him room! Give him room," Cheyenne shouted, shoving people back.

Lungs heaving, heart pounding, Jackson eased the teen onto his back on a patch of grass beside the corral. Johnny's eyes were closed, his mouth slack.

Cheyenne dropped to her knees beside him and swallowed a sob. "How bad is he hurt?"

Jackson looked up. Her face was ice-pale, her eyes filled with pure fear. When he reached and squeezed her shoulder, he discovered his hand was trembling. "One of the bull's hooves caught his left arm. It's probably broken."

"God." Blake Fallon crouched beside Jackson, his mouth clamped in a hard line. "Someone saw Dr. Kent getting a drink at the dining hall. I sent a couple of the ranch hands to find him and drive him here."

Cheyenne's hand shook as she brushed dark hair off the boy's pasty forehead. "We tried to get to you," she said softly. "We tried."

Jackson studied her with grim assessment. She had known. She had known ahead of time the cowboy would fall. That the outraged Brahma would surge out of control. That Johnny would topple into the path of its deadly hooves. She had known. How the hell had she known?

He looked toward the corral where several wary-eyed ranch hands twirled lassos over their heads as they approached the bull from all sides. The echo of a memory stirred in Jackson's mind, bringing with it the picture of a young Cheyenne trailing after her brother around the Colton stables. And with that memory came tales, rumors—

"Make way for the doc!" The shout from behind him jerked Jackson back to the present.

"Let's see what we've got here." Dr. Nicholas Kent was tall and powerfully built with thick silver hair and a matching mustache. A network of lines pulled at the flesh around his blue eyes. Having spent most of his growing-up summers in Prosperino, Jackson had been ministered to a number of times by the man.

"Doctor Kent."

"Jackson." Kent crouched just as Johnny's eyelids fluttered open. He thrashed, his eyes half-open, the whites showing, straining.

"Easy, Johnny." Jackson placed a hand on his chest, held him down.

"Just relax, son. We'll get you taken care of." Kent's evaluating gaze swept the boy's arm, then lifted. "What happened?"

Jackson used a forearm to wipe the sweat off his forehead. He had to force every word past his dirt-dry throat as he related events of the accident. "One of the bull's hooves caught him in the left elbow," he finished.

The doctor nodded. "I sent one of the hands to drive my car over here. My medical bag's in the trunk."

A thick moan rose up Johnny's throat.

Kent placed a practiced hand on his shoulder. "I know it hurts. I'll give you something for the pain in just a minute. Then I'll drive you to the hospital. I need a couple of pictures of that elbow."

"Gotta…go…to…hospital?"

"That's right, son."

The teen's dazed, half-shut eyes met Jackson's. "You…go, too?"

"Sure." The knot in Jackson's chest tightened. Over the past week, he and Johnny had developed a camaraderie while they'd worked side-by-side.

Dragging in a steadying breath, Jackson inclined his head toward the boy's arm, which was bent at an almost impossible angle. A bloody slice ran down the length of his forearm, which was already turning black and blue. "Listen, Collins, there are easier ways than this to get yourself taken off my paint crew."

"Yeah. I'll remember that…next time."

Blake furrowed a brow. "I'll follow you to the hospital and take care of the paperwork." He looked at Cheyenne. "You'll let the other counselors know what happened? Take care of things here?"

"Of course." Her voice hitched. "Don't worry about anything."

A ranch hand barged through the circle of onlookers and handed Dr. Kent a black bag.

While Kent tore paper off a disposable syringe Jackson patted Johnny's good arm. "Cheyenne and I need to talk for a minute before I leave. I have to make sure she's got everything lined up to judge the target shooting in my place.''

Johnny rolled his head, gazed up though dazed eyes at Cheyenne. "I guess I messed up. Can't...be on your archery team."

"You're on my team." She cupped a hand against his cheek. "You just get to take a break from practice for a while."

Jackson rose, held out a hand to help her up. She hesitated, then slid her hand into his.

He pulled her through the maze of onlookers, stopping a few feet away. Turning, he placed his hands on her shoulders. Beneath his palms, she felt as taut as a coiled spring.

"You okay?" he asked quietly.

"Yes. It's good Johnny asked you to go with him, Jackson." She kept her eyes on the injured boy while she spoke. "He trusts you. For Johnny, that doesn't come easy."

"For a lot of people, I think."

"If someone could call from the hospital, let us know how Johnny's doing..." Her voice broke. "You saved his life."

"*We* saved his life." Jackson cupped her chin in his hand, nudged it up until her gaze met his. Her eyes were huge and dark in the pallor of her face. "I'm not sure how we did that. When I get back, you and I have to talk. I need to know what just happened."

"I know." For a brief instant, the wrenching sadness in her voice closed around him. "I know you do."

Hours later, Cheyenne stood alone on her dark porch. Under the pale light of the moon, her small front yard was a mix of subdued shades of gray and black, with occasional patches of white. Leaning a shoulder against the porch rail, she wondered if she had actually thought she could open herself intimately to a man, yet keep secret the gift of her heritage. A gift that coursed through her veins.

"Idiot." Her quiet voice drifted on the warm night air, blending with the music coming from the far-off bandstand. After Johnny's accident, she had forced herself to work, carry out the duties required of her. Yet, she had drawn the line at going to the dance, so she'd asked another counselor to take her place. She had opted for the coward's way out by refusing to watch couples move beneath the dance floor's twinkling lights while the memory of Jackson's voice replayed in her head.

Save me every dance tonight. After that, I'm going to take you home and make love with you. All night.

Her throat tightening, Cheyenne shrank away from the thought. Instead of dwelling on what might have been she had to face what was.

Johnny would recover, that was the important thing. Blake had called after the teenager had been wheeled out of surgery, with two pins in his elbow. Dr. Kent predicted a full recovery. For that, Cheyenne was grateful.

What made her heart clench was the knowledge that Jackson had witnessed what he had that afternoon. At this point he didn't know any specifics, but he had seen enough to know she had willfully deceived him.

He would walk away, just as Paul had. The blame was all hers. She had intentionally kept the truth from Jackson and fate had taken a hand.

He had been honest with her. He'd come to her, told her the police suspected him of two attempted murders. By doing so, he had given her a choice of accepting or backing away. Because she'd been afraid of the outcome, she had denied him the truth about herself.

"Idiot," she said again.

"Are you talking to me or yourself?"

Jackson's voice caught her like a slap in the face, had her spinning around. When he moved across the lawn through a swath of weak moonlight, the grimness in his face had her nerves jittering.

"Myself," she managed. "How's Johnny?"

"Out like a light." Jackson came up the porch steps, then paused. "Blake's spending the night at the hospital. Dr. Kent says we can bring Johnny home tomorrow."

"Good. That's good." She wrapped her arms around her waist, cupped her elbows in her hands. "I owe you an explanation."

He moved toward her like a shadow, controlled and observant. "I'm not sure you owe me one, but I would appreciate one." His voice was even, his eyes intent. Unnervingly so.

She took a deep breath. "I've mentioned to you that my mother died the night she gave birth to me. I never heard her laugh. The only memories I have of her are through the stories River and Rafe tell me. Even so, I feel she is always with me because she passed a gift to me, through the blood. The gift of sight."

"Are we talking ESP?"

"A form of it."

"I'd say it's a pretty exacting form. Today you saw the accident before it happened. You knew Johnny was in danger before that bull kicked the fence."

"Yes. I have visions. I see certain things and events before they happen." She put an unsteady hand to her throat. "I know what I'm telling you is hard to believe, but it's true."

"If I hadn't been there today, I wouldn't believe it. But I was a part of what happened. Johnny would probably be dead now if it weren't for you."

"Us. We were both meant to be where we were."

Jackson raised a hand, let it fall. "I chose the oak tree as a place for us to meet off the top of my head. I could have just as easily asked you to meet me at the shooting range."

"You didn't. We were meant to be near the corral."

"So, you're saying fate put us there so we could save a life?"

"Yes."

"Do you know how incredible that sounds?" he asked, his voice taking on a hard edge.

"Of course I do. And I know you would like me to give you a rational explanation for everything, but I can't. Any more than I can explain why the visions that come to me don't always have a clear purpose, like the one did today. I sometimes don't know why I see the things I do, why I sense them, or what they mean. I just accept what I see and deal with it the best I can." She pulled in a ragged breath. "I'm sorry, Jackson."

His eyes narrowed. "Are you sorry that you have visions, or that you failed to mention them to me?"

Pride stiffened her spine. "I'm not ashamed of my gift. My mother's people revere my visions for their power to do good. I am sorry I wasn't truthful with you."

"So am I." He took a step toward her, his hands clenched. "That first night we ran into each other, when we went for coffee, I told you I remembered something about that shy, skinny little girl who used to follow River around like a shadow. I asked if you read palms or minds." His fingers flexed, fisted again. "You said no."

"That's because I don't do either. I can't look at the lines in your hand and predict your future. I can't gaze into your eyes and read your thoughts, only imagine them, like now."

He angled a rigid shoulder against one of the porch's columns, crossed his arms over his chest. "What do you imagine I'm thinking right now?"

"You're angry that I kept this from you. You feel betrayed and hurt." She shut her eyes. "I never meant to hurt you, Jackson. My intention was to help."

"Help?"

"Do you think we met in the lobby of the movie theater by chance?"

"Hell, yes," he answered, even as something flickered in his eyes. "I walked out of the police department and started driving. I didn't know I was going to wind up at the movie until the minute I whipped a U-turn in the street." He leaned in. "Why were you there?"

"I was meant to be there," she answered quietly. "The last thing I planned to do that evening was see a movie. I was at home, writing a grant for funding of a new vocational work-training program for the ranch. Then a vision came to me of a man's eyes, hard and gray. I didn't know whose eyes they were. All I knew was he was in trouble, that he needed my help and that I would find him at the movie theater. I went there, bought a ticket and waited in the lobby. I didn't know the man in my vision was you until I saw your eyes."

"So you just dropped everything and headed to the movies?" Although his voice remained steady, raw emotion flickered in his gaze. "You didn't know why or how, you just came?"

"My visions are always for good. I don't question them. I accept and respond. I still don't know how I'm meant to help you, Jackson. The answer will come in time." She turned and stared out at the moonlit yard. She could smell the poignancy of the yellow roses that edged against the porch. "It always does."

"Is that why you've let me hang around you?" He jerked her around to face him, forcing a stunned breath from her lungs.

"I—"

"Is that why you let me kiss you?" His hands clamped on her upper arms. "Agreed to make love with me? So you can bide your time until some vision lets you know how you can *help* me?"

She blinked. "I... No, I... No—"

"You claim you wanted time for us to get to know each other. We've had a hell of a lot of long talks lately, Cheyenne. I even managed to squeeze in that the police suspect me of trying to kill my uncle. I told you that little tidbit because I couldn't in good conscience let you walk deeper into a relationship with me without knowing how things stood."

"I know—"

"You had plenty of opportunity to tell me about this... gift." His fingers tightened like steel rods on her arms. "Instead, you kept it to yourself. Dammit, Cheyenne, it hurts that you don't trust me."

"I know, and I'm sorry." Guilt weighed like a stone, dead center in her heart. "I thought about telling you, even sometimes imagined myself doing that. I was afraid to take a risk, so I stopped myself."

"Why? Why couldn't you just tell me?"

"It would have changed everything."

"You don't know that!"

"I do know!" Jerking from his touch, she fisted her hands against her jeaned thighs. "What you've learned about me tonight changes how you look at me. What you think of me. I'm *different,* Jackson. Too different to have a normal relationship.''

His dark brows slid together. ''Who the hell told you that?''

''No one told me. I learned it. My father left me with my aunts on the reservation because he couldn't handle the fact I was different. He was a drunk, he beat my brothers, but I didn't know that when I was little. All I knew was my mother was dead and the father I needed didn't want me.'' She felt tears she'd thought she had finished with years ago stinging her eyes. ''At the Anglo schools I went to, the other kids called me names, shunned me because I wasn't like them. In college, I told the man I loved about my visions. He looked at me as if I had some terrible disease. He told me to stay away from him—*stay away*—then he walked out.'' Her voice hitched with the memory. ''You can stand there and tell me that being different doesn't matter, Jackson. I know better.''

''All right, so you know.'' A muscle worked in his jaw. ''You thought that was what I would do? If you told me about your visions, you thought I would walk away?''

A single tear spilled over and ran down her cheek. She turned her head so he wouldn't see her swipe it away. ''Look at history. People have hanged, burned or drowned those who seemed different. These days they mostly avoid them.''

''Dammit, Cheyenne.'' He scrubbed his hands over his face then dropped his hands and stared out at the dark yard. ''Dammit.''

They stood in silence, thoughts and space separating

them while music from the bandstand floated, soft and sensuous, on the breeze.

"I'm not your drunken father or the moron you dated in college," Jackson said finally.

She slid him a look. "What?"

"I saw what happened today. A boy is alive because of you. Maybe I had a hand in things, but I wouldn't have been there to pull Johnny out of harm's way if it hadn't been for you."

As he spoke, Jackson reached out and took her arm, then turned her to face him. "I'll concede your gift of sight makes you different from most everyone else. Since I've seen it at work, I know it also makes you special. Very special."

She opened her mouth, closed it on a shudder and felt the first tingle of relief loosen the fist around her heart. "Special."

"I don't like secrets, Cheyenne. I've seen what they do to relationships. I wish you could have trusted me enough to tell me your secret."

"I didn't want this to end. What we have, what we maybe could have." She closed her eyes for a brief instant. "I care about you, Jackson. I was selfish. I didn't want you to walk away."

"Like most every man you've cared about."

"That's right."

"Just when I think I get my footing, you knock me off-balance again." He gently traced the line of her earlobe, idly fingering the simple gold hoop she wore there. "I'm not used to a woman doing that to me."

Her heart began to pound. "You're not?"

"No. This gift of yours—the way you are—is new to me. I need time to take it all in." Slowly, he pulled her into his arms until his body brushed hers. "That doesn't mean it changes how I feel about you."

Her throat went dry. She still couldn't quite believe. "Doesn't it?"

"We've stayed in each other's minds since the night of my uncle's party because you and I sparked something in each other that's impossible to ignore. *I* don't want to ignore it. I want to find out what that something is and exactly how I feel about you." His eyes stayed on hers as he lifted a hand to her cheek and stirred her heart. "Is that what you want, too, Cheyenne?"

"Yes." The word came out on a shaky breath. The band's steady, sensuous beat matched that of her pulse.

His mouth took a slow, quiet journey over her jaw, down the line of her throat, back to her trembling lips. Even as a shiver coursed through her she felt her body warming, melting. The air seemed to go very still, very suddenly. Now the only sound was her own uneven breathing.

"You were supposed to save me every dance," he murmured against her mouth.

Her hands wound into the fabric of his shirt. Her mind blurred. "I can't...hear the music...anymore."

"To hell with dancing, then." One of his hands slipped beneath her loose braid to cup the back of her neck as she arched her head back. In the moonlight, reckless need glinted in his eyes. "I want you." His other hand cupped her breast, kneading, tormenting. Her nipple budded, strained against the silk of her bra. "I've never wanted a woman the way I want you."

Her arms slid up, and she dug her fingers into his hair. The remembered vision of candlelight glowing gold against their joined bodies played back in her head. Destiny, she thought dimly. This man was her destiny.

"Candlelight." Her breath caught in gasps as she raced greedy kisses down his neck.

His hand shoved beneath her blouse, her bra, seeking flesh. Heat flashed so fast and hot, it incinerated her skin. Her body strained and trembled against his. When her legs went weak, she clutched at him for balance. "I want candlelight. And sweet wine. But first, I want you."

"You'll have them. You'll have all that and more," he said, then latched his mouth onto hers.

Eight

"**I**nside," Cheyenne managed to moan before Jackson's mouth clamped against hers in a dazing, dizzying kiss that heated her blood until it flash-fired beneath her skin, roared in her head.

"We...can't do this...on the front porch."

She scraped her teeth over his jaw and felt him tense like a runner on the mark.

"We're going inside." His voice was rough, urgent while one of his hands worked at the buttons on her blouse. "And we're not coming out. Ever."

"Fine. Good."

They staggered together across the porch, hot, hungry mouths locked. When she took a stumbling step backward, he swept her up into his arms and jerked open the screen door. Her fingers plunged into his hair, her body straining against his with urgent need.

He carried her inside the small house, then kicked the

front door closed behind him. A weak wash of light coming from the lamp she'd left burning in her bedroom illuminated the small living room in silver light and shadow.

When Jackson set her on her feet, Cheyenne discovered her knees were loose, her head filled with blinding light and colors. If he hadn't shoved her back against the nearest wall and trapped her body with his, she knew she would have crumpled to the floor.

Against her belly, she felt him pulsing with need.

His breath a harsh rasp through his lips, he caught her face in his hands. "Tell me." Eyes the color of the storm-tossed sea bored into hers, searching. "Tell me you want this, Cheyenne. You want us."

"Yes." Her throat was so dry the word was barely audible. "I want us." His warm, musky scent filled her head, made her heart thud. "I want to feel you." Her unsteady fingers worked to free the buttons on his shirt, then shoved material aside. "Touch you." Frantically, she tugged his shirttail out of his jeans, then rose on tiptoe to nip at the pulse in his throat. "Everywhere at once. Here. Now."

His eyes glimmered in the weak light as he fought the shirt off his arms, flung it aside. "You've got a bed—"

"Now." A hum of pleasure surged up her throat while her exploring hands slid across his chest, savoring the power of sinew and muscle, soaking up the feel of him. "Here, Jackson. Right here." With a light fingertip she traced the swirl of coarse, dark hair that circled one nipple, then her mouth replaced her fingertip.

He tasted dark and dangerous and so very male.

"Holy…" Beneath her lips, she felt his heart jolt, then thunder.

Wrapping her braid around one hand, he arched her

head back to expose her throat to his mouth. He dipped his head, his lips scalding hot against the point in her throat where her pulse hammered.

"All right, Cheyenne, here." When he raised his head and met her gaze, she felt a shocking jolt at the burn in his eyes. "The first time, right here." His voice seemed to throb the words across her skin, making the flames in her blood rage hotter. "We'll find the bed later. And use it."

Lust clutched deep in her belly while he helped her fight off her boots. He shoved her shirt off her shoulders, down her arms, then to the floor. With an expert flick of his fingers, he unhooked her silk bra, dragged it off and found her flesh.

"You're beautiful." Gazing down at her, he cupped her breasts in his rough, clever hands, his thumbs performing a slow, erotic massage of her nipples. "Perfect."

The flash of passion, the fury of need that darkened his eyes filled her with a sense of decadent power as she stood before him, naked from the waist up. Time and place became nothing against a hard, driving desire for him. Only him.

Urgency made her fingers clumsy, and she fumbled with the button on his jeans. She whimpered when he caught her wrists in his hands, stilled her movements. "Not yet," he murmured. "We'll get to me."

Need raged, clawed inside her when his teeth seared a hot path across her exposed flesh. She drew in a sharp breath at the sensation of his mouth trailing down her ribs, then lower to the waist of her jeans.

She felt the insistent tug of his fingers at the button, then heard the rasp of the zipper, followed by the exquisite torture of his mouth moving lower still. His hands stroked over her hips, slipping beneath the loosened waist of the jeans. Denim whispered against her flesh as he skimmed them off. Then he went down on his knees, his hands locked at her waist, and nuzzled her through the thin silk of her panties.

Desire flooded her veins like flame leaping along a trail of gasoline.

"Jackson…" Her knees threatened to buckle, and she had to cling to his shoulders for support.

She writhed against the first touch of his tongue, the tender stroking, the feather-soft flicks. When he lightly nipped the crest of flesh where her lips joined she thought she would shatter into a million pieces. The pressure of his mouth intensified as his lips suckled her through silk. The air around her thickened; her breath snagged in her lungs while the wet pulse between her legs pounded.

Inch by inch he peeled the heated silk down her legs, then pulled her to the floor with him. Beneath her back she felt the softness of the rug that pooled in the center of her living room.

Her mind went hazy when Jackson leaned over her, blocking out everything else. Nothing existed for her but him. Only him.

His mouth began feasting on her flesh, his greedy hands racing over her quivering body in ruthless exploration. Heat pumped through her blood; she felt herself going warm and soft, melting into his touch, becoming one.

Her hot, hungry mouth nipped his neck, his chest. Her nails dug into the hard ridge of his shoulders. She couldn't get enough of him, of his taste, his touch. He seeped into her, pore by pore.

She whimpered when he eased away to pull off his

boots; her fingers tangled with his as he stripped off his jeans and briefs.

In a heartbeat of time, she gazed at him through the dim, silver light. His body was beautiful, tanned and strong, with muscles that rippled and tightened as he moved.

He came back to her, his greedy mouth claiming one breast to feed, suckle, devour, his teeth scraping erotically over her aching, budded nipple. Words strangled in her throat, images exploded in her brain and she arched back, her fingers digging into his shoulders. Minutes, or maybe hours, later, his mouth shifted to her other breast and reworked its torrid magic.

He fanned his long fingers low over her belly then cupped her, his hand molding against her already sensitive flesh with intimate possession. She writhed under his touch, her hands raking into his hair, fisting. His fingers moved against her wet heat, relentlessly driving her up, the need for release building, clawing viciously inside her.

"Look at me," he said when her eyelids fluttered shut. "I want to watch your eyes when you become mine."

"Yours." The shadows around them seemed to shift while his fingers stroked. Sensation slid over sensation, building inside her in trembling, shuddering layers, then exploded. Her vision grayed; his name tore from her lips in a half sob.

Strength gone, her hands slipped from his shoulders. She lay motionless, sweat slicking her flesh, helpless to do anything else but gasp for breath.

One of his hands slid beneath her, his fingers splaying at her back to lift her hips.

His body was like iron over hers.

A sob of pure, overwhelming pleasure eased up her throat when he pushed inside her. Her body opened to his, joined with his. Arching, she buried her face in the hollow between his neck and shoulder and brought him in deeper. She gave herself over to him completely, moving with him, welcoming the deep, smooth strokes of his body inside of hers.

In that fleeting moment before they plunged together into the roaring dark, Cheyenne understood that she was his. There would never be room for another man in her mind, in her heart. Jackson was the one. The only one.

Eventually, they found Cheyenne's bed. And made good use of it.

Now, hours later, Jackson lay awake, propped on one elbow, watching her sleep while the heady scent of her drifted through his senses. They'd turned out the light earlier after he had lit the candles scattered around the bedroom. The flames had since drowned out in their own wax. The only light left was from the moon, pale streams of it slanting over the bed, turning Cheyenne's skin a warm, seductive gold.

She lay sprawled on her stomach, her breathing slow and even, her hair a glorious blue-black fell on the white pillow. He reached out, grazed his palm along the length of her body.

A sigh rose up her throat.

Even now that he'd had her, he was half-wild to get his hands on her again, to feel her under him.

Emotions that he was helpless to put a name to or understand surged through him. Before tonight he had accepted he had feelings for her. But he hadn't known, couldn't have known, that a woman's touch—*this woman's*—could sever the knots of his control so quickly. Thoroughly.

They had known each other only a short time. Before that they knew of each other, walked around the edges of each other for years. That was why he had carried with him the faint memory that something was different about River's shy little sister. Something mystical.

He understood now what those secrets were he had seen in her eyes. Visions, he thought. Much more than mere wisps of intuition—she had proven that today when her actions had saved Johnny Collins's life. The power she possessed seemed something more akin to subconscious dreams rooted in some sort of surreal reality.

Frowning, Jackson blew out a breath. He had no true understanding of what powers she possessed. But he did recognize that, by telling him about the gift of her heritage, she had pushed aside caution, exposed herself, made herself vulnerable. For that, he was responsible. He watched her, lying curled beside him, warm and soft and trusting, and hoped to hell he could handle the responsibility.

That he didn't know for sure didn't come as a surprise. Responsibility meant commitment—where relationships were concerned, he had always involved himself in straightforward affairs, no gray areas, no untidy emotions. No woman had ever made him feel the need to dip below the surface. With Cheyenne, at some point when he wasn't looking, he had gone fully under.

Reaching out, Jackson stroked his fingers along the silky softness of her hair. Logic told him that his being the suspect in two attempted murders was reason enough to keep their relationship as it was now—no strings attached, with walking away an option. The thought of her doing that had his fingers clenching in her hair. It didn't seem to make a difference that he didn't need more complications in his life right now. All that mattered was that Cheyenne James wasn't just any woman. She was *his* woman.

To his profound amazement, he was beginning to think he meant to keep her.

Cheyenne woke just after dawn feeling achy and sated…and totally decadent from having spent most of the night being ravished and ravishing. Stretching like a contented cat, she shoved her disheveled hair out of her face. The corners of her mouth lifted at the memory of Jackson loosening her braid, working his fingers through the long, thick strands, then fisting his hands in her tangled tresses while he eased himself into her wet depths.

Twin surges of fulfillment and excitement swam through her. She and Jackson had shared more than passion during the hours they'd spent together. There were feelings that ran deep below the surface, too. How deep, she wasn't sure. All she knew was that they existed. Eventually they would have to be faced, then dealt with.

Turning her head on the pillow, she gazed through the weak dawn light. Jackson lay asleep on his side, his face half turned toward her. Against the white pillowcase, his face looked deeply tanned, shadowed by jet-black stubble. His hair was a rumpled mess, his mouth slightly open, his lips relaxed.

Thoughts of how that mouth had destroyed her control sent a shudder of pure longing through her. Easing out a trembling breath, it was all she could do to keep from reaching out and raking her fingertips through the dark hair that dusted his chest, then letting her hand slide lower….

She closed her eyes. It wasn't just passion she felt stirring in her belly, she realized. Last night Jackson had accepted her as no man ever had. She had opened both her body and her soul to him and he had not turned away.

He had touched her heart simply by understanding, by seeing what was inside her. He had seen, and he had accepted.

She loved him.

Her eyes widened as the realization settled around her. Oh, God, she was in love with him! It was that simple. That staggering.

That terrifying.

Although she'd shared her body with Jackson, given him her trust, she wasn't sure what to do about sharing her emotions. Gnawing her bottom lip, Cheyenne thought back to their youth, to the seemingly unending stream of high school girls he'd entertained during weekends and summers at the Colton ranch. Then there was Sophie's comment about the number of hearts Jackson had reportedly broken after he'd moved to San Diego. Cheyenne knew it wasn't his nature to want to hear a woman's declaration of love. Most likely it would put the fear of God into him.

It came close to doing the same to her.

Swallowing past the tightness in her throat, she slid out of bed. She needed time…and space to think.

At one point during the night when they'd taken a breather from pleasuring each other, Jackson had gone into the living room and retrieved their clothes. Now Cheyenne stepped shakily around the pile where he'd dumped them, grabbed her robe, then padded across the hall to the shower.

* * *

A sharp hammering noise woke Jackson. With his face pressed into the pillow, he could smell Cheyenne. Her soft, seductive scent brought a dreamy image that both aroused and soothed.

The hammering grew louder.

His mind still hazy, Jackson shifted, reached for her— and discovered he was alone in bed. Raising his head, he caught the sound of running water. Cheyenne, he reasoned, was in the shower.

Another burst of ungodly noise brought the realization that someone was banging on the front door. Blinking, he decided if the racket was going to stop, it was up to him to see to it.

"Hold on," he muttered.

Groggy, he sat up, raking a hand over his stubbled jaw. He retrieved his jeans off the floor where he'd piled them last night, pulled them on. On his way down the hall, he tugged on his hopelessly wrinkled white shirt.

"I'm coming," he said as the thudding continued. Jackson reached the door and yanked it open. His heart stopped.

"Detective," he said evenly.

Thad Law, dressed in a blue suit, blue tie and white shirt, stood on the porch, the morning sunlight sparkling clear behind him. "Mind if I come in, Colton?"

"Would it matter if I did?"

"Nope."

Jackson stepped back, pulling the door open wider. Law followed him in, his gaze flicking toward the dim kitchen, then across Jackson's shoulder toward the hallway. "Where's Miss James?"

"In the shower," Jackson said, although he no longer

heard the water running. "Are you here to see me, or her?"

"Both. I'll get my business with you taken care of first." As he spoke, Law shoved back one flap of his suit coat and pulled a pair of handcuffs off his belt. "Jackson Colton, you're under arrest for two counts of attempted murder."

Jackson's stomach knotted. "If you're basing this arrest on the evidence you presented me a week ago, you don't have a case. You and I both know that."

"New evidence has come to our attention."

"What new evidence?"

"We'll get to that. Downtown. Turn around and put your hands behind your back."

The knots in Jackson's stomach turned to pure acid. He knew he had no choice but to do what Law said. The cop patted him down for weapons. When the cold steel bands snapped around Jackson's wrists, his body gave a compulsive jerk.

"You have the right to remain silent—"

"I'm an attorney. I know my rights. I don't need to hear them—"

"Jackson!"

With her hair wrapped in a towel and a white terry robe belted at her waist, Cheyenne darted from the hall. Eyes wide, her face pale, she looked at Law. "Why are you doing this?"

"Why else?" Law asked. "I've got evidence that points to Colton's guilt."

"Of what?"

"I figure you have a pretty good idea, Miss James. Just in case you need it spelled out, the charge is the attempted murder of Joe Colton. Two counts."

She took a step forward. "I don't care what evidence you think you have. Jackson is innocent."

"Doesn't look like it from where I'm standing."

"Jackson." She turned to him, her already pale face bloodless now. "Tell me what you want me to do."

"Call my Uncle Joe." Jackson gritted his teeth. It was all he could do not to jerk away when Law clamped his fingers around his upper arm. "Tell Uncle Joe I've been arrested, and the charge. Have him contact my cousin, Rand—he's a criminal attorney in D.C."

"All right."

"I've got business with you, too, Miss James," Law said. "I need a formal statement from you. After you make that call, get dressed and drive to the station."

Jackson saw something dark come and go in Cheyenne's gaze. "After I talk to Joe Colton, I'm calling my attorney. He'll be in contact with you, Detective Law."

"By all means, consult counsel. Bring him to the station with you. Just make sure you show up."

"Like I said, my lawyer will be in touch."

Jackson felt Law's fingers tighten on his arm. "You don't want to get on my bad side, Miss James. Trust me on that."

Frustration began to rise in Jackson, and with it anger. Cheyenne was playing with fire, trying to protect him. This was *his* problem, he needed to make her understand that.

He met Law's stony gaze. "Let me talk to her before we leave." He dipped his head toward one corner of the living room. "Over there."

Law narrowed his eyes. "You're an attorney, Colton, you know what I can do if she refuses to cooperate. You going to clue her in?"

"That's exactly what I intend to do."

A muscle working in his jaw, Law aimed a hitchhiker-like thumb in the direction of the living room's far corner. "Five minutes."

As he moved, Jackson tried to block out the cold, desperate feel of the cuffs that secured his wrists behind his back. He couldn't dwell on that. Nor could he lose himself in the rush of useless emotions—anger, outrage, a hated sense of vulnerability—that bubbled in his blood. He had only a short time to make Cheyenne see that she couldn't protect him. That he didn't *want* her protection.

When they reached the end of the couch, she turned to face him. "Jackson—"

"We don't have much time," he began in a low voice. "I need you to listen to me. First, do you even have an attorney?"

Her gaze flicked past his shoulder to Law. "No. There's one who handles legal matters for the residents of the reservation. I'll call him."

"Don't bother, chances are he doesn't know much about criminal law. When you talk to Uncle Joe, tell him you have to make a formal statement, that you need one of his attorneys to go with you to police headquarters."

"I don't want to make a formal statement."

"Cheyenne—"

"I can place you in almost the exact spot where the shooter stood at your uncle's birthday party. That can only hurt you. I don't *want* to make a formal statement."

"You can't *not* make one," Jackson countered through his teeth. "You don't have the right to refuse to talk to the police. You only have the right not to incriminate yourself when you do talk to them." He paused, took a deep breath. "You're trying to protect me, I understand that. There's a part of me that even appreciates it. But in doing so, you're putting yourself in jeopardy. That's not how we're going to do this, Cheyenne."

"Law intends to use me to make you look guilty." Anger flashed in her eyes. "You're not."

"You're right, I'm not. But my guilt or innocence isn't the point here. The point is what he can do to *you* if you try to put him off for long."

She lifted her chin. "I doubt he can do a lot."

"That's where you're wrong. Law might let you drag your feet for a day or two, but the bottom line is, he has to make his case so he can present it to the D.A. Your statement is part of his case. If you refuse to cooperate, Law can arrest you on a charge of material witness to an attempted homicide. If he feels like it, he can also add withholding evidence and impeding an investigation charges. He can go before a judge, say that you're an unwilling witness—which you are—and because of that you might be a flight risk."

"I'm not going anywhere."

"Law doesn't know that, and neither will the judge. So, if Law asks the judge to hold you without bond, chances are the judge will grant the request. For a while anyway, you'll be stuck in jail with no way out."

Color flooded her cheeks. "That's blackmail."

"It's also law enforcement." Jackson leaned in. "No way in hell are you getting locked up because of me, Cheyenne. Do you understand that?"

"A vision sent me to *help* you." She placed an unsteady palm against his cheek. "I need to help you, Jackson. I don't know how I'm supposed to do that."

"Start by calling Uncle Joe." The tears swimming in her eyes almost brought him to his knees. "Have him call Rand. Tell him to get you a lawyer. Come in and give a statement to Law." Jackson turned his head, placed a soft kiss against her palm. He wanted to hold her, touch her. All he could do was savor the taste of her.

Nine

"Look, Law, I've told you the truth," Jackson said two hours later. "Repeatedly. There's nothing else I can tell you. I don't know who tried to kill my uncle. All I know is, it wasn't me."

He and the detective were in the same small room, sitting in the exact spots at the scarred table where their initial interview had taken place a week ago. Burns still tattooed the tabletop; the air carried the same stale odor of cigarettes and sweat. As it had a week ago, Law's small recorder sat beside the notepad that the cop had placed in front of him.

The difference was that Jackson was now under arrest. The cops had fingerprinted him. Photographed him. Placed him in a bleak, sterile holding cell. The thought of going back to a cell, just the thought of it, had his blood icing.

He clenched his hands, still smudged with the remnants of fingerprint ink, and met Law's steely gaze. "I wish to hell I hadn't been alone in that service hallway when someone took a shot at Uncle Joe during his birthday party. And if I had known four months ago what I do now, I wouldn't have driven in from San Diego and arrived at the house just minutes after the second attempt on my uncle's life. I would have waited until the following day and flown to Prosperino with my father. But I didn't. I drove. And I arrived at Hacienda de Alegria right *after* the shooting. Those are the facts. The truth."

When Law pursed his lips, the small, paper-thin scar on his left cheek turned even whiter. "No, Colton, I don't believe you've told me the truth."

"What you believe doesn't matter." Jackson leaned forward. "It's what you can *prove.* So far, all we've done is rehash what we went over a week ago. Yes, I was the attorney of record on Amalgamated Industries vs. Jones. I helped my former college roommate take control of his family's business away from his father, who was addicted to alcohol, drugs and gambling. That doesn't *prove* I planned to kill my uncle and take control of Colton Enterprises from my father. And I don't know who the hell it was who walked into that L.A. insurance company and bought a policy on Uncle Joe's life that names me as beneficiary. My guess is it was some starving actor who'd do most anything for the right money. All I know for sure is that man wasn't me."

"You're correct, Colton, all we've done so far is rehash. It's time we made some progress." Law pushed back his chair and stood. Sometime after their arrival at the station, the detective had shed his jacket. Now his white shirt looked almost as rumpled as Jackson's. The cop had opened his collar, loosened his blue tie. Rays from the room's stark fluorescent lighting glinted dully off the gold badge clipped on his belt beside a holstered automatic.

"Let's talk new evidence." Law moved to a small table beside the door, retrieved the manila envelope lying there. "I'm looking forward to hearing your explanation for this."

He strolled back to the center of the room. Easing a hip onto the table, Law opened the envelope and pulled out a large plastic bag. Inside the bag was a blue-steel automatic.

"Tell me about this," Law said, holding the top of the bag between a fingertip and thumb.

Wariness tightened Jackson's chest. "I can't tell you about it. I've never seen that gun in my life."

"Nine-millimeter German Luger. Ballistic tests confirm this is the gun used in both attempts on your uncle's life." Law's mouth curved into a feral smile. "Ring any bells?"

"No."

"So, you're telling me you've never seen this gun?" Law extended his arm to give Jackson a better view of the weapon. "Never shot it?"

Jackson stared at the Luger, noting the notch in one of its dark grips. "That's what I'm telling you."

"How do you suppose your prints got on it?"

Jackson felt the muscles in his shoulders tighten. "No way in hell are my prints on that gun."

"They are." Law shrugged. "I don't know, Colton, maybe the evidence fairy put them there."

Jackson took a breath, braced himself. "Look, I told you last week someone has gone to a lot of trouble to set me up. The Luger is another piece in that setup."

"Yeah, I remember your theory. Trouble is, you're

the only person swimming in the suspect pool. I've tried, but I can't eliminate you.''

"That's because when someone gets set up, they look guilty.'' Jackson narrowed his eyes. ''Where did you find the Luger?''

"In a Dumpster, a couple of blocks from the PD.''

"You just happened to look in the Dumpster and got lucky?''

"Dispatch got an anonymous call yesterday, telling us where to look. We dusted the Luger for prints, then ran them through the system. You're in there because you were fingerprinted when you joined the California bar.'' Law leaned in. ''If I were you, I'd confess and get everything over with.''

"Don't hold your breath.''

The cop sighed. ''I figured you'd say that.''

A knock sounded at the door. ''Company.'' Law slid the bag holding the Luger back into the manila envelope. He rose, walked to the door, opened it and stuck his head out. Seconds later, he looked back at Jackson. ''Your lawyer's here, says he wants to confer with you.''

Jackson blinked. He didn't know what time it was— he'd left his watch on Cheyenne's nightstand. But he was sure his cousin Rand hadn't had nearly enough time to make the trip from Washington, D.C. to Prosperino.

"I'll talk to my client in private.''

Jackson leaned back in his chair, surprised to see his father stride through the door. Graham Colton was dressed for business in a pristine needle-thin pinstripe suit, perfectly tailored to fit his lean, wiry build. Thatches of gray edged the temples of his thick, blond hair.

Jackson rubbed a hand over his face. He remembered now his uncle saying that his parents had planned on arriving last night at Hacienda de Alegria. Great, this was all he needed.

Graham waited to acknowledge Jackson until Law stepped out of the room and closed the door behind him.

"Quite a mess you've gotten yourself in, son."

"I didn't get myself into it." *Unlike you when you slept with Aunt Meredith and fathered Teddy.* "Someone shoved me into this mess when I wasn't looking."

"Hmm." Graham pulled out the chair Law had occupied. He sat, steepling his long fingers that sported a pair of gold rings. Jackson noted there was no concern in his father's eyes, just speculation.

"Before we get into things," Graham began, "I'll tell you what's going on from my end. Your current fling— I forget her name—called the house this morning."

"Cheyenne," Jackson said through his teeth. "Her name is Cheyenne James, and she's not a fling."

Graham's brows arched over cool blue eyes. "I see. Anyway, when *Cheyenne* called, I answered the phone. She wanted to speak to Joe. Since he was out riding and hadn't taken his cell phone, she had to settle for me."

Jackson propped his elbows on the table and rubbed at the headache that snarled in both temples. "Did you get her a lawyer? Has she come in yet to give Law a formal statement?"

"No, on both counts."

Jackson smashed a fist onto the table. "Dammit, she needs a lawyer! I want her to make a statement. No way in hell is she going to jail on my account."

"Calm down," Graham said mildly. "After Cheyenne told me everything, I had her drive to the house. Joe was back by the time she arrived. He thinks you're innocent, by the way, and he's incensed you've been arrested. He called Rand's office, got hold of his new wife..." Graham raised a hand. "I can't remember her name."

"Lucy."

Graham waved the information aside. "She said Rand was in Sacramento attending to some business. Apparently, he had planned on surprising Joe and Meredith with a visit before he flew back to D.C. Anyway, Joe contacted him, then sent the corporate jet to pick him up." Graham glanced at his watch. "Rand should have arrived by now. Joe's meeting him at the airport. They've got an appointment with Yale Williams to arrange your bond."

"Good." Yale Williams was a judge who'd been Joe Colton's friend for years. Jackson felt the tension backing off knowing that chances were good he wouldn't have to spend the night in a cell.

He rubbed his gritty eyes while fatigue pressed down on him like a lead weight. "What about Cheyenne?"

Graham angled his head. "I get the idea you care about this woman."

"I do. She needs a lawyer to bring her in so she can make a statement."

"I disagree. She should hold off—"

"I don't give a damn—"

"You're wasting time getting angry. Your Uncle Joe and Rand agree with me. In fact, Rand talked to Cheyenne on the phone while he was on the way to the airport. She told him she can place you at the party, in the vicinity of where the shooter stood when he tried to kill Joe. At almost the exact time of the shooting."

"That's right, she can."

"No way does Rand want her giving Law a formal statement. As of their conversation, Rand is also representing Cheyenne. He told her to stay at Hacienda de

Alegria. Once we get you out of here and back to Joe's, we'll put our heads together. Have a strategy session, so to speak.''

Jackson blew out a breath. Except for the two summers he'd interned in the L.A. County D.A.'s office, he'd had little experience with criminal law. On the other hand, Rand was one of the country's top defense attorneys. A master at strategy, he was considered lethal in a courtroom. Jackson trusted him explicitly.

"Okay. Good." He met his father's dispassionate blue gaze. "I appreciate you handling things."

"I should mention that your mother is staying at Hacienda de Alegria for a few days. Since she's also an attorney, she considered coming here with me. I told her you only need one lawyer at a time. She agreed."

Typical, Jackson thought. The woman who'd barely acknowledged his presence while growing up would never consider he might want—or need—a mother's emotional support.

He gave his father a sardonic look. "I doubt an entertainment attorney would do me much good right now."

"Probably not," Graham agreed. "Your uncle gave me a rundown on the evidence the police had as of last week. That doesn't sound like much. What did Law base the arrest on?"

Jackson closed his eyes, opened them. "He says they received an anonymous call telling them where they could find the gun—a Luger—used to shoot at Uncle Joe. They looked in a certain Dumpster and found the gun. Ballistic tests match the Luger to the slugs found at both murder attempts."

"That still doesn't explain why you're under arrest."

"Law claims my prints are on the Luger."

Graham sat silent for a moment. "Did you do it?" he asked quietly.

Control kept Jackson in place, made his eyes flat, held his voice even. If he got out of the mess he was in, there was no way he would spend another day working with the father who had so little faith in him.

"Our business is done, Graham. You can leave now. And don't bother making that strategy session tonight."

On long-ago weekends when Cheyenne visited her brother, River, at Hacienda de Alegria, she had spent hours curled up in Joe Colton's paneled study, made warm and vibrant by deep rugs and polished brasses. She'd expended most of her time leafing though the collection of Colton family photo albums that Meredith had meticulously maintained. Young and desperately shy, Cheyenne had turned the heavy pages slowly, mesmerized by the faces that smiled back at her, the locations pictured, both familiar and exotic. And always, always her young girl's heart had sighed over the pictures of Jackson Colton flashing his bold, reckless, irresistible grin.

Tonight there was no humor in Jackson's face.

He had settled in the maroon leather wing chair that was a twin to the one she'd chosen, both angled in front of Joe's massive mahogany desk. The Colton patriarch, along with his attorney-son, Rand, had persuaded the judge—an old family friend—to grant a bond for Jackson's release. The three men had arrived grim-faced at the house in time for Jackson to shower and change before dinner. Now he wore tailored slacks and a black linen shirt that deepened his tan and turned his gray eyes the color of a storm-tossed sea.

With so many people around, Cheyenne had barely

had a chance to talk to him, certainly hadn't had a moment alone. While Jackson was in the shower she had met with the tall, dark-haired attorney. She had once heard that seeing Rand Colton argue a case in court was like watching a wolf circling a potential kill and losing patience. Even so, Rand's eyes were oddly gentle in such a strong-featured face. Cheyenne supposed that was why it had been easier than she thought it would be to propose the strategy she had worried over for most of the day.

She doubted Jackson would react with equal calm.

"The Luger with your prints on it is our major concern." Rand spoke as he walked to the wet bar built into a small alcove between towering bookcases. He poured a snifter of brandy, then glanced over his shoulder. "Does anyone other than Dad want a drink?"

"I'm off alcohol," Jackson said while Cheyenne declined the offer with a shake of her head.

Rand arched a dark brow. "Since when?"

"Since the one drink I had at Liza's wedding reception knocked me for a loop."

"It's best to keep a clear head now anyway while we figure out how to deal with the Luger." Mouth pursed, Rand carried the snifter to his father who was leaning back at his desk, glancing occasionally at the bank of security monitors built into the nearby wall.

Cheyenne sat in silence, breathing in the scent of leather and beeswax. She wondered whether Graham and Cynthia Colton, both attorneys, had opted not to join them for this brainstorming session or hadn't been invited. All she knew for sure was that Jackson's parents had both been quiet and subdued at dinner. As had Meredith. Even the usually rambunctious Joe, Jr. and Teddy had eaten their meal in almost total silence. They'd slipped away the first chance they got and dashed into the kitchen where Inez had their favorite dessert waiting.

Rand eased onto the edge of the desk and met Jackson's gaze. "Do you remember ever seeing that Luger?"

"No."

"Have you been at a firing range since the second attempt on Dad's life? Maybe someone laid the gun down and walked off. Maybe you picked it up, returned it to them? A scenario like that would be enough to get your prints on the gun."

Jackson shoved a hand through his dark hair, leaving it appealingly rumpled. "I've racked my brain about that Luger since Law pulled it out of that envelope. I don't remember ever laying eyes on it. I sure as hell never shot it."

Joe scowled into his snifter as he swirled his brandy. "There's got to be some logical explanation for your prints to be on that weapon."

Jackson raised his chin. "Uncle Joe, I give you my word, I didn't—"

"Boy, don't you even start!" Joe's blue eyes sparked when he leaned forward in his chair. "I *know* it wasn't you who took those potshots at me. Only a fool would think that. I'm a lot of things, but not a fool."

"Thanks. Your belief in me means a lot."

Cheyenne's heart went out to Jackson when she saw the effort it took for him to smile.

Rand plucked a brass paperweight shaped like an oil rig off the desk, weighed it in his hand. "I plan to file discovery papers tomorrow so I can get a look at all the reports and evidence the police have. I'll arrange for my experts to conduct independent ballistic tests and fingerprint comparisons on the Luger. I also want my handwriting specialist to examine the signature on the insurance policy someone bought in your name. Those tests will take a couple of days. In the meantime, we need to address Cheyenne's dilemma.''

''That's right, we do,'' Jackson said.

Cheyenne's heart clenched when he rose, stepped to her chair and placed a palm on one of her shoulders. ''She isn't going to spend one minute in jail on my account. I want that understood up front.''

She placed her hand over his, then looked up and met his gaze. ''I don't want to give Law a formal statement about where I saw you at the party.''

Jackson's fingers tightened on her shoulder. ''Dammit, Cheyenne, we've talked about this. I told you what Law can do to you. Your being stubborn isn't helping.''

''I disagree,'' Rand said mildly.

Jackson slid his cousin a narrow-eyed look. ''She's trying to protect me by putting herself in a situation where Law can arrest her. That's not going to happen. Deal with it.''

''Cheyenne's testimony doesn't prove you pulled the trigger, but it places you at the location—at almost the exact time—from where the shot was fired at Dad. It won't help our case to have a jury hear that.''

Jackson reached down, hooked a finger under Cheyenne's chin and nudged it up. ''This morning Thad Law as good as told me he'll arrest you if you don't make a formal statement. He's not bluffing. He'll toss you in a cell. Trust me, it isn't a pleasant experience. I know.''

Swallowing hard, she took the leap. ''He can't arrest me if we're married.''

''What?'' Jackson stared in astonishment as her face began to burn.

''I've… In college, my roommate was in pre-law. I remember her talking about how a wife can't testify against her husband. That the police..." Cheyenne's voice hitched. "I'm not trying to force you into something you don't want, Jackson. It's just that if we were married, Law couldn't make me testify against you. You're innocent. I *won't* testify against you."

His mouth thinned. "In other words, you're giving me permission to use you to try to keep my butt out of prison."

Cheyenne's stomach jumped with nerves. "I don't see it that way. Someone's trying to make it look like you're guilty. I'm trying to even the odds."

Rand slid off the desk and walked to Jackson's side. "You're not looking at this objectively, cousin. The protection angle works both ways."

Jackson dropped his hand from her chin and faced Rand. "The two of you have discussed this?"

"Cheyenne mentioned her idea to me while you were in the shower."

"In that case, you should have *mentioned* to her that certain situations aren't covered under the marital privilege law. One situation being that the criminal act in question can't have occurred *prior* to the legal marriage of the spouses to each other. The first attempt on Uncle Joe's life was nearly a year ago. The second one four months ago."

"True." Rand slid a hand into the pocket of his slacks. "However, the law being the law, there are always exceptions. I made a couple of calls before dinner. A California appeals court ruled just last month that a woman who witnessed a crime committed by her then-fiancé can't be forced to testify on the grounds that the man is now her husband. The court felt that if she were forced to testify, her testimony could jeopardize their existing marriage."

Jackson's eyes narrowed. "A higher court could overturn that ruling."

"It's possible. If that happens, it won't be for years. In the meantime, citing the court's ruling is enough to prevent Law from getting his statement. Cheyenne will no longer be in danger of being arrested and charged with impeding an investigation." Rand placed a hand on Jackson's shoulder. "There's another aspect to this. With everything you've been through today, I imagine you haven't had a chance to think things through."

"What things?"

"If Cheyenne gives a statement to Law, the D.A. will plan to call her as a witness for the prosecution. He may even consider her his star witness. If that's the case, I can't represent both of you. She'd have to find another attorney."

Jackson nodded slowly. "Which means you'd get a shot at cross-examining Cheyenne."

"Exactly. And, as I do with every prosecution witness, I'd look for the peel."

"The peel," Jackson repeated, his mouth tightening.

Not understanding their use of the term, Cheyenne met Joe's gaze. "Lawyer talk," he said quietly.

Rand kept his eyes locked with Jackson's. "I believe you know I would find what I need in Cheyenne's background."

"Yeah, I know." Jackson clenched his fists. "Forget it, Rand. I won't let you do that."

"Would you rather go to prison?"

Jackson ran a hand over his face. "Dammit—"

"If you and Cheyenne get married, she'll remain my client," Rand pointed out. "She can claim spousal privilege. That will give us more time to concentrate on finding who set you up. Whoever did that had a very well-thought-out plan. It's going to take some effort on our part to unravel that plan and find who's behind it.''

Rand glanced across his shoulder. ''Dad, why don't you and I clear out and give Jackson and Cheyenne a chance to talk? Everyone's had a long day. We can meet back here in the morning.''

''Sounds good.'' Rising, Joe moved around the desk to stand at Jackson's side. ''You've got quite a woman here, son.'' He winked at Cheyenne. ''If you don't marry her, I just might.''

Jackson arched a dark brow. ''I'll keep that in mind.''

Joe slapped Rand on the back. ''You didn't have a chance to say more than a hello to your mother when you got here.''

As she rose from her chair, Cheyenne saw a shadow flicker across Rand's eyes as he said, ''You're right, I didn't. I'll have to be sure and mention to her that I had some business in Sacramento.'' He turned and followed his father out of the study.

Cheyenne waited to speak until the door clicked softly behind them. ''I'm sure you feel like I've pushed you into a corner, Jackson. That wasn't my intention.''

He gazed down at her, his eyes unfathomable. ''No, your intention is to protect me. Because you believe I'm innocent.''

''I know you are.''

''You know that because a vision sent you to me.''

''Yes. My visions are only for good.''

''I'll tell you what isn't so good. You heard Rand mention finding the peel in your background?''

She furrowed her forehead. ''I don't know what that means.''

''It's Rand's term for his ability to get under some aspect of a story, or of a witness, so he can 'peel' the testimony back and damage the witness's credibility.'' Jackson reached, ran a hand down her long hair that she'd left loose and flowing. ''Growing up, Rand heard the same rumors about you that I did. He's got a memory that won't quit.''

Cheyenne blinked. ''You're talking about my gift.''

''Yes. If you become a prosecution witness, Rand will conduct a background on you. One visit to the reservation and he'll know all about your visions. In court, he'll call witnesses to testify that you're known to 'see things.' When he gets you on the stand he'll ask if you're *sure* you saw me near the service hallway just before the shooting. When you answer yes, he'll suggest that, instead of actually seeing me, you just pictured me there in your head. Like you do so many other things. By the time Rand gets done, the jury will look at you as if you're just some crackpot visionary.''

Cheyenne felt herself go pale. ''I hadn't thought of that.''

''No, all you've thought about is protecting me.''

''A vision sent me to you because you need my help. That's what I intend to do, Jackson. Help you.''

He cupped her cheek, his flesh warm against hers. ''Is anyone else in your family this stubborn?''

Pride flared, had her angling her chin. ''Mokee-kittuun means People of the Red River. The blood of my mother's ancestors turned a river red before they surrendered to the white man.''

''Well, that explains it,'' Jackson said, his gaze locked with hers. ''I've never wanted a wife, Cheyenne. I can't honestly tell you I want one now. That's because of a lot more reasons than there might be a cell in my future. I grew up watching my parents' hollow marriage. I saw

Uncle Joe and Aunt Meredith's relationship disintegrate. All that makes staying single look good.''

She took a deep breath. "I understand how you feel."

"No, you don't." His hands settled on her shoulders. "I care about you, more than I've ever cared about another woman. Right now, I don't know how deep those feelings go. All I know is that you're who I want to be with. Make love with. I just don't know if I can give you what you need."

The lightning response of her body to his words no longer surprised her. "What I need—all I need—is for you to believe in me. In who I am."

His eyes turned eloquent. "The same way you believe in me? In my innocence? No questions asked."

"Yes. No questions asked."

For the first time that evening, his expression softened. "How could I not believe in you?"

She raised on tiptoe, brushed his lips with hers. "Make love with me, Jackson."

"We'll get to that." He nudged her back, yet kept his hands tight on her shoulders. "If you refuse to give Law a statement, you'll wind up in jail. If you cooperate and testify for the prosecution, Rand will tear you apart in court. All because of me. The thought of either of those things happening to you ties my gut into knots. This isn't your fight, Cheyenne, it's mine. It may not be the right thing to do, but if the only way I can keep you out of this is to marry you, that's what I'll do."

Her heart turned over. What would she give to hear him say those words under other circumstances? "It sounds like we're protecting each other. I can't bring myself to think that's wrong."

"A man ought to be able to give his wife guarantees. Make her promises. I can't do either of those, Cheyenne.

Even without your testimony, I could wind up in prison.''

"If that happens, we'll deal with it.''

"If that happens, you'll file for divorce. No way are you going to be saddled with a husband who's locked in a cell.''

Reaching up, she cupped her hand against his cheek. If the thought of him going to prison terrified her, she could imagine how it made him feel. "Now's not the time to think about that.''

He rested his brow on hers and slid his arms around her waist. "You're right, I don't want to think about it.''

"Then don't.'' She smelled the scent of his soap, his own spicy male tang, and nuzzled her face against his neck, wanting to absorb it. "Kiss me, Jackson. Tonight you don't have to think about anything else but kissing me.''

He lowered his mouth and plundered. Need and pleasure burst through her in one sizzling ball of heat. Her arms wound around him, banded around him until it seemed his heart wasn't merely thundering against hers but inside hers. The mindless pleasure she'd felt the previous night was back, and she surrendered to it.

"I can't get enough of you,'' he murmured. "Never enough.''

His lips left hers, but before she could protest, he pressed them to her throat. "Stay with me tonight,'' he breathed against her flesh. "All night.''

Her breasts ached for his touch, her thighs trembled. "All night,'' she promised.

He caught her face in his hands and stared down at her, his eyes dark and searching while his hard, lean body pressed against hers. "We'll get married tomorrow, if you're sure that's what you want.''

She sighed and rested her head on his shoulder. To even consider that their nights together might be numbered, that he would wind up in a cell for years—maybe even for life—had a terrible dread curling inside her belly.

She closed her eyes against the prospect. "Yes, Jackson, marrying you is what I want."

Ten

Patsy knew that Graham habitually rose before sunrise and took a walk on the beach. For that reason, she had crept out of her bedroom when the first thready light of dawn slid over the horizon. Now she stood on the beach, positioned out of sight from anyone who might peer over the rocky cliff that edged the rear of the Colton property. She knew damn well if Graham saw her he wouldn't venture down the wooden staircase built against the cliff's rocky face.

The air was lush with ocean spray as foamy waves slipped onto the wet sand. In her haste to leave the house she had pulled on snug slacks and a cashmere top, and forgotten to grab a jacket on the way out the door. The predawn chill prickled her skin, but she didn't dare go back for something warm to wear.

She *needed* to talk to Graham.

With so many people staying at the house, this was

the first chance she'd had to get him alone. And after Rand's nonchalant mention last night that he'd been conducting business in Sacramento when Joe summoned him to Hacienda de Alegria, she had to do whatever it took to force Graham into resuming the blackmail payments.

At Rand's mention of the city in which Meredith had attended college and worked, Patsy had murmured something about how lucky it was he'd been so close to Prosperino when Jackson got arrested. Smiling until she felt her face would crack, she then told him she was tired and going to bed. She'd had to wash down two Valiums with three fingers of vodka just to calm down. She hadn't slept a wink all night. How could she?

He knew. The bastard had sent her the message through those cold-as-glacial-ice eyes of his. When she'd first taken over Meredith's identity, Rand had treated her with deference, like a loving son. Over the years he had pulled away, grown distant. She no longer expected a hug and kiss on the cheek when she saw Rand. Lately a perfunctory nod was all she got. None of that had prepared her for the edgy suspicion she had seen in his eyes last night. It was as if he were waiting for something he knew would happen. Just waiting.

All of her senses screamed that he was close to putting the pieces of the puzzle together. He was a criminal attorney, for Christ's sake. All it would have taken for him to start digging in the right places was one phone call from that runaway bitch, Emily. The thought had Patsy's nerves slithering like restless snakes. What if Emily *had* remembered seeing her "two mommies" the day of the accident? What if, after that idiot Pike bungled killing Emily, she'd run to Rand for protection? He was smart and cunning and, like all lethal predators, he knew exactly when to bide his time and when to move in for the kill.

Patsy stared out at the sea, her eyes narrowing while her blond hair danced in the wind. She might still have some time to do damage control. After all, the cops already knew Meredith had a twin sister. Patsy closed her eyes and gave silent thanks that Meredith had saved the letter she, Patsy, had forged announcing her own death years ago. Lucky for her that the fire in the mental clinic's basement had destroyed all of her records.

Still, Rand had gone to Sacramento for a reason, and he'd made a point to let her know he'd been there. What if Meredith had been fingerprinted when she was hired on at the nursery school she'd worked at? What if Rand had gone to Sacramento because he'd discovered what the police hadn't—that some obscure nursery school had his mother's fingerprints on file?

Identical twins didn't have identical fingerprints.

Patsy put an unsteady hand to her throat. All Rand had to do was take a glass she'd used, or maybe go into her bedroom and retrieve a bottle of perfume, and he would have her prints. He could then have them compared, and he would know she was not Meredith. He would know she was Patsy, Meredith's twin who had killed a man named Ellis Mayfield when she discovered he had sold their sweet baby, Jewel. Because goody-goody Meredith wouldn't agree to lie for her, Patsy had been tried, convicted and sentenced.

Twenty-five years to life.

The vicious resentment she felt for Meredith bubbled up instantly. Her loving sister, her *twin,* had left her in a cell to rot for all those years. There was no forgiveness for that. Just revenge. Patsy had been taking that revenge, parading as Meredith, enjoying the Colton wealth and power for ten years.

The pinpricks of unease that surged up Patsy's spine told her that her life as Meredith Colton might soon end.

If Rand suspected enough, if he got Meredith's fingerprints and compared them with hers, he would know the truth.

She needed money—a lot of money—and she needed it now. Any minute she might have to pack up Teddy and Joe, Jr. and take off. She couldn't do that, couldn't *survive* without a stake. Dammit, Graham Colton had promised to pay her to keep her mouth shut about his being Teddy's father. Pay was exactly what he was going to do.

She had gotten Jackson out of the way—just because Joe had cried to some judge to get his nephew out of jail on bond didn't make a difference. Her getting Jackson's fingerprints on the gun ensured that he was headed to prison, maybe for life. Served him right for sticking his nose into her business and putting a stop to Graham's payments to her. Now that the son was essentially out of the way, it was time to deal with the father.

Her gaze drifted to the small, rocky alcove where she'd seen the person who'd actually tried to kill Joe hide the gun. She would love to see the shooter's amazed face when the news came of Jackson's arrest...and that *his* prints were on the gun.

The clatter of footsteps coming down the wooden staircase brought up Patsy's chin. She leaned, her mouth curving when Graham came into view. She took a moment to appreciate his strong good looks, the thick blond hair threaded with gray, that evidenced a stylist's touch. Even this early in the morning he was perfectly groomed, his heavy sweater and pleated chinos a complement to his well-toned body.

Just as quickly, she pushed Graham's sinfully handsome looks out of her thoughts. She hadn't come to this secluded apron of beach for seduction. She was there for money. Her whole future, and that of Joe, Jr. and Teddy, might depend on the next few minutes.

The instant Graham's feet hit the sand, she stepped into view.

"Jesus, Meredith, you scared me!"

"You're a smart man, Graham." She leaned forward fractionally to make her point. "You'd better be afraid of me."

Wariness slid into his eyes. "What the hell do you want?"

"You're a guest in my home, darling. I'm just trying to make sure your stay is comfortable."

"The next time I feel comfortable around you, I'll be laid out on a slab. Just tell me what the hell you want."

"Money. You promised to pay me to keep quiet about our little liaison. I have. Joe doesn't know you're Teddy's father, which means you're still named in Joe's will. I expect you to keep your end of the bargain."

He lifted a hand to his neck for a quick, impatient rub. "You know as well as I do that Jackson found out about the payments I made to you. He wasn't bluffing when he told you if you keep leaning on me for more money that he'll go to the police. In case it hasn't occurred to you, what you're doing is called blackmail. It happens to be illegal. You could get arrested."

"Yes, well, Jackson knows all about getting arrested, doesn't he? And because he has his hands full taking care of his own problems he's too busy now to pay attention to yours. It's time to stop trying to hide behind

your son, Graham.'' She gave him a sugary smile.
''There's one way, and only one, that will get you off
the hook. You pay me one million dollars. In cash. If it
makes you feel better, we'll call it a loan—which I'll
never pay back, of course. That's the only way you'll
be free of me.''

He stared at her for a long moment. ''I can't get my
hands on a million dollars in cash.''

''You've got stocks, bonds, other investments.'' Patsy
lifted a shoulder. ''Sell them.''

''I can't just *sell* them,'' he said with more than a
touch of annoyance in his voice. ''They're in Cynthia's
name, too.''

''I'm sure you'll figure out some way to get around
the ice-bitch you're married to.'' Patsy narrowed her
eyes. ''I expect you to be smart this time. If you tell
Jackson about this conversation, I promise you, you'll
be sorry. More than sorry.''

''Save the threats, Meredith. Jackson's gone.''

''What do you mean, he's *gone?* He's out on bond
for two attempted murders, his half-breed girlfriend is
set to testify against him and the police have a gun with
his prints all over it.''

''He and Cheyenne left the house this morning the
same time I did. They're going off somewhere to get
married.''

Patsy blinked. ''Don't you think this is a strange time
for that?''

''Not when you know the reason. Once they're married, Cheyenne can claim spousal privilege. That means
she can decline to testify against Jackson, which helps
his case. Immensely.''

''That doesn't change the fact that the police have the
gun with his prints on it.'' Patsy gave silent thanks that

she'd been forward thinking enough to set that up. "Your eldest son is going to prison, Graham. Maybe for the rest of his life. He won't be around to protect you and threaten me. All I want is a measly one million dollars. I need it to take care of your *other* son. If you don't pay, I'll go to Joe and tell him you're Teddy's father. You'll lose millions, *millions,* when he writes you out of his will."

"You act like this is all my doing, but we both know you came on to me, hotter than a cheap pistol." Hands clenched against his thighs, Graham turned his head and stared out at the ocean. "You're a conniving bitch, Meredith. I wish to hell I'd never laid my hands on you."

Abruptly furious, she grabbed his jaw, making sure to dig in her nails when she jerked his head around and locked her gaze with his. "Don't you dare stand there acting like you're so much better than me. I was more than good enough for you the night you cornered me in that rest room and had me." She felt herself vibrating with the anger he'd sparked in her. "Actions have consequences, you bastard. Your having to buy my silence is one of them. Pay up or your brother will be the next Colton you'll have to deal with. Compared to Joe, I'm a walk in the park. And you know it."

"Yeah." He shoved her hand away, rubbed his jaw where her nails had left half-moon imprints. "All right, you'll get your money. In cash. I just need time to get it together. Cynthia can't find out."

Patsy smiled and felt the tension in her stomach unknot. "Good boy," she crooned. "Just don't take too long. And be sure you keep Jackson out of this."

"That's not a problem," Graham said. "I'm not exactly his favorite person these days."

* * *

"I'm sorry, Cheyenne. As weddings go, ours wasn't much of one."

"It was fine." Gliding her hands up Jackson's bare chest, she stood on tiptoe, making no effort to avoid the stream of warm water that beat down from the shower's spray. "The honeymoon is shaping up to be much better."

He lowered his head to rub his wet lips over hers. "There is that."

While steam rose around them, he pulled her against him, one hand resting on the curve of her waist, the other pushing through her thick, wet hair to the back of her head. He kissed her deeply, thoroughly; she tasted the warm water that had beaded on his lips, felt it on his fingertips as his hand curved low over her.

It was surreal to think that this man whose touch made her tremble was her *husband*. Surreal, maybe, but true.

She and Jackson had risen early that morning and driven south along the rocky, rugged coast to Mendocino. They stopped at the courthouse and obtained a marriage license. One hour later, they had stood beneath sparkling sunlight on an ocean cliff with a justice of the peace and his smiling wife. There, they exchanged vows while gulls swooped and whales played in the distant surf.

Mr. and Mrs. Jackson Colton had then checked into an inn known for its isolation and beauty. Once in their cozy, paneled room, they'd barely stripped off each other's clothes before tumbling into bed. Hours later, Jackson had carried her into the shower. Now, with her entire body trembling from his touch, Cheyenne was certain he would have to carry her out, too.

"Cheyenne." He murmured her name over the hiss of water and curling clouds of steam. His hands glided gently over the curves and sleek planes of her body, as if he were discovering her all over again. She wrapped her arms around his neck as she lost herself to sensations—the wet heat of his body sliding against hers, the dark hair plastered across his chest, the taste of him in her mouth.

"I need you," he whispered hoarsely against her lips. "Just you."

"And I need you."

One of his hands moved down her belly, his long fingers cupped her, circling and kneading her sensitized skin until her legs threatened to give out. Just when she was sure she could no longer stand, he lifted her, guiding her legs around his waist as he pushed inside her.

The pure physical sensation of the act made her feel as if she had ceased to exist alone, and now existed as a part of him. For her, it was a joining that went beyond the physical to the spiritual, until body and soul became one. She loved him, yet she held that knowledge close to her heart. She knew Jackson cared about her, yet she was well aware the events of the previous day were the reason he was now her husband. Those events had not changed the man he was. That man had never before chosen to let a woman into his life. He hadn't had much of a choice when he'd let her in.

Cheyenne pushed away the thought. She loved him. He needed her. With so many shadows hanging over their future, thinking about what might happen was useless. She and Jackson were together. That was enough for now.

Slowly, he lowered her to her feet, nuzzled her throat. "I think if we don't get out of this shower now, we'll both drown."

"Save yourself," she said as she slumped against the wet tiles. "I can't move. I'll never move again."

"No way I'm leaving you," he said, then pulled her from beneath the warm spray.

Fifteen minutes later, Cheyenne walked out of the bathroom, wearing one of the inn's heavy velour robes. She had towel-dried her long hair and gathered it over one shoulder. She smiled when she saw that Jackson had already lit the logs in the fireplace built into one of the paneled walls. She glanced out the window that led to their private balcony. An early evening fog had rolled in, obscuring the inn's grounds and the ocean beyond. The whole world seemed to have turned a cottony gray cloud.

"After you dry your hair, we should think about getting something to eat," Jackson said as he stood before a small antique bookcase and uncorked the bottle of local wine he'd bought at a nearby store. He had pulled on casual slacks and a light sweater that was a shade darker gray than his eyes. His black hair was still damp, slicked straight back from his tanned face.

She slid him a look as she knelt in front of the fireplace and started finger-combing the tangles from her waist-length hair. "Food sounds good. I was beginning to think you didn't plan to do anything on this trip, except ravish me."

His mouth curved. "Certain appetites take precedence over others. It's the law." He moved across the room, crouched beside her and handed her a glass of red wine. "You thinking of suing me?"

"Could be. I have a really good attorney, you know." The words weren't totally out when she realized what she'd said. "Jackson, I'm sorry."

"You were just kidding."

"Yes, but considering the reason I have that lawyer..." She dropped her gaze to her lap where she'd clenched her hands. It was a jolt to see the plain gold band that circled her left ring finger. Taking a deep breath, she closed her eyes. As though they had agreed silently not to, neither she nor Jackson had spoken today about his arrest, or the real reason she now wore the gold band.

Last night, when they'd conferred one last time with Rand, he had suggested they get married as soon as possible, then take the next twenty-four hours to just be together. In the meantime, he would deal with the necessary paperwork. That paperwork included advising Detective Law and the District Attorney that Cheyenne James was now Mrs. Jackson Colton. Further, she was claiming spousal privilege and, therefore, could not be compelled to make a statement or testify against her husband.

"Cheyenne." Using a finger, Jackson nudged her chin up while he settled beside her in front of the fire. "I've got pretty thick skin. After all that's happened between us, I have to figure you're on my side."

"Yes." She raised the glass of wine, took a sip and felt her flesh warm. "I just wasn't thinking. And I didn't intend to remind you of everything."

"I haven't exactly forgotten." He glanced at his watch. "I'm planning on checking in with Rand before we leave to eat. By now he will have informed Law and the D.A. that they can't force you to give them a formal statement. I want to make sure no glitches have surfaced." He reached for her left hand, entwined his fingers between hers. "You're my number-one supporter. I'm not going to let anything bad happen to you."

She took another sip of wine, her brow furrowing as

she set the glass aside. "Speaking of supporters, I'd like to ask you a question."

"So, ask."

"I've been wondering about your parents."

His eyes narrowed. "What about them?"

"Why didn't they join us last night to talk strategy?"

"I didn't ask them to join us."

"They're both attorneys. Maybe one of them might have thought of something the rest of us didn't."

"Don't count on it. Neither of my parents has ever given my sister or me much thought. I don't expect that to change just because I'm facing prison." He paused. "At the police station, my father asked me if I tried to kill Uncle Joe."

"Oh, Jackson—"

"My sister, Liza, and I grew up in a house where manners took precedence over love. In fact, there wasn't any love, not where our parents were concerned. They never gave much of a damn about us. They left our upbringing in the hands of nannies and housekeepers. Uncle Joe and Aunt Meredith were the ones who cared. Meredith intervened, told my parents that Liza and I would be spending most of our time at the ranch with them. We basically grew up at Hacienda de Alegria."

Cheyenne's heart went out to the man who as a child must have thirsted for his parents' love. "On the weekends I spent there visiting River, your uncle always let me sit in his study and look through the photo albums. He always took time to tell me a joke and tweak my nose. Your aunt let me help her cut flowers from her gardens and showed me how to arrange them in crystal vases."

"I doubt Meredith has even looked at a flower bed in the past ten years. She sure hasn't spent the time promoting family unity.'' Jackson angled his head. ''I'll stop before I'm tempted to tell you all of the sordid Colton secrets. I don't want to make you sorry that you married into the family.''

''I won't ever be sorry.''

''I hope not.'' Jackson shifted, rested his back against the love seat upholstered in a soft raspberry-colored fabric. ''Speaking of family, do you want to call River and Rafe and let them know they have a brother-in-law?''

Cheyenne shook her head. ''I asked Rand to talk to both of them and to tell them I'll explain things when we get back.''

''I plan on talking to them, too. Considering the situation, I doubt either of them will be delighted.''

''My gift passed to me from our mother, from the blood to the blood. She taught my brothers to understand the power of her visions. They understand mine. River and Rafe will accept what we have done.''

''Accepting doesn't mean they have to like it.'' Jackson rubbed his jaw. ''Both might feel like going a few rounds with me, just for the principle of things.''

She arched a brow. ''Think they'll drag you behind the barn and gang up on you?''

''It's possible. I keep thinking about your ancestors, how a river ran red with their blood before they surrendered to the white man. Your brothers have that same blood running through their veins.'' Jackson flashed her a grin. ''And I thought my family was scary.''

Laughing softly, Cheyenne resumed finger-combing her damp hair and shifted her gaze to the fireplace. Flames danced. A spark popped. Thin curls of smoke rose toward the chimney.

In the next instant, she no longer heard the greedy lapping of the flames against wood, no longer smelled the heady scent of wood-smoke. All had been replaced in her mind's eye by a nearly blinding slash of light. Illuminated in the glare was a man's hand, clenched into a tight fist. Beneath the skin, the knuckles showed white. In her hazy, half-dreamed dream, Cheyenne could see—*feel*—the searing anger that had caused that hand to clench. Fear tripped in her heart, beat wings in her stomach.

"Cheyenne, what is it?"

"He's…" The air turned stale and hot, making it difficult for her to breathe. Her heart faltered; the fear she had felt transformed in an instant to cold, hard rage. "He wants…to kill him."

"Steady."

She knew the voice she heard was Jackson's, yet it seemed to come from far away. Everything around her was fuzzy and disjointed, except the man's fist, lit in that painfully bright slash of light. Something dark lay beyond the light, a form whose edges seemed to waver. She reached out her hand, desperate to touch. The form shifted, retreated. Straining, she leaned forward. If she could only touch. She *needed* to touch—

"Cheyenne!" Jackson's hand locked around her wrist, jerked it back. "You want to set yourself on fire?"

The images slid into one, fractured again before her eyes, then were gone.

"Cheyenne."

Shuddering, sweating, she struggled up from the depths of the vision, following the sound of Jackson's concerned voice. "Jackson…"

"I'm here." She hadn't known he'd put his arms around her, hadn't realized he'd pulled her onto his lap. All she knew was he was there, holding, comforting.

"Oh, God." She blinked, trying to clear the blur.

"It's okay, I've got you." His voice was soft, with a hint of steel beneath. "You had a vision, I take it."

His eyes came into focus, gray and waiting. "Yes."

He watched her, his face somber as he smoothed his palm down her damp hair. "That didn't quite have the same effect as the vision you had before Johnny got hurt."

"No." She forced a swallow past the dry knot in her throat, then looked for her wine. "I spilled it," she said quietly when she saw the glass lying on its side beside the crimson liquid that had pooled on the wood floor in front of the fireplace.

"*I* knocked the glass over when I grabbed your wrist. You kept leaning closer to the fire, reaching." He shook his head. "I was afraid you might stick your hand into the flames."

She took a breath that wasn't quite steady. "I'm not sure what I was doing."

"I'll clean that up and pour you more wine."

"No." Being held in his arms felt like she'd landed in a safety net. "Later. Just hold me."

"All right." He placed a soft kiss against her temple. "You want to tell me about what you saw?"

"It was more than just what I saw." She frowned. "I've never had a vision like that. Never *felt* one like that."

"How did it feel?"

"Horrible. There's a burning hatred. A fury." Her voice hitched. "He wants to kill your uncle. He hates him and he wants to kill him."

She felt Jackson's body stiffen beneath her. "You *saw* who tried to kill Uncle Joe?"

"No. I'm sorry." She could almost feel the hope slide through Jackson's fingers like cold, dry sand. "I saw his hand...and a slash of bright light. Something else was there, just beyond the light, something dark. Black, maybe. It was too bright and I couldn't see. That's what I reached for. I thought if I could just touch it..."

A chill racked her body. Feeling drained, she rested her head against his shoulder. "It's there, Jackson."

"What is?"

"The answer we need to clear you. It's there, beyond the light."

Eleven

Three days later, Jackson stood on Hacienda de Alegria's sprawling back terrace, hands jammed into the pockets of his slacks. The noonday sun shone down with blazing intensity while he watched Cheyenne, her movements smooth and controlled, walk across the stretch of manicured lawn toward the sea.

A tug of worry had him narrowing his eyes. He wasn't sure if it was simply her trim black slacks and blouse that made her look impossibly thin, or if the stress of the past few days had resulted in her losing weight she couldn't afford to shed.

She paused when she reached the staircase that led down the face of the rocky cliff to the beach below. Standing motionless, she stared out at the wind-tormented sea where wave swallowed wave. Her long, black hair blew around her face like a veil, but she made no move to control the thick tresses.

Something was happening. Something was building inside her that Jackson didn't understand. *Needed* to understand.

She had slept only in fits and starts since the vision first came to her at the inn. Later that same night he had felt her slip from his arms, had watched her move soundlessly across the moonlit room to the love seat. She had sat curled there the remainder of the night, staring into the dark depths of the fireplace.

Each night since they had returned to his aunt and uncle's house, Cheyenne had repeated the process, only now she left not only their bed, but their room. Because he sensed she needed to be alone, he hadn't followed her. Where she went, he didn't know. All he knew was that each time she moved from the circle of his arms, a part of his heart went with her.

Each morning when she returned to their bedroom, her face was pale with fatigue, her eyes shadowed. Haunted.

She spoke little of the vision, except to tell him that the light had grown brighter, as had the man's hatred. "The answer is there, Jackson," she had told him moments ago before she'd left to take a solitary walk on the beach. "It will come. You must have faith. You must believe. With time, the answer we need will come."

Inside his pockets, his hands fisted as he watched her move to the staircase, then descend the first few steps. Seconds later, she disappeared from sight. He felt the loss as keenly as a punch in the gut.

He couldn't avoid it any longer. Could not continue to deny how he felt about her. He knew those feelings had probably started settling inside him the moment he laid eyes on her at his uncle's birthday party. Had intensified steadily every hour he'd spent with her. No other woman, at any other time, had ever come close to taking root in his heart. Hell, he hadn't even thought it was possible. Not until Cheyenne had looked at him with simple, unquestioning faith in her eyes.

How could he not love her?

That no scrabble of panic accompanied the thought was a mild surprise. He dragged in a deep breath, bringing into his lungs the scent of salt spray, sunshine and the tea roses that bloomed in nearby planters. He had spent his life avoiding relationships, running from them because he hadn't understood what it was that made the rare ones work. Now he did. Vividly. The key was finding the unique woman, the one who could stir his heart where no other could.

Cheyenne, his wife, stirred his heart.

He loved her.

Even as the knowledge raced through his mind, he quelled it. He could not, would not, tell her how he felt.

He knew her intimately now, knew how her mind worked, had seen for himself the stubborn slant her jaw took when she'd made up her mind about something. Although she hadn't told him how she felt about him, he was almost certain her feelings mirrored his. If that were the case and he wound up in prison, she would refuse to file for divorce. Knowing that he loved her, she would fight for their marriage, sacrifice for him, perhaps waste her entire life. For him.

The absolute helplessness of his situation had his jaw locking. He couldn't change anything about the evidence the police had against him, but he could damn well do something about her. It was best, for both their sakes, that Cheyenne not know his true feelings. That she continued to believe he was a man ready, able and willing to walk away from any relationship. Even their marriage.

She *should* believe that, he thought. He wanted her to believe it. Because if he wound up in prison, that was exactly what he would do. Walk away. Legally and emotionally. For her sake.

The sound of footsteps approaching from behind had Jackson turning.

Rand, dressed in a dark suit, white shirt and crimson tie, strode toward across the terrace. "You don't look like a man who's having pleasant thoughts," his cousin commented.

"You got that right, counselor."

"Detective Law sends his regards." Rand settled into one of the padded, black wrought-iron chairs that dotted the spacious terrace. Reaching up, he loosened the knot on his tie and flicked open his shirt's top button. "So does the D.A."

"I'll bet." Jackson dropped into the chair nearest his cousin's. "They still making noise about Cheyenne claiming marital privilege?"

"Yes. The D.A. plans to file a challenge with the court. He'll probably do that this afternoon. Tomorrow at the latest."

"You have an opinion on how that'll turn out?"

"I believe our position will be upheld." Rand slid him a look. "It wouldn't hurt, though, for you to keep your fingers crossed. And your toes."

"Yeah." Jackson shoved a hand through his hair. "You and I need to get something settled between us. If it winds up that Cheyenne does have to testify for the prosecution, I don't want you going after her during cross-examination."

"Jackson—"

"It's not negotiable."

"It's suicide."

"Maybe. Look, I won't—*can't*—let you go for her jugular while she's on the witness stand. I've seen you work, Rand. By the time you were done with Cheyenne, you'd have the jury on the edge of their seats, waiting to see what magical Indian potion she was going to stir up. That would destroy her."

"Going to prison wouldn't have the same effect on you?"

"We're not talking about me."

"Answer a question." Leaning in, Rand rested his elbows on his knees. "Are Cheyenne's visions *real,* or just real to her?"

"I can't tell you I understand how they work. All I know is that I was there when one of her visions saved a boy's life. I'd say that's real enough."

Rand pursed his lips. "This vision she says she's having now about a bright light and a man's fist and a dark object she can't quite make out. Do you believe her claim is true? That the vision will eventually lead us to the man who took the shots at Dad?"

A fist of fear squeezed at Jackson's gut that she wouldn't find the answer. "Cheyenne says it will. She keeps telling me to have faith." He shifted his gaze to the staircase at the top of the ragged cliff where he'd last seen her. "With my butt on the line, I'd be lying if I said I'm content to sit back and wait for the answer. I'm not. I'd prefer to have some rock-solid evidence of my innocence to take to the police. All I can say is, Cheyenne knows a hell of a lot more about visions than I do."

"Well, let's hope she knows what she's talking about on this one." Rand raised a hand, let it drop. "You're an attorney, pal. I don't have to tell you that our case has its weak points."

"You're right, you don't have to tell me." Frustration pushed Jackson to his feet. "Any word from your experts yet on the results of the ballistic, fingerprint and handwriting tests?"

"Not yet." Rand checked his watch, then rose. "I'll go make some calls now." His hand settled on Jackson's shoulder, strong and firm. "Maybe one of them will come up with something solid we can use."

"I hope to hell you're right," Jackson muttered while he watched Rand stride across the terrace.

Just as his cousin reached the house, the door swung open. Jackson raised a brow when Johnny Collins, clad in baggy jeans, T-shirt and a red baseball cap, stepped out the door. Emmett Fallon followed behind him, sunlight glinting off his gray hair. After shaking hands with the twosome, Rand swept a hand Jackson's way, then disappeared into the house.

Jackson tucked away the frustration churning inside him and forced a smile.

"The patient is up and around, I see." While he spoke, Jackson shook hands with Emmett. "Too bad Uncle Joe's in Prosperino on business. I know he'd have liked to have seen you."

Emmett nodded. "I saw Joe at Hopechest Ranch on Memorial Day. He said to drop by anytime." Emmett's gaze swept the trim, jewel-like grounds and color-laden flower beds that sprawled toward the sea. "I'd heard he hired a security company to patrol the grounds after someone took that second shot at him. I bet I had to answer twenty questions when they stopped my car coming up the drive. Good thing Meredith answered the phone when they called the house to check on me, or we'd never have gotten up here."

"They take their job seriously," Jackson commented.

"Yeah." Emmett shrugged. "Anyway, Johnny here's going stir-crazy not being able to do any of his regular activities." While he spoke, the older man dug a pack of cigarettes and a book of matches out of his wrinkled denim shirt. "He wanted to thank you again for saving him. Since Blake's tied up today with Hopechest Ranch business, I volunteered to drive Johnny over."

"Glad you did." Jackson offered the teenager a hand and arched a brow at the cast molding the boy's left arm. A bright red sling with the Hopechest Ranch's logo looped around Johnny's thin neck, cradling the injured arm tight against his chest. "Last time I saw you, that arm was pointing the wrong way."

"Yeah, that Brahma sure packed a punch." Johnny shifted the brim of his baseball cap. "Thanks again for getting me out of the corral before that bull hammered me into dog meat."

Jackson hid a wince at the image. "You're welcome. How long do you have to wear the cast?"

"Doc Kent said at least a month," Johnny responded. "He'll take more pictures of my elbow then." He hesitated. "I was sort of wondering…are you and Cheyenne coming back to Hopechest?"

Jackson slid a hand into the pocket of his slacks. Because he wanted to clear the air, he said, "I don't know. I assume you've both heard I'm in trouble with the law."

Johnny's gaze slid away. "Yeah. I guess most everybody's heard."

Emmett exhaled a puff of gray smoke then swiped the side of one finger across his white mustache. "I can't figure that out, Jackson."

"What part of it can't you figure out?"

"I heard on the radio the police found the gun used to shoot at Joe. They're saying your prints are on it."

Jackson expelled a slow breath. Leaking information to the media about a suspect's alleged guilt was a standard law enforcement ploy. When it came time to pick a jury, almost everyone had their mind made up about the defendant's guilt, whether they admitted it or not.

"That's what the police say. Problem is, *I* didn't put my prints on that gun."

"I've known you a long time, son," Emmett said, his gaze going to the teeming ocean. "I've never known you to say anything that wasn't true."

Johnny shifted from one foot to the other. "We heard that you and Cheyenne got married."

"That you can believe." Jackson angled his chin at the boy's serious expression. "You have a problem with that?"

"No. Unless it means she won't be coming back to work at Hopechest. By the looks of this house, I guess you've got a lot of money and she doesn't have to work, but what if she wants to? You won't stop her, will you?"

Jackson fought a smile. He doubted he could stop Cheyenne from doing anything. "Cheyenne talked to Blake and he approved her taking a leave of absence. As far as I know, that's just until things settle down."

"I'd hate to see her not come back," Johnny said, then looked toward the house. "Is she here?"

"She's walking on the beach. I'll take you down to see her if you feel up to some pretty steep stairs."

"Sure, I'm game."

Jackson turned to Emmett. "What about you? Want to go with us, or would you rather wait for us here? I can ask Inez to bring out some iced tea."

Emmett dropped his cigarette, ground it beneath the

toe of his scuffed boot. "I wouldn't mind the walk. Haven't been on a beach in a while."

"Let's go, then," Jackson said.

After dinner, Cheyenne took refuge in Joe Colton's empty study. Over the past days, the vision had turned relentless, images sliding into one another, tormenting her thoughts, robbing her of sleep. The picture that came regularly now to her mind's eye had strengthened. Through the bright light she could now make out the man's shape. Though his face was a blur, she had a clear picture of his weathered hand fisted against his waist.

The black image just beyond the light would not sharpen into focus. It formed over and over in her fatigued mind like wax, melting, then reforming into hazy, muted shapes. The deep-seated instinct she'd always trusted told her that small, shadowy fragment held the answer she sought.

The answer that would prove Jackson's innocence.

With fatigue pressing down on her like a lead weight, she drifted half asleep in the chair where she'd curled. The study was barely lit by a single dim light, the air around her cool and quiet with the heavy hush of the advancing night. Her tensed muscles relaxed. As if a mental static had invaded her brain, images stirred, flitting in brilliant bursts of color across the back of her eyelids, exploding into the white light that illuminated the fisted hand. The shadowy fragment fled through the shifting light, and she followed it in her mind's eye until it plunged her into a black, dank pit.

She felt the man's emotions as surely as if they were her own—grief, fear and hatred. Searing hatred, years old and vicious in strength.

Cold struck her like a knife, cutting through her

clothes and into her flesh. Terror dug sharp claws into her throat.

Her breath sobbed through her lips; the quick, instinctive fear of a cornered victim had her lunging to her feet. Rocking a bit, she clung to the chair, waiting for her heart to slide back down in her throat while she dragged in quick gulps of air.

She closed her eyes, desperate to freeze the vision in her mind, to see the man, his face. The black, hazy image.

All were gone, like letters wiped off a chalkboard.

"You'll come back to me," she whispered, her raw voice trembling. "You *have* to come back."

Tears welled up, ran in hot rivulets down her cheeks. She loved Jackson and she needed to help him, had been sent to help him. But so far, she'd done nothing. He was her husband, charged with crimes he didn't commit, facing prison, maybe for life.

Her gaze dropped to her left hand, clenched into a fist against the chair's back. The gold band Jackson had placed there blurred through her tears. He had not married her out of love, she reminded herself, but out of a need to protect her. *Protect her.* She was the one with the gift, the legacy. It was on her shoulders to protect him. She had failed.

No, she instantly countered, battling control back into place. Not failed. She just hadn't yet succeeded.

She lifted her trembling hands to her face and wiped away her tears. She was trying too hard. Attempting to force the vision to come to her when she had learned long ago that no measure of force could stir those things she saw in her mind's eye. Still, that knowledge didn't stop the weight of all the sleepless hours from descending around her. She rubbed her burning eyes and struggled to clear her brain. Useless, she told herself. She was so tired, she could no longer gather up the force to focus her concentration.

"There you are," Jackson said as he swung open one of the study's double doors. "What are you doing in here in the dark?"

She took a deep breath, made one last attempt at swiping away the wetness from her cheeks. She would not let him see that she was terrified for him.

"I fell asleep." It was close to the truth, she told herself, forcing her mouth to curve when he flicked on the overhead lights.

"You've been crying." His expression clouded as he walked to her. "And you look exhausted."

"I'm fine."

He nudged her braid behind her shoulder. "Meredith has tranquilizers. You should take one tonight so you can sleep."

"No." She knew in her heart that the vision would return, perhaps tonight. The man would come back. She had to step into the vision, go beyond the light to the dark shadows. She could not do that with a mind dulled by tranquilizers.

"Cheyenne—"

"Trust me." She reached up, cupped a hand against his jaw. "I have to do this my way, Jackson. My way."

"Your way is to wear yourself out?" Beneath her palm, she felt a muscle tick in his jaw. "To exhaust yourself to the point that the shadows under your eyes have shadows? To agonize so much that you lose weight? All because of me, dammit. You think that's easy for me to swallow?"

She measured the mix of anger and frustration in his eyes and realized how helpless he must feel. "I don't think any of this is easy for you." She closed her eyes, opened them. "Things are the way they have to be. Fate doesn't alter its course, or change its speed, just because we wish it to."

He opened his mouth to respond, then snapped it shut when Rand walked in. "Good, you're both here."

The attorney closed the door behind him. He strode behind the desk that he'd commandeered from his father and settled into the high-backed leather chair.

The grim set of Rand's mouth put a hard lump of dread in Cheyenne's stomach. She dropped her hand from Jackson's jaw and turned to face the desk. "Has something happened?"

"I've got the faxed reports from my experts."

Jackson crammed his hands into the pocket of his slacks. "I take it from the look on your face the news isn't good."

"The results pretty much match the evidence the police say they have." Rand shuffled through papers. "The document examiner states that the signature on the insurance policy is close enough to your own that he can't say it *isn't* yours. All he can say is the comparison is inconclusive."

"Hell," Jackson muttered. "What about ballistics?"

"Tests confirm the Luger the police recovered from the Dumpster is the gun used in both attempts on Dad's life. There's no record the Luger has ever been registered to anyone."

"And the fingerprints on the Luger?" Jackson asked evenly.

Rand paused. "They're yours."

"Dammit, they can't be!"

"They are."

"There's no way in hell I've ever touched that Luger."

"There *is* some way, and we need to figure it out." Rand's dark brows slid together. "Here's where things get interesting. My expert used Super-Glue to fume the Luger."

"Fume?" Cheyenne asked.

Rand nodded. "Fumes from Super Glue react to components in human perspiration. Your skin leaves traces of your perspiration behind on anything you touch. Labs have glass tanks in which they place items needed to be analyzed for fingerprints. The tanks are filled with fumes from Super Glue. Those fumes, which adhere to ridge detail, appear after a few minutes as a white latent fingerprint."

Rand looked back at Jackson. "Except for your exact prints, the gun is absolutely clean. Like somebody wiped it before you picked it up—"

"I didn't pick it up—"

"Or printed your fingerprints onto the Luger when you were unaware. There are no smears or partials or smudges on the gun's background surface like there should be when someone handles something. There's just one set of very clear prints. Too clear, too careful. They have to be deliberate."

Cheyenne stepped to the desk. "Are you saying someone *pressed* Jackson's hand around the gun?"

"That's the logical assumption."

Jackson settled his palms against the top of the desk and leaned in. "You want to tell me how come I don't know about that?"

"I'm working on it," Rand stated. "What about a medical condition? Have you ever blacked out? Woken up and not known how you wound up there?"

"No."

"Ever seen a doctor for any symptoms even remotely resembling those?"

"No."

"All right." Brow furrowed, Rand stared down at the papers spread across the desk. "We're missing something. We've overlooked the piece that will put this puzzle together so it makes sense."

Jackson shoved a hand through his dark hair. "It looks like I'll have plenty of time to work on that when I'm locked in a cell."

"Cousin, I've got a hell of a lot more plays to make before that happens. I don't care how well this was planned, there's no way the person who pulled off this setup could think of everything. No matter how well he or she covered themselves, there's some way they're not covered. The devil is in the details. Mistakes, accidents or random chance can ruin even the best-planned crime. Trust me, there are too many details on this setup for the person to have anticipated them all. We'll find what we need. Eventually."

Cheyenne slid a look at Jackson. She saw the tension in the way he held his shoulders, the strain about his eyes.

Rand glanced at his watch, then rose. "Time for me to hole up in my bedroom and call Lucy before it gets too late. Let's meet back here first thing in the morning. We'll put our heads together on this and come up with something."

Cheyenne waited until Rand closed the door behind him, then placed her hand on Jackson's arm. She could feel the frustration, the sense of helplessness shimmering inside him. "Rand's right, Jackson. You can't give up hope."

"Too late, babe." Shaking off her touch, he turned and paced to the far end of the study, where he stood before a bookcase with several shelves crowded with framed photographs. "I'm already there. Somebody decided I should take the fall for two attempted murders. That's exactly what I'm going to do."

The certainty in his voice had her heart thudding in her throat. "No, you're not. Not if I can help it." She wrapped her arms around her waist. "You must have faith. The answer will come, you have to believe."

He stared at the photographs for a long, silent moment, then turned to face her. His gray eyes were dark, unreadable. "What I *have* to do is start thinking about spending the rest of my life in prison." He angled his head. "And while we're on the subject, it's time you accept how bad things are. I know you believe you'll see the answer I need, but I'm not counting on that. Neither should you. There's too much evidence against me. I don't have an alibi for the time of either shooting. My fingerprints are on the Luger. No vision is going to change those facts. Period."

She felt the blood drain from her face. "You don't believe in my visions?"

"Hell, yes, I believe in them. I just don't happen to have much faith in this particular one you say you're having."

"I *say* I'm having?"

"That came out wrong." Swiping a hand across his face, he walked to her. "I know you want to help get me out of this jam. You have no idea what that means to me. But I can't stand watching you tear yourself apart because you feel some obligation to help me." He reached out, settled a hand on her forearm. "Just because you believe something will happen doesn't mean it will. All you're doing is wearing yourself out. Losing weight. Sitting in here in the dark, crying. All on my account.'' As he spoke, his fingers tightened on her arm and he gave her a small shake. ''Dammit, you need to think about yourself. You need to back off. Accept the inevitable before you make yourself sick.''

''You don't believe.'' A razor sharp blade of hurt pierced her heart. She took a step back, then another, forcing him to drop his hand. ''You don't believe the answer you need will come to me. You don't believe in my gift.''

''Dammit, quit twisting my words around.'' He moved forward; impatience flicked in his eyes when she retreated backward two more steps. He raised a hand, took a deep breath. ''All I'm saying is that you need to think about yourself. From where I'm standing, there's no way out of this for me. I could wind up in prison for years. For the rest of my life, maybe. We'll both be better off if we accept that. Deal with it. Then figure out where to go from there.''

''Do you think I'm playing parlor games here?'' Her chin lifted while anger boiled through her like water in a pot. ''That maybe for my next trick I'll pull a rabbit out of a hat?''

His brows drew together. ''What?''

She fisted her hands, her muscles taut enough to snap. ''Do you think my gift works according to some schedule? Demand an answer, then immediately get one?''

Wariness slid into his eyes. ''I guess I don't understand exactly how it works.''

''I guess you don't.'' It hurt to think about everything she felt for him. Everything she had begun to wish for. ''And there's something else you obviously don't understand, Jackson. From day one, I *believed* in you. In your innocence. Do you know why? Because a *vision* sent me to you. I trusted it. Believed in it. Just like I believed in you. Totally.'' She set her jaw. The sense of betrayal was huge, overwhelming. ''All I ever asked of you was equal belief in me.''

''I do believe—''

''Not enough,'' she said in a voice that had gone very cool. Very calm. ''Not fully. And that's what matters.''

''Cheyenne, please.''

She turned, walked to the door, then paused and gave him a searing look across her shoulder. She had given him her heart, and now it was bleeding. She could feel it.

''I can't—*won't*—be with a man who doesn't accept me for what I am.''

Twelve

Jackson discovered that a man could lose his mind in the space of a single night.

After Cheyenne had walked out on him in the study, he spent hours prowling the dark house and grounds, searching for her. Her white Mustang had remained parked in its usual spot near the five-car garage. When questioned, none of the security team on patrol had caught a glimpse of her. He couldn't even spot her with the help of his uncle's state-of-the-art video system that surveilled all of Hacienda de Alegria, including the stables, barns and other buildings. Having run out of places to look, he had gone to their room, where he'd tossed restlessly in bed until dawn. Waiting for her.

Even now, as he sat brooding in his uncle's study, he told himself what had happened between them was best. If he was going to prison, this was as good a time as any for Cheyenne to pull away. To avoid him. To not even step one foot into their bedroom the whole damn night.

A vicious case of frustration had him surging to his feet, roaming the length of the paneled room. He was going out of his mind with worry. And fear. He closed his eyes on the image of her walking away from their marriage, from him, but that didn't stop white-hot panic from burning through his belly.

It didn't seem to matter that he had resolved to walk away from her if he wound up in prison. In his mind, the situation was different. Totally. It was a way—the only way—for him to protect the woman he loved so that she didn't waste her life waiting for a man who could never give her anything but heartbreak.

He had not considered that he would die on the inside if she were the one who turned her back.

He paced to the study's far wall then back again, scrubbing his hands over his whisker-stubbled face while guilt and misery rolled through him. His mind was so fatigued that he wasn't sure he was even thinking logically. How the hell could he think when in all his life he had never been so afraid? That fear had nothing to do with the prospect of going to prison and everything to do with the fact he might never again step into Cheyenne's arms and feel her complete, unconditional acceptance.

Which was all that she had ever asked of him.

He cursed himself for the idiotic way he'd handled things. More precisely, fumbled them. She had trusted him with all that she was. Opened herself to him. All he'd done was show doubt, try to convince her the gift that was her legacy, a part of her soul, couldn't be counted on.

Dammit, he *did* believe in her. In her visions. All he

had to do was make her understand that. He was an attorney, adept at delicate negotiations. The minute he saw her he would force—no, request—that she sit with him, then he would calmly ask if a man who was about to have a mountain of irrefutable evidence avalanche on him shouldn't be allowed to voice a momentary lack of faith. Surely he could compel her to view the situation reasonably, and admit it was human nature for him to have doubts, even if she had never once doubted him.

"Lame, Colton," he muttered as he paced the length of the room. "Totally lame."

Okay, he would forgo the attempt at logic, and beg. Promise to do whatever it took to make things right again. Swear he would never again doubt her and all she was.

The sound of the study door opening had him jerking around in midstride. Hope that Cheyenne would walk through the door died like a flamed-out match when Rand stepped into view, a mug of steaming coffee in one hand. Jackson filled the air with a stream of graphic oaths.

Rand raised a brow. "I sense I'm not who you wanted to see."

"Nailed that one, counselor."

Rand moved to the front of the desk, leaned against it and sipped his coffee. His speculative gaze met Jackson's over the mug's rim. "You look like hell."

"Since I'm headed there, I'll fit right in."

"I told you, we've got a lot of hands to play before you need to worry about going to prison."

"To hell with prison." Striding to the desk, Jackson took the mug from Rand's hand and swallowed a gulp. The coffee scalded his tongue. "Dammit, I'm talking about Cheyenne."

"Ah." Rand glanced around the room. "Where is your lovely bride?"

"You tell me."

"You lost her?"

"She lost herself."

"I'm not lost."

The sound of Cheyenne's voice jerked Jackson's head around. His heart shot into his throat when he saw her face, pale as ice, her bloodless lips. Her hair rained messily down her shoulders; her black blouse and slacks made her look desperately thin, as fragile as glass.

He shoved the mug at Rand, who staggered sideways to avoid the coffee that sloshed over the rim and onto the wood floor.

"Where have you been?" Jackson reached her in two strides, grabbing her forearms as if to confirm she was really there. His stomach knotted when he felt her tremble against his touch. "Are you all right? We need to talk."

"Not now."

"Cheyenne—"

"I see the gun." She stared up into his face, her eyes dark and hard. Lines of exhaustion etched the corners of her mouth. "In my vision. The dark shape—it's a gun. He wears dark clothing, like a hunter's. The gun is against his waist, slipped beneath a brown leather belt."

"Come sit down." Wrapping an arm around her shoulders, Jackson drew her across the study to the leather couch. She was shaking so badly he was afraid her legs would give out.

"This is the man who tried to kill Uncle Joe?" he asked after he'd nudged her back onto the cushions. Out of the corner of his eye, he saw that Rand had moved to the bar and was adding a shot of whiskey to the coffee.

"Yes. He hates your uncle. Viciously. The hate has festered for years."

Crouching beside the couch, Rand slid the mug into her hands. "Drink this," he said quietly. "It should make you feel steadier."

"Thank you." Cheyenne took a sip. Then another. "Rand, he hasn't given up trying to kill your father. He still wants to. There's security here now. The patrols. That's why he hasn't tried again. He's just waiting."

Rand angled his chin. "Do you know who the man is?"

"No." She closed her eyes, opened them. "I can't see his face. I tried. All night, I tried...." Her voice hitched. "It's not Jackson. Even though I can't see the man's face, I know it isn't Jackson."

"Cheyenne..." Jackson's heart turned over at the thought of how carelessly he'd handled her faith in him. He cupped his palm against her cheek. "I'm sorry."

She shifted away. He wouldn't exactly describe it as a cringe, but it was close enough to lock his jaw.

"In my vision, I see the gun clearly," she said after a moment. "The metal is dark, its barrel long and thin. It's older, carries marks of use. It has a notch—one notch—in the top of its grip."

Jackson felt his throat close. He pictured Thad Law, holding the plastic bag that shrouded the Luger. Even through the plastic, he had noticed the distinctive notch in the Luger's grip.

"A notch." Rand's voice remained even although his eyes had widened. Jackson knew his cousin had read the description of the Luger in both the police report and the information Rand had received from his ballistics expert. He would have read about the notch in the Luger's grip.

He and Rand exchanged a silent look. Jackson shook his head to indicate he hadn't described the gun to Cheyenne.

Her brow furrowed as she stared down into the coffee's golden depths. "I have seen the man before, standing with his hand fisted at his waist, sunlight reflecting off the gun's metal. I've *seen* him in this setting." She lifted a hand, rubbed at her temple as if to massage an ache. "I just don't have a sense of being *there*. Of being near him."

Jackson wanted to reach for her hand, but he was afraid she would pull away again. "You've seen this?" he asked. "Not just pictured it in your mind?"

Her gaze slowly rose to meet his. "Yes."

Rand stood. "So, now we have to figure out where it was you saw him." He paused. "Could it have been here? On the reservation, maybe? Hopechest Ranch?"

"I don't know." Cheyenne raised a hand, let it drop to her thigh. "I just don't know."

Jackson's spine straightened on a thought. "You've seen him, but don't have a sense of being near him. Cheyenne, the other night at the inn, you mentioned how, on the weekends you came to visit River, Uncle Joe would let you sit in here and look through the family photo albums. Maybe this man is in one of the pictures. You would have seen him with the gun even though you weren't there when the picture was taken."

Her lips parted. "Yes, that would explain it." She set the mug aside. "I could have seen him in a picture."

"Let's get at it." Rand turned, had the bottom door on one of the bookshelves open before Jackson and Cheyenne made it across the study. "We'll each take a couple," Rand said, jerking albums off the shelves and handing them to Jackson.

Twenty minutes later, Rand was muttering about the number of photographs his parents had taken over the years. "If I'd known they'd kept all these ridiculous pictures of me with various teeth missing, and opening every Christmas present they've ever given me, I'd have gotten rid of them long ago."

"Same here," Jackson said from the place he'd taken on the couch. At the other end, Cheyenne sat in silence, leafing through the pages of an album. Although the color had returned to her face, he saw no warmth in her eyes when she looked at him—which was as seldom as possible. His fingers tightened on the pages of album he was flipping through. He would rectify that, he promised himself. The minute he got her alone.

"My God," she whispered, then looked up from the album in her lap. "It's him! It's the pose I see in my vision. *It's him!*"

"Who?" Jackson and Rand asked the question in unison as they both moved to stand behind her.

"He's dressed in dark hunting clothes and holding a rifle," she said, almost to herself. "I didn't see the rifle in my vision."

"Just the Luger tucked into his belt." Rand settled a hand on her shoulder and leaned in to examine the photo. "With the distinctive notch in its grip." He looked at Jackson. "He and Dad used to hunt together all the time. Mother made a habit of snapping their picture when they were in full hunting garb."

Cheyenne rose from the couch, handed Jackson the open album. "I spent hours looking through these albums. I must have seen this photograph a hundred times."

"And remembered it," he said quietly.

"In my subconscious, yes."

Jackson gazed down at the photograph. A much younger Emmett Fallon smiled up at him. The eyes that were now so often bloodshot from alcohol glittered with pride. Then, his shoulders held an aggressive squareness, his chin a proud slant. And there, tucked into his brown leather belt beside his fisted hand, was the Luger, sunlight glinting off its metal surface.

"I need to take a look at something." Rand took the album from Jackson, laid it open on the desk. He slid a fingernail beneath the photo and lifted it off the page. "Perfect," he stated, his mouth curving.

Cheyenne peered around his shoulder. "What's perfect?"

Rand flipped the photo over. "Mother habitually wrote the date on the back of all the pictures she and Dad took. Once, when I was a brilliant teenager, I informed her it was a waste of time for her to do that. She told me some day I would be glad she wasted her time." Rand's smile turned into a glowing grin. "Thanks to Cheyenne, that day has come."

She placed a hand on Rand's arm. "Is the photo enough to clear Jackson?"

"Close." Rand put a hand over hers, squeezed it, then walked around the desk and pulled open a drawer. "This shows Emmett Fallon in possession of the weapon used in the commission of two attempted murders. It's more than enough probable cause for the police to bring Emmett in for questioning. With that notch in the grip, he can't claim the Luger stuck beneath his belt isn't the same one the police have in evidence. If he were my client, I would advise him to confess and try to work a deal."

"Why Emmett?" Jackson asked. "He and Uncle Joe served in the army together." Leaning, he picked up the brass paperweight shaped like an oil rig off the desk's blotter. "Emmett gave this to Uncle Joe when the first Colton well hit. That had to have been forty years ago."

Rand nodded. "I guess Emmett will have to be the one to explain his motive, among other things."

"One being how he got my prints on the Luger," Jackson said.

"I'm not looking forward to telling Dad that his oldest friend in the world is who took those shots at him."

"Or Blake." Jackson laid the paperweight back on the desk then turned to Cheyenne. "Your boss lived here for a while when Emmett and his mother got a divorce. Blake worships Uncle Joe. What's it going to do to him when he finds out what his father did?"

Cheyenne raised a hand to her throat. "He'll be hurt. Terribly."

"I guess we'll have to deal with a lot of things." As he spoke, Rand slid the photograph into an envelope. "The first order of business is to get my client cleared. Jackson, you and I need to visit Detective Law."

"Glad to." Jackson stared down at Cheyenne for a long moment. "I need time with my wife first."

"Later." She shoved her hair behind her shoulders. "I'm so tired, I can't think. I have to get some rest." Nothing in her voice, in her face, offered him the slightest opening. She walked to the study door, hesitated, then turned. "Your clearing yourself is the most important thing, Jackson."

"Not by a long shot," he muttered as she hurried out the door.

"We got a confession out of Fallon," Thad Law said nearly six hours later when he strode into the small conference room at the Prosperino PD. To Jackson, the cop looked harried with his shirt collar unbuttoned, sleeves rolled up and tie askew.

"At first, he denied having anything to do with the attempts on Joe's life," Law continued. "Then I showed him the photograph you brought in of him in possession of the Luger. After that, Fallon folded like a cheap tent in a strong wind. Turns out, his grandfather won the Luger in a poker game. That's why the gun wasn't registered."

"Why?" Jackson nudged aside the foam cup that held the coffee he'd let go cold. "Why the hell did Emmett try to kill Uncle Joe?"

Law settled a hand on his waist near his gold badge and holstered automatic. "He claims Joe Colton owes *all* his success and wealth to his guidance. Because of that, part of Colton Enterprises is rightfully his."

Rand leaned forward in the chair beside Jackson's. "It's true Dad took some guidance from Emmett. In fact, he contributed a lot to the start-up of Colton Mining. But Dad's the brains behind Colton Enterprises and all its subsidiaries. Knowing Dad, you can bet he's compensated Emmett generously over the years for whatever he contributed."

Law raised a shoulder. "From what I've found out about Fallon's past, I have to wonder if the guy even knows the meaning of the word *stability*. He's been divorced three times. His four kids were shuffled from household to household while they grew up. It doesn't sound like any of them get along very well with him now. Plus, he has a drinking problem that apparently started early."

Jackson thought about how bloodshot Emmett's eyes

had been when they re-roofed the barn at Hopechest Ranch. "I worked with him last week on a couple of jobs at Hopechest to help out Blake. Emmett still has the drinking problem."

"Speaking of his son, Blake." Law pulled out a chair at the table and settled into it. "It sounds like he has a lot of good things to say about Joe Colton."

"That's right," Rand said. "When Emmett divorced Blake's mother, Blake came to live with my parents. He's told me more than once that living at home was hell, and he credits the Colton family with saving his life."

Law nodded. "That's the ironic part. Blake's the only one of Emmett's four kids that'll have much to do with him. Emmett told me he got sick of hearing Blake talk about how he respects and admires Joe Colton. Emmett already carried this burning hatred for Joe over the way he perceived Joe cheated him out of his share of the company. Believing that Joe also stole his son's affection had the effect of pouring gasoline on that fire."

"Why now?" Jackson asked. "Blake's been singing Uncle Joe's praises for years. Why did Emmett suddenly decide to shoot him at the birthday party?"

"Fallon's drinking problem worsened last year. It got so bad that your uncle had to pressure him to retire. Fallon couldn't deal with the shame of that. Plus, without a job or a real family, he realized for the first time how alone he is. He filled his time focusing his resentment and unhappiness on Joe. Fallon decided the sixtieth birthday party would be the perfect place to kill him. When that attempt failed, he waited a couple of months, sneaked onto the grounds of Hacienda de Alegria one evening and took the potshot at Joe through his bedroom window."

"Which, unlucky for me, occurred just a few minutes before I drove in." Jackson rested his forearms on the table. "Does Blake know about this yet?"

"Yeah. I called him, told him what was going down and that he might want to hire a lawyer for his dad."

Rand pursed his lips. "We're not going to let Blake carry this weight on his shoulders alone. Emmett's sick and he needs help. I'll meet with Blake and give him the name of a criminal attorney in San Francisco I've worked with. He'll know how to work a deal with the D.A. that will include getting treatment for Emmett."

"That's what Uncle Joe will want," Jackson agreed, then shifted his gaze back to Law. "Okay, why me?" he asked. "Why the hell did Emmett choose me to set up? And how did he get my prints on that Luger?"

"That's the curious thing." Leaning back in his chair, the detective rubbed a fingertip along the thin scar on his left cheek. "Fallon says he didn't set you up. He claims someone else did all that. I tend to believe him."

Rand looked at Jackson. "Think about it. Is the Emmett Fallon you know sharp enough to pull all that off?"

Jackson pressed the heels of his palms to his gritty eyes. He'd been awake for over twenty-four hours; his body ached with fatigue and his brain felt numb. "Now that you mention it, no."

Law crossed his arms over his chest. "Fallon claims that when he took the second shot at Joe, he was worried about getting stopped by the cops on his way home, so he dashed down the stairs to the beach and supposedly hid the Luger in the alcove that's carved out of the cliffs. He planned on coming back for the gun but first there were too many cops on the grounds, then Joe hired his own security patrol. Fallon never did retrieve the gun."

Jackson blinked. "Emmett brought Johnny Collins—

one of the Hopechest kids—to the house yesterday. We went down on the beach to talk to Cheyenne. At one point, Emmett wandered off. When I looked around for him, he was just walking out of the alcove.''

"That squares with what he told me," Law said. "He couldn't believe it when he heard on the radio that you'd been arrested for the attempts on your uncle's life, and that we had the Luger with your prints on it. He arranged to drive the kid as an excuse to get onto Colton property without the security people hassling him. He wanted to make sure that someone had taken his Luger out of the alcove."

Jackson raised a palm. "So, if Emmett is to be believed, we're back to square one. We don't know who the hell set me up."

"I wouldn't exactly call it square one," Law commented. "You're in the clear now. That ought to make you rest easier."

"There is that."

"We've got to track down whoever it is who's intent on putting you behind bars." Law leaned forward, his eyes grim. "You have any idea who that might be?"

Jackson shook his head. "All along, I thought it was the same person who tried to kill Uncle Joe."

"It's not. Anyone have a personal grudge against you? Might make you want to pay for something you did?"

Jackson's thoughts skittered back to the conversation he'd had with his aunt the previous month. He had seen resentment spark in Meredith's eyes when he promised to go to the police if she continued blackmailing Graham over the fact he was Teddy's father. Would she do it? Jackson wondered. Had the woman who had taken Liza and himself into her home, nurtured them and loved them changed so much over the years that she was now capable of setting him up to take the fall for two attempted murders?

Jackson slid Rand a look. Meredith was his mother, for God's sake. At this point, he had no proof that she was behind the setup. Until—and if—he ever did, he couldn't in good conscience give her name to Law.

Jackson re-met the cop's gaze. "If I come up with anything, you'll be the first to know."

"All right." Law rose. "In the meantime, watch your back." The cop relaxed enough to smile. "I'm glad this worked out for you, Colton. Heather isn't exactly thrilled at my suspecting one of her friends of attempted murder. She's given me a lot of grief over this."

"Good." Jackson grinned at the thought of his friend defending him. "Give Heather a big kiss for me."

"I'll give her a big kiss, but not for you," Law murmured as he checked his watch. "I have reports to write. If anything else comes up that either of you need to know, I'll call."

When the detective strode out, Rand nudged a fingertip against the foam cup Jackson had set aside. "The other night, you mentioned you'd quit drinking."

"That's right. I had one drink at Liza's wedding reception. One. It threw me for a loop. I've been off booze ever since."

"Did you pass out?"

"No." Jackson frowned. "I just got tired. Real tired, real fast. I finally went to bed. Slept like a rock until morning."

"Has alcohol ever hit you like that before?"

"Never."

"You slept like a rock," Rand repeated. "What if there was something more than alcohol in that drink?

Instead of sleeping, maybe you were drugged. With you sedated, that would have given someone plenty of time to sneak into your bedroom, press your hand around that Luger, then leave. That would explain why your prints on its surface are so exact.''

Jackson closed his eyes. He already knew Rand's next question.

"Who gave you the drink?"

Jackson hesitated. "Meredith."

"Good old Mom."

The derision that settled in Rand's eyes had Jackson's spine going stiff. "Look, it's obvious you and your mother don't get along the way you used to. You want to tell me what's going on?"

"Not right now. Does Meredith have any reason to set you up for two attempted murders?"

Jackson rubbed at the nerves that shimmered in the back of his neck. "Maybe."

"What reason?"

"Jesus, Rand, we're talking about your mother."

"Don't let that get in your way."

Jackson rose, walked to the room's lone window and stared unseeingly out at Prosperino's main street, busy with the usual tourist traffic. "I'm like Blake Fallon—I think your Dad walks on water." Jackson turned to face his cousin. "If Uncle Joe found out about what I know, it would hurt him. A lot. I love the man, so the last thing I want to do is cause him any pain." And, Jackson thought, if the truth got out, his half brother, Teddy, would suffer even more than his uncle. The kid deserved better.

Rand stood, walked around the table to Jackson's side. "Certain things are going on that I can't talk about right now. Things that, if they play out the way I think they will, are going to rock this family to its core. Chances are, whatever it is you know will just add another blast to a series of explosions.''

"Well, that's clear as mud." Jackson expelled a slow breath. "Let's you and I agree to hold off on telling each other what we know until we see how things play out.''

"Fair enough.''

Jackson checked his watch. He had called Cheyenne thirty minutes ago. Inez had answered the phone, advised him Cheyenne had been asleep for hours, was still asleep. He wanted to be there when she woke up.

"I need to get back to Cheyenne." All day he'd battled a rippling panic at the thought that she had already slipped through his fingers. "My wife and I have some unfinished business to take care of.''

"And I need to get with Dad and tell him about Emmett.'' Rand settled a hand on Jackson's shoulder. "I hope your business is more pleasant than mine.''

"Don't count on it.''

She hadn't meant to sleep so long, Cheyenne thought as she crammed clothes into the suitcase that lay open on the big bed covered in a thick emerald comforter. She had intended to be up hours ago, packed and gone from Hacienda de Alegria long before the afternoon shadows slanted toward evening.

Long before Jackson returned from the police station.

Still wearing the rumpled shorts and T-shirt she'd slept in, she crossed the bedroom, her bare feet sinking into pale ivory carpet so thick it would muffle the sound of a jackhammer. Stepping into the bathroom, she scooped up the few cosmetics she owned, then did a last check of the gleaming tile surfaces to make sure she'd gotten all of her belongings.

She had.

She wasn't running away like a coward, she assured herself as she headed back to the bed. Her relationship with Jackson had simply run its course. Served its purpose. Moments ago, Inez had knocked on the bedroom door to report that Jackson had called earlier and said he was cleared of all charges. The threat of Cheyenne having to testify against him no longer existed, nor did the reason for their marriage.

He didn't love her. Didn't *believe* in her gift. Her legacy.

Blinking back tears, she stuffed the cosmetics into her suitcase, her hands trembling with a sense of urgency.

She loved Jackson, but she would get over that. Hadn't she also loved Paul, who was now only a faded memory? So, too, would Jackson be. Someday. All she needed was time to mend her fatigued mind and ragged soul.

Grief ripped viciously at her heart. Who was she trying to kid? Even now, she knew she would never get over him. Never rid herself of the sense of loss, the bittersweet wish for what might have been. If only he had loved her, believed in her.

She slammed the lid on the suitcase, the gold band on her left hand shimmering through the haze of her tears as she snapped the locks into place. After she'd woken, she had taken time to call the attorney on the reservation. He had referred her to a divorce attorney who had agreed to prepare papers for her signature. Loss scraped at her as she worked the band off her finger and laid it on the nightstand.

"You can just slide that ring back on your finger, Mrs. Colton."

She jolted at the sound of Jackson's voice coming

from close behind her. She hadn't sensed when he'd opened the door, hadn't heard him cross the bedroom. Taking a deep breath, she blinked back her tears, then turned to face him.

His eyes, darkened to the color of tarnished pewter and combined with the heavy black stubble that shadowed his jaw, gave him a cold, dangerous look. His slacks were rumpled, as was his shirt, and his fists were clenched at his sides.

Leaving the gold band where it lay, she lifted her chin and met his gaze. "Our marriage was a pretense, Jackson. A necessity. That necessity no longer exists."

"It does for me."

"I can't imagine why. And if that's the truth, it's your misfortune because I no longer want to be bound to you. I have an appointment tomorrow with an attorney who will take care of the divorce."

He grabbed her arms, his fingers digging into her flesh. "Dammit, Cheyenne, you can't leave me."

"I can and I will." She slapped her palms against his chest, shoved from his grasp. It hurt too much to be touched when her defenses were shattered. "I believed in you, Jackson. You didn't extend the same to me. As a matter of trust, it comes down to that."

He held up a hand, palm toward her. "I admit to a momentary lapse in faith. I was angry, frustrated and going slowly crazy watching the visions tear you apart. And for what? All I could see was the rock-solid evidence the cops had that pointed to my guilt. That meant a prison cell was the only thing in my future. The fact that you wouldn't even accept that as a possibility tore at me. I wanted you to be prepared." He closed his eyes for a brief instant. "I do believe in you, Cheyenne. In your gift. In everything you are."

Weary, she raised a shoulder. She was too worn out to fight about it. Too many hours of lost sleep, too many images sliding into her head had left her numb. "All right, you believe. When you come down to it, that doesn't really matter at this point." The ache inside her was like a burning. "What does matter is we've outlived our usefulness to each other."

"You think I'll let you walk out? Just like that?"

The feral look in his eyes shot her heart into her throat. In defense, she took a step backward. "Jackson—"

"I don't care if I have to tie you to the bed, you're going to listen to what I came here to say."

Nerves jittered up her spine and down again. "All right, have your say."

"You're right when you say we got married when we did out of necessity. If this whole setup business hadn't happened, there's no way I'd have asked you to marry me—"

"That's my point."

"It's not mine!" He blew out a breath between his teeth. "There's no way I would have asked you to marry me *this soon.* But I'd have gotten around to it eventually because I'm in love with you. I can't get through ten minutes without thinking about you, wanting you." He shook his head. "Dammit, Cheyenne, nobody's ever gotten inside me this way. I've never wanted anyone else inside me this way. I can't let you walk away."

"You love me?" Her voice thickened, and she swallowed to clear it. The shaft of hope was almost too painful. "You...never told me. You could have told me."

"How? How could I have told you when all I could do was envision myself seeing you, wanting you, *loving* you with a set of bars separating us?" He reached for her, his hands gentle now when he pulled her close and buried his face in her hair. "If I'd gone to prison it would have been easier for both of us if I had never said those words to you."

She tilted her head back, wanting to accept, but afraid. "So much has happened, so fast. Maybe too fast. Maybe we need time to see if we can work."

"I'll tell you what doesn't work." As he spoke, he cupped her face in his hands. "Me without you. I found that out over the past twenty-four hours. Nothing in my life is right without you. Dammit, nothing *works*. I want a life with you, Cheyenne. I need that life. I'm sorry I hurt you. If you'll give me a chance, I'll spend the rest of my life showing you how much I believe in you."

She stared into his eyes—those same gray eyes that had brought them together in a vision—and knew the words he spoke came from his heart. Suddenly, she felt the strength of his love flowing into her and her own heart opening to him.

"Jackson..." Her arms wrapped hard around him. "You love me."

"More than anything," he murmured as he rained kisses over her face. "And I've got to wonder if I'm crazy."

She lifted a brow. "Because you fell in love with me?"

"No. Because here I am married to a woman, holding her, wanting to make love to her, and I'm wondering if she loves me back."

"She does." Touched, she lifted her hand to his cheek. "I knew you felt cornered enough without my telling you my true feelings." She raised on tiptoe, brushed her lips against his. "I do love you, Jackson. More than anything."

He cupped her face in his hands, his eyes intent on hers. "Will you marry me?"

"We're already married."

"Again." He nuzzled her throat. "For all the right reasons this time. After that we can have a big blowout, invite the whole town, if that's what you want."

"Another wedding with our families there sounds good, but I'd rather have our own private celebration." Her gaze slid to the bed, its comforter looking like a soft, peaceful valley. "Right here. Now."

"My pleasure." He kissed her long and hard, then tumbled with her onto the emerald softness.

Epilogue

The next morning, Patsy sat across from Joe at a glass-topped table in the courtyard, the morning sun streaming down on the newspaper propped in front of her. Behind her huge concealing sunglasses, her eyes narrowed as she read the slashing black headline that all but screamed Emmett Fallon had confessed to the two attempts on the life of Prosperino's favorite citizen.

With disgust fountaining inside her, Patsy dropped the paper, then picked up her coffee cup while she watched the man sitting across from her. His expression grim, Joe stared out at the sun-kissed sea while he sipped coffee from a thick-handled mug. A slight breeze lifted strands of his dark hair, but he didn't seem to notice. No doubt, he was mulling over the fact that a man he'd considered his friend for forty years had tried to kill him.

Contempt twisted in Patsy's stomach. If Emmett

hadn't been such a total screw-up he'd have killed Joe long ago and *she* would have inherited his fortune. She wouldn't be sitting here now, worried about collecting money from that bastard, Graham Colton.

The good news was that she seemed to have gotten away with setting up his son. Even though Emmett had probably claimed he had nothing to do with framing Jackson, the police couldn't be absolutely sure. Still, Emmett had confessed to the crimes, they had their prey in the trap—that was what the police would focus on. If she backed off, did nothing else to Jackson, she would stay in the clear.

Which was fine, because she needed to focus all her attention on Silas Pike. She would call him this morning, tell him he had better find the prey he sought if he expected to get more money out of her. Dammit, he *had* to find Emily!

Diamonds winked on her fingers as Patsy shoved her blond hair off her shoulder. Emily was out there somewhere. How hard could it be to find her? *Kill* her?

"Good morning, Dad. Meredith."

The sound of Rand's voice had Patsy tightening her fingers on her cup as she glanced across her shoulder. He wore black slacks, a charcoal-colored shirt and sunglasses with lenses as dark as hers. She didn't have to see his eyes to feel them boring into her.

Remaining silent, she watched Joe swivel in his chair and smile. "Morning, son. You still insisting on leaving today so you can get back to that wife of yours?"

"I am."

Joe nodded. "Need a ride to the airport?"

"Jackson's driving me."

Patsy gave him a tight smile. "It's been wonderful having you home, son."

"Thanks." He placed a hand on her shoulder and leaned in. "I'm hoping to be back soon. Very soon."

She gave Joe a quick glance to see if he'd picked up on the thread of menace in Rand's voice. Joe's smile told her he hadn't. Her hand trembled on the coffee cup; sweat beaded between her breasts. She closed her eyes. Get hold of yourself. You're a good actress. Act.

Reaching up, she patted his hand. "Soon is good."

Patsy caught movement out of the corner of her eye and turned her head. Jackson strode across the courtyard, looking disgustingly happy. She still couldn't believe the explanation for how he'd managed to clear himself of the charges. His wife had a *vision!* Patsy wished both him and Cheyenne a speedy trip to hell.

"About ready to go, Rand?" Jackson asked.

"Yes. I was just telling Meredith I hope I'll be back soon."

Patsy felt the weight of the world lift when Rand moved his hand from her shoulder.

Jackson nodded. "If that's the case, you'll have to come see Cheyenne and me at Hopechest Ranch. I told Uncle Joe last night that I've accepted a job offer from the Hopechest Foundation to act as legal advocate for the kids at the ranch. Cheyenne and I will live in her house there, for a while anyway."

Joe shook his head in acceptance. "Hopechest's gain is Colton Enterprises' loss."

Patsy watched Rand shake hands with Joe, saw the tenderness in the way the son squeezed his father's shoulder. In contrast, she had felt only a threat.

"Take care, Dad. I'll be in touch."

Joe engulfed his oldest son in a bear hug. "You'd better be."

"Yes," Patsy murmured. "Stay in touch." She reached for the coffeepot to refill her cup just as Cheyenne stepped out of the house.

Jackson turned his head, following Meredith's gaze. He pursed his lips when he saw his wife rushing across the courtyard. Five minutes ago, he had left her trembling and sated in the shower. Now, she was dressed in the hopelessly wrinkled shorts and T-shirt he'd stripped off her and tossed across the bedroom the evening before. Her long, black hair hung in a wet curtain across her shoulders, her eyes glowed with awareness.

When she reached his side, he took a handful of her wet hair and tugged her head back for a kiss. "You miss me so much you couldn't wait to see me again?" he murmured against her mouth.

"That, too," she said, smiling up at him. "Right before I got out of the shower I had a vision."

He flashed a devil's grin. "So did I."

A blush started at her throat and rose to two bright spots on her cheekbones. "Hush."

Joe put his head back and laughed. "Jackson, I *told* you it'd be a smart move to marry that girl."

Jackson nodded, staring down into the face of the woman who in so short a time had become precious to him, vital to his life. "Best advice you've ever given me, Uncle Joe."

Cheyenne slid her hand into his, then turned to Rand. "I wanted to catch you before you left. The vision I had was about you."

Jackson scowled when Rand sent him a smug smile before saying, "Cheyenne, I'm flattered. But do you think it's wise to let your husband in on this?"

Cheyenne gave an exasperated shake to her head. "Has anyone ever mentioned that all Colton men think alike?"

"I've noticed that," Meredith murmured.

Cheyenne looked back at Rand. "In my vision, I saw that you'll receive wonderful news when you get back to Washington. I wanted to let you know you have something to look forward to."

Rand touched her cheek. "Any idea what that news is?"

"No." Smiling, Cheyenne nuzzled against Jackson's side. "Just that it's something you've been waiting for a long time."

Cheyenne was as good as her word, Rand thought as he stood at his desk in his Washington D.C. office, his suitcase sitting in the middle of the room. Face grim, he listened for the second time to the message Austin McGrath had left on his answering machine only fifteen minutes ago.

"I've found Meredith." The private investigator's recorded voice echoed through the still air. "She's in Jackson, Mississippi, going by the name of Louise Smith. Apparently, Meredith's a victim of some form of amnesia. She's being treated by a Dr. Martha Wilkes, a specialist in repressed memory."

With a hand not quite steady, Rand jotted down the phone number for the doctor the P.I. gave. He clicked off the machine, then picked up the phone and dialed a number he'd recently memorized.

When the soft voice answered, he said, "Emily, it's Rand. Austin found our mother. Meet me in Jackson, Mississippi."

*Don't miss the continuation of
the Colton family saga in
THE TROPHY WIFE
by Sandra Steffen.
Look for it in March 2002.*

One

"**W**hy Tripp Calhoun! I didn't know you were here."

"Amber Colton. It's been a while."

He cast a cursory glance at Amber. From this position he could see the tan line along the inner swells of her breasts. The flesh exposed to the sun was golden, the portion hugging her swimsuit, pearly white. It wasn't easy not to stare. He could see the narrow ridges of her lower ribs, but she certainly had curves in all the right places. Her hips flared just enough to entice a man's imagination. Her legs were long. He tried to remember how tall she was.

"You're probably thinking I remind you of my mother."

His eyebrows arched before he could stop them. That wasn't what he'd been thinking at all. "I don't recall ever seeing your mother pull weeds wearing a purple bikini."

As if she was suddenly aware of the view she was inadvertently awarding him, she rose almost shyly to her feet. Amber Colton, shy?

She glanced at the bottle of sunscreen in his hand. "Did Inez send you out with that?"

Inez. Ah. So this was what she'd had up her sleeve. "That woman is trying to start something."

"With you?" Amber asked.

He nodded.

No, Amber Colton definitely wasn't shy. She *was* very blond, extremely pretty. He'd wondered how tall she was. Now that she was standing he'd put her at close to five-six. A leggy five-six.

He jerked his gaze away before he got caught looking. "Very funny. Obviously, Inez doesn't know that I'm not the type to have a tête-à-ête with a rich little heiress out by the mansion's pool."

A blind man would have caught the haughty lift of Amber's chin. Tripp figured he probably deserved the scathing comment that was certain to follow. After all, he hadn't exactly been nice. Truthful, but not nice.

There was a terse silence. But the scathing comment never came. She didn't accept the bottle of sunscreen from his outstretched hand, either. Instead, she strolled to an ornate bench and reached for a white cover-up. When she'd fastened the last big button, she said, "I still say your name should be Chip, not Tripp, to go with the mountain-size chip you carry around on your shoulder."

They stared at each other, unmoving.

A memory swirled over Tripp, and he smiled, a rarity for him. "That was the first thing you said to me the summer I stayed here." She'd been what, nine or ten?

That would make her twenty-six or seven now. "You've grown up, Amber."

Amber found herself gazing into Tripp's dark brown eyes, and wondering... Oh, no she didn't. After that last comment of his, she wasn't about to give in to the curious swooping sensation tugging at her insides.

Stark and white, his smile did crazy things to her heart rate. She dragged her gaze away. It was bad enough that his look sent a tingling to the pit of her stomach. She would be darned if she would let him know it.

She remembered the first time she saw him. He'd been fifteen, lean and belligerent and street-smart. He was still lean today, but his shoulders were wider, his chest thicker. His jet-black hair wasn't as long as hers anymore, but it was still too long to be considered reputable. There was more than a hint of Latino in his features, passed on to him from one of his grandfathers, who had immigrated to America when still a boy. The first time she'd laid eyes on Tripp, she'd thought he looked like Zorro, the legendary superhero her brothers used to pretend to be when they were kids.

With his looks, he could have acted on one of those modern-day medical dramas or police-detective shows. Tripp was a pediatrician now. Her gaze caught on the gold stud in his ear; he certainly didn't look like the pediatricians she'd visited as a child.

The good manners and etiquette instilled in her from the cradle dictated that she stride to the table and pour iced tea into the waiting crystal glasses. His fingers brushed hers as he accepted the glass. Their gazes met, held. For a moment, neither of them moved.

That tingling was back in the pit of her stomach, stronger than ever. She didn't know why she glanced at his knuckles. His hands were large, his fingers long, his knuckles bony, especially the first two. She reached out with her other hand, covering the hard ridge of the largest one with her finger. ''So these broken bones healed.''

He drew his hand away from hers very slowly, and took a sip from the glass. Ice jangled, his Adam's apple bobbed slightly as he swallowed. A bead of perspiration trailed down his neck, disappearing beneath the collar of his white dress shirt. He seemed nervous.

WYOMING WINTER

by bestselling author

Judy Christenberry

In preparation for the long, cold Wyoming winter, the
eldest Randall brother seeks to find wives for his four
single rancher brothers...and the resulting matchmaking is
full of surprises! Containing the first two full-length novels
in Judy's famous *4 Brides for 4 Brothers* miniseries,
this collection will bring you into the lives, and loves,
of the delightfully engaging Randall family.

Look for WYOMING WINTER in March 2002.

And in May 2002 look for SUMMER SKIES,
containing the last two Randall stories.

HARLEQUIN®
Makes any time special ®

THE COLTONS

If you missed the first eight exciting stories from
THE COLTONS, here's a chance
to order your copies today!

0-373-38704-0	BELOVED WOLF by Kasey Michaels	$4.50 U.S.☒	$5.25 CAN.☐
0-373-38705-9	THE VIRGIN MISTRESS by Linda Turner	$4.50 U.S.☒	$5.25 CAN.☐
0-373-38706-7	I MARRIED A SHEIK by Sharon De Vita	$4.50 U.S.☒	$5.25 CAN.☐
0-373-38707-5	THE DOCTOR DELIVERS by Judy Christenberry	$4.50 U.S.☒	$5.25 CAN.☐
0-373-38708-3	FROM BOSS TO BRIDEGROOM by Victoria Pade	$4.50 U.S.☒	$5.25 CAN.☐
0-373-38709-1	PASSION'S LAW by Ruth Langan	$4.50 U.S.☒	$5.25 CAN.☐
0-373-38710-5	THE HOUSEKEEPER'S DAUGHTER by Laurie Paige	$4.50 U.S.☐	$5.25 CAN.☐
0-373-38711-3	TAKING ON TWINS by Carolyn Zane	$4.50 U.S.☐	$5.25 CAN.☐

(limited quantities available)

TOTAL AMOUNT	$ _____
POSTAGE & HANDLING	$ _____
($1.00 for one book, 50¢ for each additional)	
APPLICABLE TAXES*	$ _____
TOTAL PAYABLE	$ _____

(check or money order—please do not send cash)

To order, send the completed form, along with a check or money order for the total above, payable to **THE COLTONS**, to: In the U.S.: 3010 Walden Avenue, P.O. Box 9077, Buffalo, NY 14269-9077; In Canada: P.O. Box 636, Fort Erie, Ontario L2A 5X3.

Name: _Heather Burton_

Address: _____ City: _Portland_

State/Prov.: _Maine_ Zip/Postal Code: _____

Account # (if applicable): _____ 075 CSAS

*New York residents remit applicable sales taxes.
 Canadian residents remit applicable GST and provincial taxes.

Visit Silhouette at www.eHarlequin.com
COLTBACK-8

Silhouette®

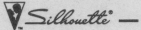

THE COLTONS

Silhouette®

Where love comes alive™

If you've enjoyed getting to know **THE COLTONS**,
Silhouette® invites you to come back and
visit the Colton family!

Just collect three (3) proofs of
purchase from the backs of three (3) different
COLTONS titles and receive a free **COLTONS**
book that's not currently available in retail outlets!

Just complete the order form and send it, along with three
(3) proofs of purchase from three (3) different **COLTONS**
titles, to: **THE COLTONS**, P.O. Box 9047, Buffalo, NY
14269-9047, or P.O. Box 613, Fort Erie, Ontario L2A 5X3.

(No cost for shipping and handling.)

Name: _Heather Burton_

Address: _____ City: _Portland_

State/Prov.: _Maine_ Zip/Postal Code: _____

Please specify which title(s) you would like to receive:

❑ 0-373-38716-4 *PROTECTING PEGGY* by Maggie Price
❑ 0-373-38717-2 *SWEET CHILD OF MINE* by Jean Brashear
❑ 0-373-38718-0 *CLOSE PROXIMITY* by Donna Clayton
❑ 0-373-38719-9 *A HASTY WEDDING* by Cara Colter

Remember—for each title selected, you must send three (3)
original proofs of purchase. To receive *all four (4)* titles, just send
in all twelve (12) proofs of purchase.

(Please allow 4-6 weeks for delivery.
Offer good while quantities last.
Offer available in Canada and the U.S. only.)
(The proof of purchase should be cut off the ad.)

THE COLTONS
ONE PROOF OF PURCHASE
COLTPOP-R2

093 KIJ DAET   Visit Silhouette at www.eHarlequin.com   COLTPOP-R2